THE SILENT DAUGHTER

KIRSTY FERGUSON

Boldwood

First published in Great Britain in 2020 by Boldwood Books Ltd.

A CIP catalogue record for this book is available from the British Library.

Paperback ISBN 978-1-83889-890-8

Hardback ISBN 978-1-80426-218-4

Large Print ISBN 978-1-83889-889-2

Ebook ISBN 978-1-83889-892-2

Kindle ISBN 978-1-83889-891-5

Audio CD ISBN 978-1-83889-884-7

MP3 CD ISBN 978-1-83889-885-4

Digital audio download ISBN 978-1-83889-888-5

Boldwood Books Ltd
23 Bowerdean Street
London SW6 3TN
www.boldwoodbooks.com

For Tarni, my partner in crime

1

Danielle Brooks awoke with a start, the dankness seeping into her cold bones. She rolled over, pulling the blanket up around her chin, her shoulders chilly in the frigid room. While she loved it most of the time, sometimes she hated the old house, the creaking of the settling wood and pipes, the third stair that squeaked sharply every time you stood on it just right, the broken bathroom doorknob that her husband Joe had meant to fix but had never got around to.

Danni sighed. Joe, snoring loudly beside her, had woken her up again, just like he had every night for the better part of two decades. She untangled herself from the blanket and swung her legs out, wincing at the cold of the floorboards as she placed her bare feet on them while she felt around for her slippers. Danni fumbled for her dressing gown, eventually finding it at the foot of the bed. Shrugging herself into the voluminous gown, she knotted the tie to fit around her waist, pulling it tight. Wondering why it was so large on her, hanging from her delicate frame, she realised she had put on Joe's by mistake. Too tired to find her own and open herself up to the cold again, she pulled the collar higher around her neck. Danni looked at the alarm clock resting on the bedside table, reminding her the dawn was still hours away.

Wearily pushing herself up from the old, sprung mattress, she slid her feet into her worn slippers, scrunching up her toes in the end, trying to magic warmth into them, the fluffy innersole long since gone.

Need another blanket. Too bloody cold in here.

Danni stumbled from the bed tiredly, yet walked without hesitation, knowing her way to the door having made her way over the floorboards hundreds of times in the darkness. She quietly went through the doorway, turning the knob and closing the door as she left. Her bladder was calling to her as she walked across the landing to the bathroom, leaving the door with the broken handle open a bit. If you closed it all the way, you became trapped in the bathroom until someone came to let you out. It happened to their son Noah more often than you'd think. Many a time Danni had found him, eyes filled with fresh tears, spent ones wetting his face, snot running down to his lip.

Danni would sit on the floor beside him and, as he crawled into her lap, she would wipe the tears from his five-year-old face. He would look up at her, love for her burning in his hazel eyes. He looked so much like his dad, with the same colour eyes and tanned skin. She would kiss the top of his head and mumble how much she loved him into his sweet-smelling hair. Her middle child Alexandra, big sister to Noah at nine and a half, would also rescue him. She never laughed at him, never made fun of him for forgetting and locking himself in again, or for crying.

Her oldest daughter, Mia, was almost a woman at seventeen years of age, as she was so fond of telling her father when he refused to let her do what she wanted. Dress how she wanted, go out with her best friend, stay up past her bedtime. Joe and Mia didn't always get along and Danni found herself playing referee more than she'd like to. They seemed to constantly be at odds with each other these days. They used to be close, Joe and Mia, but in the last couple of months they had drifted from having a loving relationship to sometimes outright hostility from Mia and anger from Joe. Danni didn't understand why, and when she broached it with Joe, he just gave her the old *she's a teenager* line. It felt wrong, but Mia refused to talk to her about it too, so Danni had no choice but to watch them grow apart, saddened by the growing divide. Danni hadn't thought about her for a long time but now, in the darkness of the home she shared with her family, the memories came rushing back. Beth, her tormentor, her abuser, her sister, flashed through her mind.

* * *

When Danni was young, she thought all families were the same and that all families lived like hers did. It was only after she went to a friend's house for a play date that she began to realise that what happened in her house was not normal. Love, laughter and no violence. That was normal. Danni couldn't get over the difference. There was love in these homes, and they were homes, not just houses full of pain and resentment. Danni had become used to her combative family life so much so that it was second nature to her to feel scared and alone.

In her family, there were clumps of hair missing, hidden by a well-placed ponytail, purple and black finger mark bruises on her upper arm, disguised by her school uniform sleeves, sprained wrists that went unwrapped, and slaps so hard she always had a headache. Danni thought this was normal behaviour but, even though she knew better now, she also knew that she couldn't tell anyone. Beth, her older sister, would just hurt her more. She'd even threatened to kill her on more than one occasion and Danni suspected she was capable of doing it. They went to the same school which made it hard for Danni to escape her. Her only saving grace was that she was in the year below her sister and didn't have to share any classes with her.

Danni couldn't remember when the abuse started, so she guessed it had always been there. She did know from overhearing her parents when she was older that they hadn't wanted her, that they only wanted Beth. She guessed that's why they didn't really care how Beth treated her, how she hurt her. They didn't want her anyway. She was disposable.

Her life was a real shit show. When Danni was a young girl, she used to have long dark hair that she would wash, dry and plait herself. Actually, it was the only thing she liked about herself, her sister having worn down her self-esteem long ago. She had hopped out of the shower, gone to her room and had just finished plaiting her hair in two when Beth barged in, one arm behind her back. She had that look on her face, the one of maliciousness and glee, and Danni knew she was in for something bad. That look meant pain and suffering for her. Her muscles automatically tensed, getting ready to fight the blow she knew was coming. She bit her lip to stop it from trembling. Danni made a dash for the bedroom door and the relative safety beyond, but Beth grabbed her by one of her plaits, halting her getaway, pulling at her scalp so hard she cried out.

'Where are you going, you little bitch?'

Danni fought back, she always fought back when she couldn't flee, not that it did her any good. Beth seemed to get off on watching her squirm. She was so much stronger than Danni and she loved proving it.

'Think Mummy and Daddy are going to save you? They don't care about you. You're just their unwanted baby. Their little accident,' she taunted, pulling on her hair painfully.

Danni had heard it so many times before that it no longer bothered her, although many times she had buried her head in her pillow and cried stinging tears that tore at her soul. She was brought back to the present by another tug on her hair. Finally, Beth removed her hand from behind her back. In it she held a pair of scissors. Danni felt the breath leave her lungs, then she dragged a shaky breath in, eyes round with fear. She knew exactly what Beth was going to do, of course Beth would ruin the only thing she loved.

'No,' whispered Danni, putting her hand up to grab her plait, trying to tug it from Beth's hand.

Beth lined up a plait between the scissors and was slowly pushing down when Danni kicked her in the shin and ran. Danni knew she'd pay for it, but she had to try for the front door at least. Beth never chased her beyond the front door. Never terrorised her where other people could see. Danni could always sleep in the drain behind their house in the vacant block if she had to. She'd done it before, no doubt she'd have to do it again.

She almost had her hand on the front doorknob, reaching out to grasp it, when she was wrenched from behind, Beth pulling her so hard that she fell to the floor. She scrambled to her feet and tried to dodge her sister again, but Beth anticipated it and grabbed her, spinning her around and quickly hacking through one of her plaits before Danni could even scream. Then Danni found her voice, shrieking as Beth held aloft her glossy hair above her head like some kind of sick trophy. Danni's hand immediately went to grab it, but she was too short, and what would she do with it anyway? Beth swung her hand down hard, slapping Danni across the face with her own plait, leaving trailing red marks of fire across her cheek and chin. It was what Danni imagined a whip felt like. She cried out, plait forgotten for now, and grabbed at her face, eyes shimmering with tears that she would not let fall.

'Whoops,' said Beth, 'that's another day off school.' She was grinning at her younger sister.

Danni had a lot of sick days because of Beth. If anyone ever cared to ask, which was rare, Danni used the standard excuses: I ran into a door, I fell out of bed, I opened a cupboard door into my eye.

She was not entirely sure the teachers that did ask believed her, but they never said anything, nor did they call child services on her parents. Yet more people who didn't care about her. Would anybody? Beth threw the plait to the floor. 'Cut off the other one, you stupid cow, you look ridiculous.'

Danni slammed the door closed and pushed a chair underneath the doorknob. It wouldn't stop her if Beth really wanted to come in, but it made her feel better. The window had been nailed shut from the outside years ago, so she couldn't get out that way even if she wanted to. She was trapped between the window and Beth beyond the door.

2

Back in the bathroom, Danni realised she was no longer sitting on the toilet. She was standing at the sink, her cold hands gripping the slick porcelain as she stared into the blackness that was the mirror above. She leaned forward and exhaled her breath onto it, drawing a love heart in the fog. Slowly it disappeared, replaced by shadows from the dappled moonlight outside, then the mirror cleared, and she could see her reflection crystal clear. Danni didn't know how long she had been standing there staring at her reflection, but she felt the prick of pins and needles in her feet, her hands aching from holding onto the sink for so long. Danni was freezing, Joe's dressing gown not doing much to keep out the bitterness of the air in the bathroom. Shuffling outside the door, Danni made her way down the stairs, careful not to stand on the third stair that squeaked. Joe and the kids had no such concern, bounding down the stairs with wild abandon, not caring about the noisy stair.

Making her way down the stairs, hand trailing behind her, feeling the old, worn banister under her fingertips, she thought about the renovations they still had to do. The to-do list was ever growing. Danni would add new things to the list every day; today it was sanding and re-staining the banister. She would ask Joe about it in the morning. That was his area of expertise. Joe did most of the chores and renovations while she ran the house and looked after their three children. She loved her kids with a fierce passion that only a mother could understand. She would do anything for them. Her relationship with Joe had changed over the years. Danni still loved him, but she felt that they were drifting apart, her longing, her loneliness overwhelming at times. Was Joe was deliberately putting distance between them? Why he would do that? He was working longer hours, often not coming home until well after dark and even when he was home, he seemed... distant, unable to connect with her. Sure, they'd been together a long time, since she was seventeen, but that was no excuse. They were supposed to be a team, them against the world. It had always been that way, ever since they had started dating.

Danni made her way into the kitchen, the night wrapping around her like a darkened shroud, the fingers of cold finding their way onto her bare skin. Danni shivered, her whole body shaking, her teeth clicking together, sounding loud in the silent kitchen. Opening the cupboard door quietly, Danni grabbed a glass from the shelf and leaned over the sink, filling up her glass with tap water that was so cold it burned its way down her throat. Outside, she heard their dog Pooch barking into the wind. His sudden barks turned into a long mournful howl that touched Danni deep inside, making her feel melancholy, filling her with a longing for something she couldn't put words to.

Danni looked at the clock. Where had the time gone? The glass in her hand had warmed from the contact with her skin. She took a sip; it was lukewarm. Pooch still howled outside, and finally Danni decided to go and check if he was all right. She pulled the dressing gown tighter around her body, already knowing that it would be inadequate once she went out into the night.

Danni unlocked the front door, stepping over the threshold, the dim and dusty veranda light doing little to illuminate the night. She walked into the darkness and it was only after the door closed behind her that she realised that she had forgotten to click the lock into the open position. She was now locked out of the house.

Damn it!

She was cross at herself, not knowing how she was going to get back inside since she knew the house was locked up tight, she had done it herself, as she did every night. She would walk around to each and every window, locking out the world. She would have to try to rouse Joe from outside the house to let her back inside, but he was such a heavy sleeper, and the wind that she could hear whipping around would steal her voice and carry it away into the night. He would never hear her. She might be sharing Pooch's bed for the rest of the night. Danni wanted to smile at the thought, but she was just too damn cold.

Pooch cried into the wind again and, deciding on a course of action, Danni gingerly walked over the uneven ground towards his doghouse. She rounded the corner of the house, the wind buffeting the length of her body, making her stagger against the force of it. Leaning into the blast of cold air, Danni made her way over to where the dog was howling mournfully.

Squatting down, trying to make herself as small a target for the wind as she could, she reached forward to touch the dog. Danni could see his wild eyes, the whites catching the faint moonlight, reflecting back at her, his head thrashing this way and that.

'You okay, Pooch? What's the matter? The wind scaring you too, huh? Least you didn't lock yourself out of the house,' she grumbled.

Pooch pushed his muzzle into her cold hand, licking it gently at first, then enthusiastically, simultaneously wetting and warming her hand. She let out a small laugh, unheard in the wild wind. She scratched him gently behind the ears, the warm creases in his skin giving her comfort. Danni put her hand against his collar and unclipped the chain. He yipped happily and as she stood, he ran around her legs in a circle, threatening to trip her up in his excitement.

'Settle, Pooch,' Danni said, her voice carrying to the dog's pricked ears. He bumped into her leg and she smiled, leaning down to pat him again.

* * *

Danni stood at the side of the house, near the doghouse, staring up at the cold stars glittering above her. Despite the frigid night, they looked beautiful, diamonds hanging high in the inky sky. She sighed, her breath puffing out in front of her. The night air nipped at her exposed face, chilling it, making her lips feel stiff, unyielding. Danni had no idea how long she had been outside. Her phone was in the bedroom, resting unhelpfully on her bedside table. She sighed deeply. She had better try to wake Joe before she froze to death.

Bending into the wind, Danni, with Pooch at her side, walked slowly around the side of the house towards the back, where their bedroom was. Mia's room was across the hall from her parents' room. She had the biggest room out of the kids. Noah and Alexandra's bedrooms were on the other side of the house. Maybe Alexandra would be easier to wake up than Joe, although all her family were heavy sleepers, just her luck. She remembered the conversation where Alexandra had brazenly called dibs on Mia's room once she went to university. The almighty argument that it had caused. It was still a good two years away, but they had been talking about it at dinner one night and Alexandra had said that she wanted Mia's room. Mia proceeded to tell her in no uncertain terms that a room swap would be over her dead body. Alexandra started to argue but Joe put an end to the girls' bickering by bashing his fist on the table, something he rarely did. It silenced the girls and erased the bemused smiled from Danni's face. She wondered what had got into her husband, but when she asked him about it later, he didn't have an adequate answer for his behaviour.

Danni could hear the roaring wind, louder as she trudged closer to the back of the house. It seemed to be getting much louder, almost as if it was taking on a life of its own. She rounded the corner, and the wind seemed warm here somehow. Danni looked up at Mia's window, and for a long moment, she couldn't comprehend what she was seeing.

Suddenly she screamed her daughter's name as she heard the great whoosh of the wind, felt its heat warming her frozen face.

The house was on fire!

Her mind screamed at her and, for a moment, she was too stunned to register what that actually meant.

The greedy flames of fire had already engulfed the back of the house, the destructive golden-red tongue licking at the upstairs windows.

'Joe! Joe, wake up!' Danni screamed, arms clutched around her belly in fright as she repeatedly yelled Joe's name again and again.

Pooch, yapping loudly, ran around her legs in a tight circle, sensing her distress. He began barking in earnest, running into her as he completed his loops, adding his voice to the cacophony of sounds.

The flames, burning into the night, ate the weather board house like it was made of paper, consuming it hungrily. The house didn't stand a chance. Danni's heart banged loudly in her chest as she ran towards the back door. Her left foot rolled painfully on the edge of garden bed, the sharp stab immediate in her ankle. Ignoring the intense feeling, Danni made it to the back door, hoping against hope that she had forgotten to lock the door this night.

But of course she hadn't. The door remained stubbornly closed and her small fists slammed on the unyielding wood as she screamed. So worried about safety and protecting what was theirs, Danni had insisted on bars on the ground floor windows. She reasoned that they lived far from town, and in the event of a break in the police would take a half hour to reach them, maybe longer. She regretted that decision now, berating herself as she ran from window to window, pulling futilely on the warming solid metal bars. She had to get inside, she had to warn her family, get them to safety.

'No, no, no, no!' she screamed into the night. Still screaming, Danni ran back to the rear of the house, the dog chasing her, thinking it was a game now. He yipped again, then lay down on his haunches, waiting for Danni to throw his ball. The flames were still eating away at the back of the house, the columns of black smoke weaving their way into the night sky, illuminated by the raging inferno. Golden embers sparked from inside the house, shooting upwards, lighting up the darkness for a brief moment like fireworks before they died in the sky. Danni ran back to the door, screaming and pounding on it, trying to get anyone's attention, trying to get inside, trying to do anything but stand there helplessly and watch her house burn down with her husband and children in it.

Danni's breathing was ragged, her screams tearing from her throat, primal with pain and fear. Ash flew into the air to come to rest on her outstretched fingers as they reached toward her family. She looked up, watched as it floated down from the burning house, staining her fingers with its ashy existence. Tears fell from Danni's eyes, soaking her cheeks, dripping off her chin. She was standing as close as she could to the house without getting burnt, screaming her family's names, feeling the heat baking her skin, turning it a ruddy red colour. She would take their places in an instant and she begged to an uncaring God above to save them. Instead, she could only watch them burn.

She couldn't call for help, her phone was upstairs, she couldn't flee to a neighbour's house because her car keys were behind the locked front door, she couldn't break in because of the barred windows that *she'd* insisted upon. Her neighbours were so far away, they probably wouldn't even see the fire unless they happened to be awake and looking in the direction of their house. Danni sank to her knees, watching as the fire engulfed her house.

Then she heard it. A single scream that cut through the roaring of the all-consuming fire. She looked wildly at the windows, trying to find where the scream was coming from. Danni ran to the other side of the house, screaming Noah and Alexandra's names, expecting to see one of them banging on the window for her to help them. The scream rang out into the night again, but it wasn't coming from her youngest children's rooms. She raced around to the back of the house again and saw Mia standing in her bedroom, in front of the window.

'Mia!' she screamed, the sound disappearing into the night, overtaken by the roar of the fire.

Mia looked around wildly until she saw her mother. Danni could see her lips moving but couldn't make out what she was saying. Mia disappeared for a second then reappeared with her desk chair and threw it at her window, the shattering of the glass swallowed up by the whooshing flames. Once she cleared the glass she stood on the veranda for a few seconds before sliding over the burning hot tin roof, then dropping heavily to the dirt. The house groaned alarmingly as Danni ran to her eldest child and pulled her back from the burning house with all the strength that she could muster. Her clothes were hot to the touch. Danni was surprised they weren't on fire, such was the heat that radiated from them. Once out of danger, Danni held her in her arms, crooning her name and rocking her back and forth as they both watched the veranda cave in, and the rest of the old two-storey house being swallowed up by the rising flames. Mia had got out just in time.

Mia coughed in her arms, struggling to breathe. But Danni could only hold her and stare at the total destruction in front of her. Her babies! Gone. She hoped with all of her heart that they hadn't known what was happening around them. That they hadn't felt the terror that Mia had. In that moment, she wished them all a peaceful and painless death.

Danni had no idea how long she sat with Mia in her arms. She was mesmerised by the raging fire that had claimed nearly all that she had. Tears made tracks through the ash on her face as she dropped a kiss onto Mia's head, her hair smelling of smoke and something else. A strong smell clung to her. It wasn't just soot and the smell of singed hair, there was something more sinister lurking beneath the fire and smoke smell.

Petrol?

A moment of clarity and pain hit Danni. Had someone deliberately set fire to her home? Had someone deliberately condemned her family to death? She was supposed to be in that house. It was only because Pooch had been barking that she was outside at all. Had Pooch been aware that all was not right? Did he sense something or someone that didn't belong? She tried to recall if anything had been out of the ordinary, but she had lost time again while outside. Had she been supposed to die too?

Danni held Mia in her arms, the young girl saying nothing. Finally, the house was razed to the ground. The flames of the fire were replaced by the flames of dawn. Gold streaks with a hint of rose blush crept across the sky, marred only by the oily smoke still venting into the changing sky. The family farmhouse, which had stood for over a hundred years, was no more.

The sun carried on its creep over the horizon, casting light over the ruined house. Finally, Danni could see the extent of the total and absolute devastation that was her home. Most of her family, gone. Her house, gone. Her heart was crushed, annihilated, gone, like the people she loved. She had no more tears left to cry. She was spent, her face swollen from the tears she had shed throughout the night. Her arms were stiff from holding Mia for hours. Mia moved after being still for so long. She turned around on her knees and buried her head into Danni's chest, her heart breaking, her sobs shattering Danni's soul. Mia was all Danni had left. She wrapped her arms around her, stroking her dirty and singed hair, whispering to her over and over.

'You'll be okay, you'll be okay,' she said, not knowing if she ever would be okay again. If either of them would be. Mia nodded against her chest and hugged her mother tighter. She had just survived a horrific ordeal, one that would be etched on her memory for as long as she drew breath. She had lost her brother, sister and father. Just like that. Mia couldn't even form words on her lips, let alone talk to her mother about what had happened.

Danni put her head down and smelt her daughter's hair again. Definitely a strong petrol smell to it. She was now sure that the fire had been deliberately lit.

Finally, someone came. Her neighbour Ryan Jamison found Danni sitting in the dirt near the smouldering ruins of their house.

Danni raised her head at the sound of an engine, yet she didn't have the energy to stand, let alone cry out for help.

'Joe! Is anyone there?' yelled a familiar voice as he ran around the side of the house, screaming out for Joe and Danni. 'Oh God, Danni! What happened?' he babbled, the shock stamped across his suntanned face. Eyes wide, his mouth hung open as he stared at the stricken woman and her daughter, and then at the burnt-out house.

'What happened?' he yelled again at the shocked and uncomprehending woman.

She stood, brushing the dirt from her dressing gown. 'I... I don't know what happened. I was locked out of the house. They're... they're gone.'

Ryan, hands in fists by his side, stared at the house. It still gave off burning heat, the pall of cloying smoke hung in the air, clinging to their clothes and hair, dirtying the pristine sky. Slowly, as if finally understanding that it didn't matter how long he took, Ryan pulled his mobile phone from his stained and faded work trousers and dialled the emergency services.

It didn't take long. Well, so Ryan said. Danni seemed unaware of the passage of time. Mia sat quietly beside her, saying nothing. Danni stared at her, willing her to say something, anything, while staying quiet herself to allow Mia time to process what had happened. That she survived the fire would weigh heavily on her.

'They're coming Danni, hold on,' Ryan said, putting his arms around her, his voice sounding strangled as he spoke. She pulled away from him and saw that he was crying.

'Who's coming?' she asked quietly, her mind a vastness of flames and ash.

'The fire brigade.'

'There's nothing they can do, is there? They're gone, Ryan. I need... I need... something... I don't know.' Danni wanted to cry. She wanted to open the floodgates again and never ever close them, but she had to stay strong. For herself, for Mia, for the memory of her family. They would want her to be strong. She and Mia were all the other had in the world now. Survivors.

Danni heard the piercing wail of the siren shattering the silence of the morning. She heard the crunch of tyres on the gravel patch in front of their house, the slamming of doors and the shouts of men calling out instructions to one another. Their voices intruded upon the almost sacred scene in front of her. This was *her* home. It was the resting place of her family. Danni looked at Mia again, sitting still as a rock, arms wrapped tightly around her knees. Danni longed to go to her, but Ryan was talking to her and, for a few moments, she had no idea what he was saying. All she could hear was a deafening roar in her ears, consuming her the way the fire had consumed the house. She watched as his lips moved, showing teeth that then disappeared behind his full lips. He stopped talking as the fire fighters, dressed in their slick and dirty yellow uniforms, started hosing down the ruined house. It was then that she realised the deafening sound she had heard was coming from the fire hose that shot a stream of water onto the burnt-out house.

Her house. Their home.

3

She was what you'd call fragile. She was delicate, easily startled. She never had any friends at school, never had anyone to giggle with behind cupped hands, never had anyone to sit with at lunch. She always wondered why no one ever liked her. She was a nice person, well, so she thought. She had nice manners, was polite and kept to herself. Yet she still couldn't make a friend to save her life.

Sitting at the lunch table by herself, eating her sandwich, she played with the small green box of sultanas in her lunch box. She hated sultanas; her mother knew that, so why did she keep buying them? She upended the box, dividing the dried fruit into two equal piles. There was one left over. One lonely sultana sitting there in the middle of the two piles, surrounded by a sea of sultanas. That was how she felt. Alone, adrift in a sea of people who looked like her, but she could never seem to find a way in with them.

She was busy deciding what to do with the odd sultana when a shadow fell over her. She looked up, face shining full of hope. Maybe someone did want to be friends with her after all.

'Hi,' she said sweetly, her voice pitched higher than usual. She closed her lunch box so they wouldn't see the sultana sitting there, trying to decide which group to join.

'Hi,' said Julie, her honey-blonde hair catching the light, dazzling in its loveliness. No matter how much she feared her, she thought her beautiful. 'How are you, baby?' she said brightly, flicking back her long hair and turning to smile at the two girls behind her.

The word *posse* came into mind. She was a well-read girl, on account of her not having any friends. Her mother had always ensured she had a book with her. But she refused to pull a book from her locker at school. She would not make herself an unnecessary target. What she wanted most of all was friends. So, when popular girl Julie had come up to where she was sitting and given her a nickname, she couldn't believe it. You only gave nicknames to friends, right?

She gave her a huge grin, hopefully not coming across as too desperate. She wanted to ask Julie what she wanted, why she was talking to her. Was she lost or had they finally decided that she was cool? She was sure she was, she just needed people to see it, and having Julie talk to her was a good start.

The popular girl spoke, smiling down on her. 'Want to come sit at our table? I see you alone every day. We want to be your friends.'

'You do?' she asked, surprised and overjoyed. Finally, she would have not one friend, but three! Could she really be so lucky? She followed the tittering girls back to their table. Bag on the floor, she sat down opposite Julie.

'What do you have for lunch?' Julie asked politely, a sidelong glance at her equally blonde friend on her left.

'Oh, I'm finished,' she said, not wanting them to see the mess of sultanas in her lunch box. 'Nothing to see.'

'Well perhaps you'd like to share my lunch,' Julie said, smiling so her dimples came out to play in both cheeks. Julie pulled out a dirty brown paper bag and her heart began to pound. She hated germs and she just knew there was something in there that she didn't want to see.

'Put your hand inside this paper bag,' Julie demanded, but sweetly so it sounded like she'd be rude if she said no.

Alarm bells started clanging in her head. She felt the need to wash her hands just looking at the bag. Her heart started racing, clickety clack, clickety clack. Her blood rushed loudly through her ears with a swishing sound. She knew this was wrong. She was wrong to trust Julie, she knew this now, but Julie grabbed her hand and pulled it towards the brown paper bag forcefully. No one came to help her. They either watched, unable to look away, like a car accident, or they studiously ignored what was going on with the blonde, popular bully and her latest victim.

In her terrified state, she looked around the lunchroom with wide eyes. Wasn't anyone going to help her? She couldn't handle mess. They all knew it. That's half the reason they made fun of her. She washed her hands about fifty times a day, she didn't like the dirty world around her with its filth trying to cling to her like a second skin.

Julie pulled her hand, hard, toward the bag. 'This is taking too long,' she said, her smile turning to an angry scowl. She grabbed the bag and pushed it towards the squirming girl's outstretched hand. She shoved the bag around her hand and cinched it closed around her wrist.

The young slight girl who hated mess let out an ear-piercing scream that rocked around the room. If everyone wasn't looking at her before, they were now.

'Oh, don't be such a fucking baby. It's just some dirt and worms. Calm down.'

But she was having none of it. Still she screamed until Julie let go of her and the bag of worms dropped to the ground, wriggling towards her Mary Jane shoes. She screamed again, rooted to the spot as one crawled ever closer. Then she looked at her hand, dirt under her nails, a worm still twirled around her finger. She shook her hand with a hysterical scream. The worm fell off and plopped to the ground.

Julie laughed almost maniacally, looking back at her two friends, who laughed along with her, although one was looking a little sorry for her. Not enough to speak of up for her, of course, but sorry enough. 'For fuck's sake, get your shit together.' Julie looked round at the room, laughing louder, trying to rile up the small crowd who stood around them watching, relief in their eyes that it wasn't them she was bullying.

Tears pouring down her face, snot leaking from her nose, she pushed through the crowd that had gathered to witness her humiliation and made her way to the toilet. She took off blindly, holding her arm up in the air. Pushing through the door, she ran to the sink as turned on the tap, running her hand under the cold water then lathering up her hands, rinsing them, then repeating the process so many times that she lost count.

She heard the bell go but she couldn't stop. Soon, her hands were red raw.

4

Danni watched as the house was doused in water that found its way from the pile of burnt rubble, rolling slightly downhill toward her. Anything not destroyed by the fire would certainly be ruined by the torrents of water gushing into the house. Looking down at her fluffy white slippers, stained with the grey ash water, she took a step backwards, but the water moved with her, as if hunting her down. Her toes were now cold and wet and soggy. The morning was chilly, the spray of water washed over her, driven into her body by the cold breeze. Ryan tried to comfort her, his hand upon her shoulder as one of the men in a dirty yellow uniform began walking towards them. Ryan stepped forward to greet him, putting out his hand to shake the man's. Was Danni expected to shake his hand too? Ryan's hand was dwarfed by the sheer size of the other man's hand. Danni tried to read the name on his coat but couldn't. It was as if her eyes were failing her, along with everything else. She heard them talking, but their words were mumbled, indistinct. She heard a squeal of laughter and looked around, her head snapping this way and that, looking for the source of such amusement at a time of mourning. Then she really listened.

It was Noah's voice. Little Noah's laugh. He laughed like that when he was being tickled, when someone had their hands on his bare belly. As a baby, he would let out this throaty chortle, a sound that Danni could still hear. Why was he laughing? Was this what madness felt like? Danni looked down at her clenched hands. She loosened them and watched as the colour returned to her white knuckled fists. Small white crescents from where her nails had dug into her flesh remained pale a second longer. She was aching. How long had she been standing there, fists clenched, teeth grinding against one another?

The men were both staring at her, mirror images of concern on their faces. Danni knew someone had asked her something, she was meant to respond but couldn't. She didn't know what to say.

'Danni, are you okay?' Ryan asked, touching her shoulder.

What a stupid fucking question. Of course I'm not okay. None of this is okay. She jerked away from his touch as if it burned like the fire that had ripped through her home and her heart. She opened her mouth to speak but nothing came out. She swallowed and tried again, her mouth feeling like she had swallowed sand followed with a chaser of ash. Ash that no longer fell from the sky like snow.

Cutting through her stupor, she heard another siren, slightly different to the first. Two men dressed in black pants and crisp white shirts headed straight for her. One of them carried a large backpack with him which he set down on the ground in front of her. Suddenly a light was being shone in her eyes, the man firing questions at her. Questions that she couldn't quite answer.

'Can you speak? Are you okay?'

Danni was never going to be okay again.

'Are you hurt?'

Yes, she was hurt. She hurt all over. Her heart was shattered. Her world now revolved around one person, Mia. Danni was all that she had left and she needed to be strong for her.

'Shock,' he said, throwing a blanket around her shoulders. She realised she was shivering. Mia must be freezing as well; she wore only her thin pyjamas and she had no dressing gown on. She turned to look at her just as the men gently grasped her arms on either side and began to lead her towards the front of the house and their waiting ambulance. The back doors were open, a collapsible gurney awaiting her. She looked around for the second ambulance but didn't see one yet.

'My daughter,' she rasped, finally able to push the words past the boulder in her throat.

'It's okay, Danni, she'll be taken care of. You're in shock, I'm going to give you something to help you sleep.'

'But I don't want to sleep,' she said as they helped her onto the gurney and slid her into the ambulance with practiced ease, closing the door behind her. She could just see the dying smoke curling through the sky out of the window of the ambulance. She felt a slight sting and looked down at her arm, the needle sliding out of her skin just as easily as it went in.

'What?' she mumbled groggily.

'Sleep now, Danni.'

'Mia,' she whispered so softly that she wasn't even sure she'd said it out loud.

* * *

Awareness came slowly to Danni. Before she even opened her eyes, she remembered the fire. Her family. Unshed tears burned the back of her eyes. She could see the bright light behind her eyelids, and she wondered how long she had been asleep for. Then she remembered Mia and her eyes sprang open. Mia was sitting cross legged on the chair in the corner, staring at her. There was a tray of food near her, untouched. Of course Mia wouldn't be hungry, not after what she'd been through. Danni breathed a sigh of relief. She was alive. Danni threw back the covers and sat up. Her head felt a bit muddled, but she supposed that was a residual effect of the medication they had given her. What *had* they given her?

'Want to get out of here?' she croaked. Mia looked uncomfortable and again Danni wondered how long she had been out for. How long had Mia been waiting for her to wake up, with nothing to do but watch her sleeping mother? She needed caring for, not a mother who could barely care for herself. She would have to put her grief aside for now. Danni was still wearing her dressing gown, the light colour now washed with grey and smelling like smoke. It filled the room with its presence and Danni wondered if they should have given her something else to wear. Then she noticed the clothes on the end of the bed. But she didn't have her purse, it had burnt up in the fire, so no money and nowhere for her and Mia to stay. They had nothing.

A nurse came into the room, inching the door open slowly. 'You're awake,' she said quietly, her voice pitched low, respectful, mindful of what Danni had been through. 'Is there anything I can get for you?' She covered the distance between them in a couple of steps, sitting on the bed beside her, patting her hand. 'Anything at all?'

'I... I want my family back. They're gone though, aren't they?' Danni's heart hurt, her head buzzing like a hundred bees were smashing at the inside of her skull, trying to free themselves.

The nurse looked at her, pity in her pale and watery blue eyes. She was an older woman with an air of empathy about her. Danni thought that if she began to cry, this nurse might cry right along with her.

'Yes, love, they're gone. I'm so sorry.' She patted Danni's hand again, her warm wrinkled hand seeking to give her comfort, but Danni could not be comforted. Not now, not ever.

'I have to go,' Danni said abruptly, pulling her hand from the old nurse's gripping fingers. She looked over at Mia who stood as well. 'Okay, we're done here,' Danni said to her daughter.

'All right, if you feel you're up to it, you can certainly leave. Your sister is here for you, she's in the waiting room.'

Danni froze for a moment that seemed to stretch on for an eternity, then nodded curtly. She looked over at Mia, silent and broken. Danni's heart went out to her. Just knowing that she walked away from a fire that took her brother, sister and father, must have been hell. She didn't want to ask, but she knew Mia must be wondering: why her? Danni reached out to hold her hand, but Mia pulled away, walking through the open door. Another piece of Danni's heart evaporated with the missed connection with her daughter. She couldn't afford to let her go.

Danni trudged behind her, walking down the hallway, following the boldly marked signs for the waiting room. She looked up at the lights in the hallway. Long fluorescent lights that hummed, and vibrated, flickering above her. They were spaced evenly and she began to count them in her head.

One, two, three... twelve.

So many pinpricks of lights behind her eyes, the shape of them burned onto her retinas as she closed her eyes. She didn't want to see Beth. Danni, Joe and her kids had never had anything to do with her even though she lived in the next town over. They kept their distance, at Danni's request. Beth was toxic and, although every now and then Danni had the desire to connect with her family, time blunting the edges of the abuse, she would remember how bad it really was; what she had survived...

5

What is a whore? Someone who sleeps around? Someone who sleeps with other people's boyfriends? Someone who will give it away to just about anyone?

She guessed she was all of the above, a whore after all. School had not been kind to her. She learned the way of the world when she first had sex. She'd been told since she was old enough to have sex that she was *that* thing. That word that had so stunned her at first once she'd learned what it meant. Did people really think of her like that? That she was a whore? She certainly didn't lose sleep over it. She could worry about it or she could embrace doing something that she enjoyed. Choosing the latter, she was happy with her life.

Her dad had run out on her and her mum when she was fifteen. They went from living in a nice house with a big backyard and cathedral ceilings to living in a caravan park with about fifty other caravans, because it was all they could afford. Her dad hadn't been kind in the divorce. She guessed she was trailer trash now, that's what the others called her anyway so it must be true. Once he left them, neither of their lives had ever been the same again. She never trusted men, instead looking upon them with scepticism and wariness. They were only out to screw you then hurt you. She learned what she knew from watching her mum. Her mum had been a stay at home mother and had never held down a job, so money was tight, and they were on welfare, so when they moved into their caravan and set up at the site, a well-meaning woman had come by and told her she could make a decent living here being a hooker, and that was all her mum needed to hear. She was a broken woman who'd do anything for money, to keep a roof over her daughter's head. She was a beautiful woman, her mum, although some of that shine wore off with each customer she slept with. It was as if the light was dimming in her soul. She hated her dad for that.

Thomas Decker has been the first; he started it all. They had found each other down at the river one warm Saturday morning, and Thomas said it was like they were the only two people left alive and that they had a duty to repopulate the earth. She knew it was corny, but she'd embraced the game up until then. So why not continue playing? Besides, Thomas was nice, and he was popular, and she really had no friends.

He'd climbed on top of her, rubbing where he thought her clit was, but she didn't care, he felt good. His hands were slightly cool to the touch since he'd been in the water before, but it compensated for the heat she was putting out, and there was some serious heat. Once he'd finished touching her, she was wet and ready, down by the bank of the raging river. Since this was her first time, she didn't realise that he had a small cock, but she instinctively knew she could take more. He put his cock inside her, thrusting into her like crazy, like his life depended on his speed and accuracy. When he did come, he pulled out quickly and wiped himself on her singlet.

The worst thing about it was she hadn't even felt anything. Was she supposed to come for real? Did this make her popular now? When it was over, she felt... unfulfilled, but of course she didn't tell him that, she didn't want to embarrass him or alienate him. After all, he said he promised that he was going to talk to her at school and he was the most popular boy there.

She smiled and murmured her goodbyes. She didn't know what to expect come Monday, but it certainly wasn't the word *whore* scrawled across her locker, the paint still running down the front of the door looking like blood.

She didn't know what to do. Should she run or should she stay and face it? People had gathered around her locker, to see her reaction, to watch her meltdown maybe.

Instead of melting down though, she strode over to her locker and unlocked it. The paint stained her hands, so she wiped it on her jeans, scrubbing her skin against the material. It was obvious to her that Thomas had sold her out, told someone, or a few someones. Either way, the word whore stuck.

People avoided her even more than usual. There were comments to her: *keep away from my boyfriend, whore. Just like her mother.* She couldn't understand why they treated her this way. She wasn't doing anything that the rest of the kids weren't doing, so why were they singling her out?

Eventually, sick of the snide comments about whores and boyfriends, she decided to fight back. There would be no more hanging her head low as she walked past girls that clung tighter to their boyfriends' arms in case she tried to steal them, no hanging her head in shame. While she sat in class one day, the girl in front of her turned and called her a whore right to her face. The boy beside her said, 'Heard you moan like a dog in heat.' She excused herself from class. She didn't want them to see her cry. She ran to the toilet before the tears came. Sitting on the closed toilet lid, she sniffed back her tears, vowing never to let her feel this way again. *Whore. Slut.*

She would lean into it. She would embrace it instead.

She would become the whore they wanted her to be.

She spent the last two years of schooling fucking everyone she wanted to. No one ever said no to her. She was hot and easy. She had cemented her reputation now and even went after guys she knew were taken. A girl in her science class had been whispering about how she passed herself around like a party favour, so she seduced her boyfriend, sending him naked selfies then giving him a blowjob behind the classroom. The next time she saw the girl from science class the bully of a girl couldn't quite meet her eye.

That's called payback, bitch. She found that she enjoyed her newfound power, it gave her a sense of control over her chaotic life. A way though the darkness.

6

Danni was in year eleven when things got even worse at home. It was so bad that when Beth had a friend over, male or female, Danni stayed in her room, holding the little knife she'd stolen from the kitchen. Danni understood how bad and premeditated it was to have the knife, but the truth was, she also knew she'd need it one day. That was a certainty.

Danni had found over the years that Beth got off on the pain she caused her. Danni had run away a few times, only to be hunted down by the police and returned to her family. She never said anything to the police about how much she suffered at home. They wouldn't believe her even if she told them. They would pull her from the back seat with a stern warning not to run away from home again and tell her that they had more important things to worry about than an attention-seeking girl. After all, Danni didn't look like she came from a family that abused their kid, and her bruises were well-hidden.

When Danni ran away, her parents would speak to the police. Nice, upstanding family, with a troubled runaway daughter. That's what the police thought. They saw Danni as a troublemaker, a liar. Danni wondered why her parents bothered reporting her missing at all. Oh yeah, they'd miss the money they received from the government for her upkeep. Nothing as simple and easy as loving her. No, not that – never.

After the last time she'd tried to get away and they'd brought her back home, Danni had gone into her bedroom and closed the door, putting the chair underneath the knob. Although it was flimsy, it made her feel better. As she lay on the bed, she listened to music through her headphones, the soothing tones calming down her rage.

For the next few days, she managed to largely avoid her family. Because she had tried to run, her parents were angry at her, and Beth, well Beth was being worse than usual. At least at school, she was invisible. No one noticed her, she blended in with the sea of humanity. She had no friends and no desire any more to have any. Anyone who got close to her would find out her secret. Find out that she was garbage, a thing to be punched and kicked, toyed with, not worthy of love.

Later that week Danni was in the courtyard at school, sitting on the steps by herself as usual, eating her lunch that she had made herself, when she felt eyes on her. She looked up and found herself looking right into the eyes of a boy who was staring straight at her. As soon as their eyes connected, she quickly lowered her head and peeled off the crust of the sandwich. Why was he looking at her? She felt exposed, vulnerable. Then she saw her sister. Her heart beat faster just at the sight of her. She'd never hurt her at school. No, she'd just wait until she got home, save up the violence then let it out on her in private. At school, her older sister was an angel, whereas Danni was invisible and ignored, which suited her; she was used to it, preferred it even.

The boy was still watching her. She knew who he was. Joe was a senior and someone her sister hung around with sometimes. She looked down at the book she was holding in her hand then glanced up again a couple of minutes later. He looked at her with interest, which made her uncomfortable so she packed up her things and hurried away before her sister could catch her looking at one of her friends. She would be punished for it. What did he want? Did he want to know why Beth Douglas's little sister was such an ugly little freak?

The end of the day came swiftly, and no one else noticed her the way Joe had, no one stared. She scurried home like the little mouse she was. As she walked through the door, her mother, lying on the couch, mumbled, 'That you, Beth?'

'No, Mum, it's me.'

'Who?'

'Danni,' she sighed. 'Your other daughter.' She knew it wouldn't make any difference in telling her, she was drunk. She walked around the couch and stared at her mum. She had a lit cigarette dangling from one hand, almost touching the worn carpet. Danni gently removed it and crushed it out in the ashtray, smoke curling up to reach her nose. Would it be the worst thing in the world if their house burned down and her mother was in it at the time? What a terrible tragedy. There would be no insurance money, of course, nothing for them to live on, but they'd give her up to the state to be a ward and she'd finally be shot of this crappy family. Her fingers reached for the pack of cigarettes and just as she touched them, she was aware that what she was doing was so very wrong. She was contemplating arson and the possible murder of her own mum. A nervous little laugh escaped her lips, not disturbing the comatose woman lying on the couch, the smell of cheap wine wafting from her open mouth like a poisonous cloud.

The front door banged open, hitting the wall. 'You little shit head,' screamed her sister, rousing their mother from her stupor. 'Stay away from Joe. I don't care how you did it but if he ever asks me about you again, I will cut you up into tiny pieces and feed you to the neighbour-hood dogs. You understand me?'

Danni couldn't even talk, she was so shocked by Beth spitting her venom.

'Answer me, bitch!'

'Y... yes.'

'You two! I have a headache, take your shit outside.'

'It's all sorted now, Mum. Isn't it, Danielle?' Beth said, trailing her fingernail lightly across Danni's cheek as she walked by her. Danni let out a pent-up breath once Beth was gone, trying to centre herself, knowing that she could never truly be centred in this house. She could never be safe. It was no wonder she sometimes just wished them all dead. She had no love for any of them, they all used her in some way, but Beth, the one who should have been an ally, was the worst of all. Danni just wanted Beth to die a horrible death or, at the very least, have a miserable life.

Marry some loser and live in a caravan in a run-down part of town, her hopes and dreams sucked away from her soul like she was doing to Danni.

She went to her room and put the chair up against the door, which usually afforded her about three seconds of precious but ultimately useless time before it was shoved aside and Beth would barge into her room.

She put her hand under the slats of her bed, feeling for the knife. She pulled it out, looked at it, knowing that sooner or later, she'd need it.

Danni smiled sadly. She'd be ready.

7

Joe Brooks was one of those popular kids who pretty much ruled the school. He was good looking, well liked, athletic and confident. Joe could have anything and anyone he wanted. The girls were lining up around the block to date him, to drop their panties for him, and the boys wanted to be him. He was an all-round stand-up guy, who seemed to have it all figured out, have his shit together.

What everyone didn't know was that Joe was just pretending and that actually he was just as insecure and unsure as the rest of them. He lived at home with his parents, was an only child and he never, ever had friends come to his house. He either went to theirs or they partied elsewhere. There was no way he was changing people's perceptions of him by letting them see what went on in his home.

Joe's bedroom was his inner sanctum. A place where he slept and daydreamed about getting out of this town. Joe had plans, but who knew if they'd ever see the light of day. Once he graduated from high school, he wanted to leave, go to the city where his life would finally start. He would never look back. There would be no more ties to this town, and he would be beholden to no one. But unfortunately for Joe, there would be someone who would always need him.

Joe came home, slamming the front door, and went straight to his room, leaving his door open in case she cried out for him. He had a maths test tomorrow and he really needed to study for it, as some parts of the syllabus may as well have been written in Latin, for all he understood of it. He wanted to hire a tutor to help him get his grades up but a tutor was a luxury they couldn't afford. He was thinking about asking some smart chick who might agree to exchange a special kind of service with him. He was popular – a date with him, a friendship even, would make the girl popular as well. It was a win for everyone.

'Joey,' came the weak cry from down the hall.

Joe looked at his maths book. He had barely sat down and he was being called to duty already. He pushed his chair back and stood, heading for the door. They weren't rich, they weren't poor, they landed somewhere in the middle. They had a roof over their heads and food in the cupboard but were still on benefits.

The voice moaned again, and he hurried his pace. He pulled his shoulders back, licked his lips and mentally prepared himself for what was to come. Already he could smell the cocktail of different scents competing with each other, but for him, shit won every time. He walked into the room, pasting a smile on his face.

'Hi, Mum,' Joe said as he walked into the room.

'Hi, my darling,' she replied in a breathy voice.

'How are you today?' he asked, knowing the answer. It was always the same.

'Not too bad, love. Could you please get me my medicine?' She licked her cracked lips.

It shouldn't have been his job. His father received a pension to look after his mother, but he usually spent the money on booze... or other things. Joe was sure that he had another woman on the side after he'd seen him hugging some random chick in the street when he was out driving around one afternoon. He hated him after that. His mum was bedridden and he was out having it off with some bitch. Joe had had many a screaming match with his drunk father as his dying mother was down the hall, lying in her own filth each day until Joe came home from school and cleaned her up. She was always so embarrassed and apologetic when he changed her sheets that she would cry. In those moments he wanted to kill his father. He was supposed to make sure that she had everything she needed, day and night. Quite often he would forget her daytime medicine and she would be in pain the whole day. Joe could see it on her face on those days. Instead it was left up to Joe to take care of her. Not that he minded, he loved his mum.

'Mum, do you need changing?' he asked in a gentle voice as he popped pills out of their silver foil blister packs and placed them in a small plastic cup where they rattled around forlornly when he moved. She turned her head, but he could still see the tear roll down her cheek. How dare his father reduce his mother to tears? What a fucking hero.

Joe pulled back the stinking bedclothes, chucking them on a pile on the floor for washing and went to get a large bowl of warm water to wash her with. He dropped the soap into the bowl then pulled a face washer from the stack that he himself had washed and folded. He could hear the TV on in the lounge, his drunk father ignoring his wife and son in favour of some inane soap opera. Her face was streaked with tears. This was the hardest part for them both. She was so weak, but his father wouldn't let her go into palliative care because his payments from the government would stop and he'd have to find a job.

Gently lifting his mother's nightgown, he undid the sticky tabs on her incontinence pants. From the weight and the urine on the sheets, it was clear that she hadn't been changed all day. He washed her down, then put cream gently on her angry red rash. He changed the sheets and his mother. He bent down and gave her a kiss on her dry and papery cheek. She grabbed his wrist to stop him from leaving.

'I know this is hard on you,' she choked out, 'I know this isn't what a teenage boy should be doing, and I want you to know I appreciate every-thing you do for me. But I want you to be a normal teenager, too, try to have a life. Promise me, promise me, Joe, that you'll get out of here as soon as you can. As soon as you graduate, you leave and you never come back.' Talking took it out of her and she fell asleep as soon as she deliv-ered her speech, without hearing his reply.

Joe walked back to his room. Would this be his life forever? No, even his sick mother wanted him out of this place, to get out and be free. Well, he bloody well would.

Freedom.

* * *

Joe had seen her before. He found out that she was the younger sister of Beth, who was a hanger on to his group of friends, overtly obvious in her play for his affections, but she wasn't his type. Too brash and too jealous of every other girl around him. Didn't stop him from throwing her a fuck every now and then. Beth was crazier than a shit house rat, meaner than a snake sometimes, to other people, never to him though. To him, she was sarcastic but in a good way, but he'd never commit to dating her. She had no ambition. She was happy to stay in this town, get married and have babies. Not going to happen, he wouldn't be tied down to a girl like that.

The sister's name was Danni. That's all that Beth would give him. From what he could tell, she was quiet and bookish. A girl with no friends. She sat by herself every day, blending into nothing, but her saw her clearly. When he sat down opposite her and said hello, she actually looked around to see who he was talking to and when she realised it was her, her eyes widened and her mouth popped open, but no words came out. It was cute and reminded him of every teenage romance movie that he'd watched in secret.

'How are you doing, Danni?' he asked, watching as she squirmed with embarrassment. People stared.

'Fine,' was all she could manage to eventually squeeze out.

He could feel Beth's jealous stare aimed at his back, but he didn't care. She could get fucked.

He came and found her every day for two weeks before he thought she was ready for him to ask her out, and every day Beth would ask him what he was doing wasting his time with her sister. He would always answer, 'Because I like her.' It never satisfied Beth and seemed to make her angrier at her sister, never him.

'Look, there's a party on Saturday night, would you like to go with me?' he finally asked Danni. He waited, wanting her to answer yes right away, but he gave her time to process.

'I'm not sure that's a good idea.' He knew that Danni didn't know about him and Beth since she never saw them interact as a couple. Friends, but never a couple.

It was clear that she was wary about going with him, maybe she thought he was going to make fun of her, like she was the punchline of some joke she didn't know about. But he was dead serious.

'Say yes, Danni. We'll have fun. New people, new experiences.' He flashed her a smile.

It took her a while to respond. She looked into his eyes as if to read his intent, then she whispered, 'Yes.'

He smiled, and she smiled back. 'Okay, I'll pick you up on Saturday night.'

He was walking back to class when someone pulled him roughly into an open classroom. He turned to face his attacker. It was Beth, squinting at him in anger, a sneer on her normally pretty face, her long hair sweeping over her shoulder. She had started wearing it like her sister recently.

'Why her?' she spat. 'Why not me?' She seemed genuinely hurt and upset. He felt bad for her, but he had to tell her the truth. He owed her that much.

'It was never going to be you, Beth.' He touched her arm as he said it gently, but she jerked away. 'I'm sorry if I hurt your feelings. I didn't mean to lead you on.' He knew he should have told her months ago that he wasn't serious about her, that there was no chance of them going beyond hooking up occasionally.

She looked like she was going to punch him and he steeled himself for it, tensing the muscles in his face. He deserved it. He had been sleeping with her on and off for six months and now he was dating her younger sister. He knew he'd hurt her, but he didn't know how deeply. He wasn't backing down. Beth could hit him or spread nasty rumours about him, but he didn't care. Danni was unlike any girl he'd ever been with, ever met. She had really opened up to him these past two weeks. He was slowly dismantling her walls, brick by brick. He saw a shy girl with glimpses of empathy, stubbornness, humour and, like him, a desire to get out of this town as soon as she could. Now *she* had ambition.

As he drove to pick Danni up from her house, he realised that he was nervous, something he hadn't felt for a long time. Girls came and they went, but none of them were like Danni. There was just something about her. When she came up the drive, he noticed how cute she looked in her tight jeans. They hugged her in all the right places. He felt himself growing hard just thinking about touching her, kissing her. He readjusted his trousers, easing his discomfort.

She opened the door and slid into the passenger seat. The interior light illuminated her face and he could see that she'd gone to the effort of putting on makeup. He looked at her incredibly glossy lips, her hair wild, free, and slightly curled. He put his hand up and tucked a long piece of it behind her ear, gently caressing the side of her face. She leaned into his hand then reached up to cover his with her own.

They had a great night at the party. Joe stayed by Danni's side all night, smiling reassuringly at her when it was obvious that she was waiting for the other shoe to drop. For people to realise that she didn't belong there, with him, with any of them. But it never happened, they accepted her because she was there with Joe. He tried his hardest to make her feel comfortable, easing her into dating him, into his life. He knew that she hadn't been invited, let alone gone to a party before so this was all new for her.

When Joe drove Danni home, pulling up to the kerb of her house with a jerk and a slam of his brakes, she giggled. It was a beautiful sound, something he couldn't get enough of. She told him that she had never had so much fun in her entire lonely existence. Before Joe, Danni had had no friends, no one to confide in, no one in the world who cared about her. She was on her own. Now she wasn't.

* * *

Soon after they arrived home, Danni picked her small handbag up from the floor of the passenger seat and Joe stilled her with a touch of his fingers on her wrist.

'Where are you going?' he asked, gently drawing lazy circles on the inside of her wrist with his fingertip.

Her warm skin became hotter as her heart beat faster, her blood rushing through her body with such force that she could hear it pounding in her ears, feel it in her chest. Danni looked down at his hand on her, then raised her head to look at him. The window was down, the night air warm, crickets chirping their song outside in the night. It was perfect.

'Joe,' she whispered, waiting. She knew what he wanted, she wanted it too.

He leaned in slowly, stopping when his body had closed half the distance between them, their bodies separated by mere inches. Danni held her breath.

'Just breathe, Danni,' he whispered as his lips met hers.

It was the softest touch, his lips barely brushing against hers, but she felt as though he had just claimed her as his own. Joe wrapped his hand through her long, dark chocolate-coloured hair, the strands tugging gently at her head as he moved his hand through them.

'You're so beautiful, Danni.'

She surprised herself by kissing him again, taking hold of his shoulders and drawing him towards her. She put her arms around him as he slid one hand under her top, stroking her back with practiced ease. Her lips parted under his, their tongues lightly dancing with each other. Danni could barely stand the feelings that were coursing through her body, invading her mind, making her feel weak yet strong at the same time. Finally, they pulled away from each other, his hand leaving her skin reluctantly.

'I have to go,' Danni said, when all she wanted to do was stay in the car with him, kissing for hours, forever. With him, she wasn't a nobody. He saw her, really saw her. They would move to the city together, start the life she'd always dreamed of.

'Okay,' he whispered, huskily, his voice breaking just the tiniest amount. She smiled in response. He desired her, needed her, he wanted to keep kissing her as much as she did, she could feel it. But Danni knew that if she didn't leave the car now, then she was never going to leave. She wanted to stay wrapped tightly in this cocoon of happiness. There was no pain, no fear, no doubt, no loneliness when she was with Joe. He was her escape and she desperately needed to escape.

She raised her hand in farewell as he pulled away from her and drove down the road, growing ever further from her. Danni stayed, standing in her driveway thinking about him; he was both her present and future. She turned to look back at her darkened house, taking one last look at Joe's brake lights before heading inside. She had shared two beers with Joe at the party. She never drank, so it felt unfamiliar to her, her head feeling the tiniest bit foggy. She had a little buzz going on from the beer and the incredible kiss, what a first kiss!

Danni opened the door quietly so as not to wake Beth sleeping inside, then locked it and put her bag and keys on the small side table just inside the front entranceway, aware of the keys clinking against each other, loud in the largely silent house, the only other sound coming from the faintly ticking old clock in the lounge room, covered in a thick layer of dust that never failed to disgust her whenever she saw it. It counted down every second that she was apart from Joe. Despite Danni's earlier misgivings about his interest in her being a prank, she was falling for him, hard and fast. She couldn't help but smile in the semi-darkness, the streetlight's pale beam reaching inside the entranceway, lighting a little halo around her.

Danni put her fingers to her lips, trailing them across the slightly bruised skin, where Joe's lips had burnt hers, branding her with his touch.

'You bitch!' The voice reached Danni's ears just as the hand slapped her across the face so hard her head snapped back, and she felt a click in her neck, pain following the sound.

At first she didn't know what was happening; it was gloomy in the entranceway. But Danni pieced it together and put her hands up to protect her face from the barrage of slaps coming from her sister. Danni's skin was stinging, as Beth was landing every slap. Danni cried out then she felt something shift within her, a power, a hunger as she cocked back her arm and let her fist fly at Beth's face, hitting her dead centre, her nose breaking audibly in the half-lit room. It sounded as loud as a clap of thunder in the quiet space.

'Oh! You fucking bitch!' screamed Beth in agony, holding her nose, which was now gushing with blood, black in the semi-darkness.

Danni didn't even feel one bit sorry. It was as if she had become a different person, one capable of retaliation and violence. Her mother stumbled down the hallway, rolling along the wall, snapping on lights as she went. The lounge light was flipped on and the true extent of their dust up was revealed. Danni, covered in raised red welts, and Beth, leaking blood everywhere.

'Elizabeth,' their mother whispered, looking at her bloodied and swelling nose, 'you poor thing.' She whirled on Danni. 'What did you do, you little fuck? Why did you hurt Beth like that?' she demanded.

'She attacked me first. I was... defending myself.' Danni's skin was on fire, and not in a good way. Beth had got a number of decent slaps in while Danni had been protecting herself.

Beth pushed out of her mother's grip and leapt at her again but Danni launched herself at her sister, throwing her to the ground where Beth grunted in pain as she landed on the thin carpet, a layer of concrete underneath.

'Danielle!' yelled her mother. She almost never referred to her by name. Sometimes Danni would have been surprised to know that they even remembered her name, so infrequently they used it.

'She knew I liked him,' hissed her sister, venom in her voice. Danni was not giving up Joe. He was the best thing in her miserable life. The only thing. 'She took him from me.'

Danni stood there, arms crossed. 'That's a lie.' Her voice rang out clear and true in the night. Danni felt invigorated and realised something had come over her when she had physically hurt her sister.

Power. She felt power.

8

Danni stood still in the entrance to the waiting room, looking at Beth as she watched her warily from the other side, arms folded across her chest in a show of hostility. Beth didn't take any steps towards her, so Danni closed the distance between them. Danni had had enough to deal with in her life without her sister's venom poisoning her children. She wanted to keep them as far away from Beth as possible, so they had never met, and she wouldn't be letting Mia get close to Beth now.

Beth turned without saying a word and stalked off, leaving her sister and niece to keep up with her long, angry strides. Beth flung herself into her nice new car and started the engine, its throaty roar loud as Danni and Mia hopped into the car.

'You can't stay at my house,' Beth said immediately, not even looking at Danni as she said it.

Despite all the arguments, physical fights and distance, Danni thought Beth would at least provide them with a place to stay after their terrible tragedy. She had lost two children and her husband. Was she really going to turn them away when they needed her?

'I got you a motel room instead,' she said decisively, finally glancing over at her sister. 'I don't want you invading my space.'

It was probably for the best; Danni didn't want Mia exposed to her anyway.

'Fine,' mumbled Danni. At least they had somewhere to go, even if it was the only motel in town. Danni knew the place, run-down, ugly and so close to the industrial estate that Danni imagined you could hear the thump of machinery through the walls.

Looking straight ahead, Beth said irritably, 'I paid you up for a month, but that's all I'm doing. You're not living off my charity forever.' This small act seemed to piss her off no end, her full lips now in a thin line. Danni hadn't seen Beth for years, and she had aged well, which surprised Danni. She wore nice clothes and her hair was swept behind her face, held with a clip, flattering her pretty face, makeup covering the smattering of freckles she knew were there. Danni remembered looking at herself naked in the mirror only a week ago, before she had lost her family. It seemed like a lifetime ago, another world even. She looked good, a taut stomach, perky breasts despite three kids and her hair was as beautiful as ever, although shoulder length where once it had cascaded down her back. She had been objective, wondering, after looking at herself, why she and Joe hadn't had sex in such a long time. By her count, it had been over a year. He had slowly been drifting from her and she wasn't sure how to fix it. She pulled herself back to the present. Beth was, as usual, totally self-absorbed, not even expressing sympathy for Danni's loss.

Danni had always wondered why Beth could be so cruel. Danni and Mia had just lost the ones closest to them. Seen them burn in the fire that consumed their house and now they had to learn to live without them. How they were supposed to do that she didn't know. Mia still wasn't speaking and when Danni looked over her shoulder and smiled at her, all she received in return were a pair of eyes, wide, too big for her petite features, filled with pain, staring back at her. With a sigh, Danni feared that she would never be able to make Mia feel safe again. She had failed her, just as she had failed Alexandra and sweet Noah.

Beth pulled into the car park of the motel and thrust the key into Danni's lap. 'Remember, one month.' With great reluctance, she handed her several hundred-dollar notes.

'Don't care how you spend it, but there's no more coming.' She seemed combative, wanting to fight. Brows lowered, painted lips pursed into a thin line, daring Danni to say something, anything. She was just looking for a reason to unleash on her, but Danni wasn't giving her a reason.

Danni didn't say a word as she and Mia got out of the car, shutting their doors at the same time. There was no point trying to talk to Beth. When all was said and done, there was nothing between them. Danni really did hate her sister. For as long as Danni could remember, they had been at war with each other, each skirmish worse than the last, causing damage to both sides, she wasn't even sure who had won the war, but it was clear that Beth still harboured hate in her heart.

* * *

Danni had heard the whispered rumours at school. She may not have had friends, but she still heard them. Quite the scandal it was, Joe sleeping with Beth when he was dating her little sister. Danni tried her best to ignore the hurtful comments. It was at times like these she wished she had made a close female friend, but she had never managed that, so she suffered in silence, until one day it all came tumbling out. She just had to know if what Beth said was true. Even Beth, who Danni knew to be an out and out liar, was telling her the juicy details of how Joe had fucked her in the very car he drove Danni home in every day. That it was hot, that he said she was better than Danni would ever be. She never let up and Danni was beginning to believe her.

It was a couple of days later when Danni had garnered the guts to confront Joe about the rumours. Joe was driving her home from school, something he had started doing ever since they had begun dating. She said she was happy to take the bus but leaving school, his arm slung around her, gave her a thrill. People were envious of her for the first time in her life, and it felt good.

'Did you sleep with Beth?' she asked suddenly, breaking the silence. She looked at Joe's profile. She saw his jaw tighten and his full lips pursed together, blowing out an irritated breath.

'Why are you asking me now? Does it even matter?' He was frustrated, she could hear it in his voice. And angry, like she shouldn't be questioning his loyalty to her.

'She keeps saying you did, giving me details, so, yeah, it matters. Did you?' Danni held her breath for a long moment, waiting for the confession that she was sure wouldn't come.

'Look,' Joe said, pulling the car over to the kerb, buying time.

Danni looked out the window at the grey afternoon. 'You fucked her, didn't you?'

'Yeah, I did,' he sighed. He didn't say he was sorry; he didn't touch her, but he did try and smooth it over. 'It's in the past, Danni. I'm yours, forever now. Beth, she didn't and doesn't mean anything to me, or to you. It won't happen again.' She wanted him to promise but couldn't ask for it, couldn't beg him to tell her something that in all likelihood *would* happen again. Why would he sleep with Beth in the first place? She knew now that they had slept together before she had started dating Joe because he'd told her, but to do it to her when they were dating was a low blow. She felt her heart harden against him slightly.

Danni stared out the window for a moment longer before turning toward him. He had an expectant look on his face.

'If you ever do this to me again, we are over. I don't care what your excuse is, or if you're sorry. There won't be any more talking, I'll just break it off.'

He looked wounded by her words as much as her tone. She looked how she felt, fucking angry. But what she said was true, no longer would she stand for it. If he wanted Beth, then he could have her.

Joe took her hand in his, placed if over his heart. 'I promise you that I'll never hurt you like this again.'

* * *

As soon as Danni had seen the farmhouse, she had fallen in love with the hundred-year-old house. It sat at the end of a long dirt driveway, stately, grand, homey. All it needed was some love, and she had plenty of love to give. Joe's mum had passed away in the night before she ever had a chance to meet her grandchildren. She had left him some money, enough for the modest deposit on the farmhouse, and Joe had found a job right out of school, working with a local contractor laying bricks. Danni and Joe worked hard on getting it ready for when their baby arrived. They were leaving the reveal of the sex up to chance, but Danni was sure they were having a girl, whereas Joe was convinced there would be a Joe Junior.

Danni was still painting and hanging curtains in the baby's room right up until she felt her contractions coming on. Joe was out in the paddock, trying to get some piece of machinery to work. The contractions came hard, and boy did they hurt. She screamed as another contraction ripped through her. The thought crossed her mind that she was going to have this baby alone, and she had no idea what the hell would happen if something went wrong.

She couldn't find her mobile to call Joe so he could get her to the hospital. By the time he came in for lunch, Danni was squatting on the kitchen floor, alternating between grunting and screaming.

His shocked then panicked face stared at her. 'What do I do?' he shouted uselessly.

'Call a fucking ambulance,' she said through gritted teeth, but in the end, Mia had been born right there on the kitchen floor. The ambulance arrived twenty minutes too late, its siren wailing, cutting through the quiet day, broken only by the mewling of their new born daughter along with it.

Danni looked down at her swaddled daughter, her heart swelling with pride and love. She had laboured to bring this beautiful little girl into the world. Had carried her for nine months and had looked forward to meeting her. Joe had been excited too, touching her belly all the time, bending down to kiss his unborn child goodnight, then standing up to kiss Danni on the lips. It was sweet and life was good.

Danni looked up from her seated position where she cradled the baby to her breast and said, 'Isn't she just the most precious thing you've ever seen?' She was in awe of her baby, which they had agreed to name Mia if she was a girl, her soft skin, the half-narrowed eyes that made Danni think she was scrutinising her surroundings, the small sucking sounds she made when Danni fed her.

He stared down at her. 'I kinda wanted a boy.'

His words cut her to the core. There was nothing else he could have said in that moment that would have been worse. Even finding out he'd slept with her sister had nothing on those few muttered words. Despite loving him, she would never forgive him for those five devastating words.

9

That particular day had started with Danni layering makeup on a blackened eye, given to her by her sister the night before. One of many from Beth. It wasn't the first time and it wouldn't be the last. Danni should have taken the day off, but she had an English exam. She waited patiently at the end of the driveway for Joe to take her to school.

She saw his car coming down the road and pulled her long hair further over her eye in an attempt to hide what Beth had done to her. He leaned over and opened the door for her and she slid into the passenger seat. She turned to face him, and immediately a look of horror crossed his face.

'Fuck, what happened to you? Who hit you?'

'Who do you think?' she asked sarcastically. 'Don't worry, it only hurts when I touch it, or you know, move my face at all.' She tried to make light of the situation. She had tried to fight back, protect herself, but Beth had been stronger and quicker than her.

'Right, this is getting beyond a joke, I'm going in to talk to her.' Joe turned and put his hand on the door handle.

'Don't, please. It will just make it worse for me. Please, Joe,' she begged, a sense of urgency in her words. She laid a hand on his arm to calm him down.

He was furious. He wiped a thumb under her eye and took off some of the makeup.

'Leave it on, please. I don't want people at school to see it.'

'Honey, the makeup isn't covering anything. I'm taking you to the guidance counsellor's office and she can help you, okay?'

'No. It'll just get me in more trouble. You don't understand. She'll kill me. I'm serious, one day she's going to kill me, I'm not even kidding.'

'All the more reason to get out now. Okay? Let me help you.' What he said made sense, but Danni admitted to herself that she *was* scared. Telling someone, a teacher, a police officer, made it real and she'd spent so long hiding it.

Danni turned back to face the front and said nothing, but by the time they had driven to school and she had fixed up her makeup, smoothing the foundation out with shaking fingers, she was coming around to his idea of getting help. She was a few months shy of eighteen, so she still had to stay at home a little while longer. Danni lived in constant fear of what Beth might do to her before she got the hell out of there.

As they pulled into the car park, she whispered, 'Okay.'

'Okay? Seriously? All right, I'll set up a meeting with the guidance counsellor today.'

Later that day, she was pulled out of class and it began. Danni honestly didn't remember much of that day. Danni didn't go home after confessing to the guidance counsellor, in fact, she didn't go back ever again. Finally, something to be thankful for. She told her story to the guidance counsellor and the welfare agency got involved from there. She knew her parents and Beth were interviewed. They all lied through their teeth, of course, saying she was clumsy and had injured herself. But Danni went for medical testing later that week which included X-rays, showing healed fractures in her ribs, wrists and fingers, which proved the abuse that Danni had confessed.

The following few days were a blur. She was put into a group home where she would stay until she was of age to leave. Joe was there for her every step of the way, offering support and love. Danni realised he must have really loved her to stick by her through all of this drama. The bruises faded, her parents weren't around to ignore her any more and, best of all, she didn't have to flinch every time she walked into a room the way she did at her house. Danni began to walk taller now she wasn't constantly waiting for an attack, she slept better, she no longer needed the safety of a knife under her bed. She may now be in a group home, but she was away from her family at last.

Three days after she was entered into the foster care system, she was walking to class at school, going down a flight of concrete stairs when someone pushed her from behind. She reached for the metal railing and her hand jammed between it and the concrete wall, jarring her to a halt. Her wrist throbbed in response.

'Hey sis, how you doing?'

Danni glared up at her as she massaged her jarred wrist, the air slowly returning to her body. 'You're not supposed to come near me,' Danni warned, looking up at her from the ground.

'Oh, is that right?'

'You're just sorry you don't have power over me any more,' said Danni, feeling brave, but they were alone, Beth could do anything to her.

'Oh yeah?' her sister said, walking down a few stairs. 'I still own your ass, Danni, make no mistake about it. You're mine to do with what I want; you always have been and you always will be.'

Trying not to wince at the pain in her wrist, Danni held her head high as she walked away. It wouldn't be the last time Beth would hurt her, she was sure of that.

* * *

The group home where she'd stay until she was able to be fostered out was a shit hole. Danni couldn't have put it any plainer. The chance of her being chosen to go and live with a family were slim. She wasn't a cute baby, she was almost eighteen, families weren't going to want her.

But there was something more sinister going on, something which came to Danni's attention very quickly. She was walking down a hallway, a little lost, when she happened to come across a tall red-haired girl talking to a small girl with mousy brown hair. As she got level with them, she could see that the younger girl's tear-streaked face begged for help. She couldn't ignore her. Not after what she'd gone through.

'Are you all right?' she asked the young girl.

'None of your fucking business,' snarled the large redhead, who was standing over the younger girl. Danni had just started a war, one that yet again she wouldn't win.

Her name was Anne. For a few days, all was silent. The young girl, Chelsea, came up and introduced herself, thanking her but telling her that she shouldn't have interfered, that it would be worse for both of them now, and she wasn't wrong. Two days after Chelsea delivered her prediction, it came to fruition.

Danni was in the bathroom taking a shower, alone. She had just lathered her hair and was rinsing it off when her legs were swept out from beneath her. She hit the tiles, face first. Immediately, she felt the hot blood leak from her nose. She didn't think it was broken but it hurt like a bitch. The blood ran into her mouth and she spat it out, choking.

'Jesus, Anne, don't fuck her up too much,' commented one of her assailant's friends in a high-pitched stressed-out voice.

'I want to make it clear to this new bitch that this is my place. I run the show here. You got that, *bitch*?' she asked Danni, bending down so she was right over Danni's face.

Suddenly Anne merged with Beth and she felt a surge of anger well up within her like wildfire. Her mind went blank and she raised her head with speed, smashing it into Anne's nose. The bigger girl started screaming, drawing the attention of one of the carers who came running at the sound of wailing. She took in the scene at once, instantly knowing what had happened and who had started it. She saw Danni naked on the bathroom floor, blood dripping from her nose.

'Finally someone stood up to you, eh, Anne?' the carer said.

Later that day, her case worker informed her that, 'For your safety, we've found an interim family that will take you straight away. I don't think it's a good idea for you to be here any more. Anne is a bully who will seek retribution and we can't watch you twenty-four hours a day, we just don't have the staff. I don't want to see that to happen to you again,' she added kindly.

Danni just stared at her, not saying a word. Yet again, she was being shifted to another place that probably didn't want her either. Joe seemed like the only bright spot in her otherwise bleak life.

'Look, you seem like a good kid who's had a raw deal in life,' she continued. 'I read your file. It's pretty nasty. I understand you're still attending the same high school as your sister. How's that going? Has she tried to contact you?'

Danni thought back to the incident on the stairs, but shook her head no. If she moved schools, she wouldn't see Joe any more.

'She hasn't come near me,' she said, absently touching her wrist that was still sore from her fall.

'Okay, good. Now, about this family. They're nearby so you can walk to school from the house. They have one son, he's fourteen and sweet as pie.'

So was Beth, around others. But Danni smiled politely.

'They're called the Johnsons, nice couple, they've taken in a few teenage kids before and it's worked out well for everyone concerned. I'm going to take you to their house straight away.'

Would she stay at this place for a while? Would it be home? Who knew?

10

Mia Brooks was a carbon copy of her mother. Tall, lithe, dark hair which she wore just below her shoulders and deep chocolate eyes that were almond shaped. A beautiful girl, well-mannered but shy. Despite her good looks, she wasn't popular. She had never had the desire to be one of the 'it' crowd, and they had never accepted her anyway. Jane was her best friend, her only confidant in the entire world. She used to speak to her mother about stuff but lately she had been off the charts weird, happy then distant the next minute. So Jane kept her secrets, of which there weren't many.

Mia was called out of English class one morning to go to the principal's office. When she arrived, she saw a good looking boy standing by the front desk looking a little lost. She walked over to him and quietly said, 'Are you okay?' She gave him a warm smile; it was obvious he was new to the school.

'Are you Mia Brooks?' he asked, his voice deep, his smile matching hers. A camera hung around his neck. He placed his hands around it and brought it up to his eye, snapping a photo of Mia.

'What are you doing?' Mia asked, a frown on her beautiful face. 'I don't like my photo being taken.'

'I'm sorry,' he said, lowering the camera, 'it's just what I do and you're so photogenic, so beautiful.'

'Ah, Mia, I see you've met our new student, Oliver Marks. I'd like you to show him around,' said the principal, smiling. Oliver smiled at her too.

Mia had a feeling, a bubbling sensation in her stomach and not in a good way. Something wasn't right here, yet she turned and began to walk away, hearing the footsteps behind her. He was following her, too closely. She stopped suddenly and turned, seeing him mere inches from her face.

'What are you doing?' she demanded.

'Just following you, Mia.' He flashed that winning smile at her again.

Her stomach roiled, like something heavy sat in there. She turned back and kept walking, Oliver following, giving her slightly more space this time.

Mia gave Oliver a quick tour of the school, much faster than she'd done in the past. Usually she took the time to take the new kid to assembly so they could get a sense of what the school was about. She skipped this part, though, wanting the tour to end. She introduced him to some of his teachers and after taking a look at his class schedule, her heart sank. He was in many of her classes.

Damn it!

She couldn't put her finger on it, but she didn't want to be around the good looking new boy. On the tour, he caught the eye of many of the girls, but instead of being distracted by them, he kept asking her personal questions.

'Are you from here? Where do you live? What do you do for fun? Do you have a boyfriend?'

Over and over, question after question, it was driving her mad. 'And that concludes our tour,' Mia said as they arrived back at the principal's office. She looked at his timetable one last time. 'You have English next period, remember where the building is?'

'My memory isn't so good. Think you could walk me to my class?' She didn't want to. Every part of her wanted to say no. He creeped her out. There was no way she'd be hanging round this guy ever again.

She was a good student, maintaining an A average, which her parents were proud of her for and rewarded her for. She was hoping to keep it up so next year, when she got her learner plates, they would buy her a car. Then she wouldn't have to catch the bus all the time.

Unfortunately, as the weeks passed, Oliver developed a real fixation on her. It made her uncomfortable, but she didn't know how to get him to stop. He always chose the seat behind hers in class. She would sit there, knowing his eyes were on her, boring a hole into her skull. Her concentration went right out the window. When called on in class by Mr Simmonds, the maths teacher, she couldn't recall the question, let alone the answer. Her tests scores gradually slid lower and eventually her teacher began to notice. Mr Simmonds kept her back after class one day.

'Mia, is there anything going on?'

'No, sir.'

'Maybe there's something going on at home that you want to talk about?'

You mean besides the fact that I'm depressed and scared, and my parents couldn't give a shit?

'I hope one day in the future you'll feel comfortable enough to come to me,' Mr Simmonds said.

Mia appreciated his offer to help her, but she couldn't talk to anyone about this right now. She walked out of the classroom and immediately saw Oliver standing near the lockers, taking a photo of her. Mia stalked over to him as he watched her coming, smiling.

'What is wrong with you?' she asked loudly, students turning to stare at her.

'Nothing. What's wrong with you, Mia? You seem stressed.' He continued to smile.

'Because of you!' she shouted, her voice echoing down the hallway.

'How about you just calm down a bit, Mia,' Oliver said, touching her on the arm.

She jerked her body away from him. 'Don't touch me,' she said through gritted teeth. 'And stop taking my photo.'

'I'm a photographer, besides I'm the official photographer for the yearbook now. I'm taking lots of photos of everyone, not just you.'

Mia felt her eyes well with tears, this was not going as she had planned. She had started out so strong, but he was wearing her down, twisting her words, twisting the story.

'I think you really need to chill out, you're acting like I'm paying way too much attention to you, and I'm not. I thought we were friends, you showed me around and were so kind to me.'

Mia's lip began to tremble. She knew that any moment she was going to cry.

'Come here,' he said, pulling her into an unwanted hug.

She pushed away from him, horrified that he had dared touch her. That she had let him touch her. Stifling her tears, she walked away from him quickly.

Mia ran to the nearest toilets and managed to hold in her tears until she had locked the stall door. Bawling, she ran her hands through her hair, chewing on a chunk of her hair, a habit she'd inherited from her mother. Thinking of her mum made Mia cry even more. How could they not see what was happening with her? Her grades had plummeted, she wasn't eating much, and she was so stressed. She pulled out some toilet paper, blew her nose then wiped her eyes coming out of the toilet stall. Looking in the mirror, her face was red and blotchy, but there was nothing she could do about that. She tucked her hair back behind her ears, smoothed down her dress and opened the bathroom door.

He was waiting there for her. Mia gasped as he grabbed her shoulders, pushing her back into the bathroom. He stood in front of the door, blocking her exit.

'What... what do you want?' She stuttered.

'I just want for us to be friends,' Oliver said, smiling broadly.

'I don't want to be friends with you. You're insane. Stop stalking me!' She gathered up her courage and barged past him, his laughter trailing out the door behind her. Mia ran down the hallway, sweat pooling at the bottom of her back, slick and cold. She wanted to go home and tell her mother, but they were in such a weird place with each other that she felt she couldn't. Oliver was her problem, and her problem alone.

11

Walking down the hallway, she checked that no one was behind her. Her drink bottle was empty and she needed a refill, but to use the water fountain was a disgusting ordeal which required many moving parts. Usually she had just enough in her bottle to last her the day, but today, sports afternoon had really taken it out of her, hence the empty drink bottle.

After the whole horrible day of the worm incident where she had thought Julie was her friend, she had kept to herself even more, ensuring she stayed away from everyone. Her footsteps echoed down the hall, keeping her heartbeat company. She looked around, fearful, looking out for Julie or her friends.

As quickly as she could, she filled her bottle, willing it to go faster. Finally finished, she turned around, only to find Julie and her friends standing in front of her. How did they get there so fast? How did she not hear them sneak up on her? They must have been hiding, waiting to pounce.

'Hey there,' said Julie, flipping her long thick hair over her shoulder.

Her insides turned to water, how the hell was she going to get out of this?

'Where are you going?' Julie asked.

'I... I just needed to fill my water bottle. I'm going back to class now.' She looked down at the floor, willing it to open up under her, swallow her whole.

'Hmm, I have something better in mind.' Julie cocked her head to the side and her two friends lurched forward and grabbed a hold of each of her arms. They began dragging her down the hallway. She took in a series of short, shaky breaths, unable to even scream she was so scared.

She had no idea what was going on. Where were they taking her? Then the lockers loomed ahead of her and she knew what they were going to do to her. She was claustrophobic, her throat beginning to close over at the thought.

Julie ripped open the locker and her friends shoved her inside, slamming the door shut behind her. Immediately she banged on the door, the sound echoing out through the hallway and back into the locker. If she kept banging, people would come, wouldn't they? They would laugh at her. She stopped banging, stayed perfectly quiet instead even though her heart was racing so hard she thought she was going to have a heart attack.

'Hey, you comfortable in there?' asked Julie, rapping on the locker. It reverberated, the noise crashing around the small space in the locker and inside her head. She put her hands up to her ears, but it was no use. She waited until it was over.

She stayed stone still and very silent. She looked at her watch, the hands glowing in the dark. An hour, two hours passed. She had pins and needles in her feet, her legs feeling heavy and dead. She wondered if Julie was still out there, waiting. After three hours, she began to need the toilet. After four hours, she was desperate.

She shifted her feet, which were numb. When she moved, she rebounded off the side of the locker, moving from side to side.

'So, you're still alive in there?'

She froze at the sound of Julie's voice. The bell had just sounded for the third class that she had been stuck in there. Julie had gone to class knowing that she had left her captive in the locker. She swallowed hard. Maybe she should have tried to leave earlier, but what if the door was locked? If Julie found her gone, she'd suffer much worse.

'I need to go to the toilet, please let me out,' she begged, hating herself for it. The whine in her voice was evident, even to her but she couldn't help it.

'No. I don't think I will.' She could hear the laughter in Julie's voice. The sniggers from other people. Julie's friends, no doubt. Maybe there were more people out there, standing quietly in the wings. What if there was a crowd waiting, waiting for her to crack?

She felt her bladder reach the point of no return. The piss ran down her leg, soaking the front of her school dress, hot and steamy, pooling in her shoes. There was nothing she could do about it. She held back the tears that threatened to overwhelm her. She was horrified, humiliated, and most of all, she could smell herself. She could hear it dripping under the door, no doubt pooling on the floor in front of the locker, shaming her. Her face burned with embarrassment.

'I can smell you from out here, you little piss ant,' Julie cackled.

She heard the lock on the door open and suddenly sunlight flooded the locker, blinding her temporarily. She put a hand up to shade her eyes from the harsh florescent lights in the hallway.

Then it started. A single laugh. High-pitched and full of teasing, then one by one, it was followed by a chorus of voices until she could hear nothing but laughter, directed at her.

'She pissed herself!' screamed Julie above all the voices. She had been set up yet again. She went to move out of the locker, to run down the hall, to escape the humiliation which she knew she'd never live down.

'Stay there,' demanded Julie. She pulled out her mobile and snapped a pic of the large wet patch on the front of her dress. She was beyond mortified.

'Julie...' her friend said.

'I think she's had enough,' said the other girl, the one who'd looked remorseful at the worm incident. Now she looked downright uncomfortable.

'You want some too?' Julie asked her friend, who shrank back. 'Okay, you're right, I guess I've proved my point. She's such a loser.'

Julie walked away, her friends trailing her, one by one. Some looked

embarrassed for her, some outright laughed at her. She just couldn't
catch a break. Julie clearly had it in for her, there was no doubt about
that, but she couldn't figure out what she'd done to provoke her. If she
knew, she'd try to fix it. School was pure torture, torture that was never
going to end, not unless something changed.

12
———

Danni put her head against the cool window, watching as the houses rushed by. As they drove along, her case worker told her a bit about her new foster family. 'Michael and Michelle and their son Andrew Johnson. Great people, very caring of their wards. You'll be well looked after. You have your own room and no one will hurt you there, I promise.' She turned to smile at her, and Danni managed a weak smile in return. She wanted to get a feel for them herself, she didn't trust anyone any more. She had been burned too many times. Really, how much more could she take?

They pulled up to the house. It was neatly maintained, a brick house with blooming flower beds bordering a concrete pathway. Danni thought it looked nice enough, but she knew looks could be deceiving. Joan, her case worker tasked with getting her settled into a new home, rang the doorbell. It was opened by an older lady with short curly hair who she assumed must be Michelle.

'Oh, you must be Danni!' the lady said, excitedly ushering her inside the house. Joan followed and was pulled into a hug by the woman. Then she grabbed Danni and hugged her too. It was the nicest contact she'd had with another woman in her whole life, and for a moment she let herself be hugged before she gently pulled backwards.

'Nice to meet you, Mrs Johnson,' Danni said politely.

'No need to be so formal here, I'm Michelle, and this is my husband Michael,' she said, gesturing to the man who'd walked up behind her. He immediately went over to Danni and put out his hand for a handshake. At least he didn't try to hug her too. She didn't think she could handle two hugs in one day.

'Hi, I'm Danni.' She tried on a smile. This was where she was going to live for the next few months, so she should make an effort.

'Nice to meet you, Danni. Andrew!' he called out.

A teenage boy ambled into the entranceway. He stopped when he saw Danni, eyes wide, and mouth open. Danni's soul shrunk a little bit. She knew that look. If he developed a crush on her, would that become a problem? Could or would he make her life here difficult?

'Let me show you to your room,' Michelle said, flapping her hand towards the hallway. The room was plain and simple, but it was enough, it was hers. She would be safe here. 'Come say goodbye to Joan and we'll get you settled in.' Danni went to say goodbye to her case worker, who was talking to Michael.

'Well, Danni, this is it until next month. I'll pop in and check on you. Now you've got my number, so call me if you need anything. Okay?' she asked cheerfully, knowing that her obligation had been fulfilled. Danni had been neatly tucked away and she didn't have to think about her any more.

13

The motel room was dank. There was no other word for it. It was the only motel in town, and their room was dark, with only one small window at the front that looked out onto another building. It had a smell to it that Danni couldn't identify, and beds so lumpy they put a bowl of porridge to shame. She couldn't imagine her and Mia staying there for a month, maybe longer. She swallowed with difficulty. She couldn't afford to be choosy, but she couldn't help but compare this horribly depressing motel to her comfortable, airy, farmhouse that was full of love. How could Mia be expected to recover here in this godforsaken hellhole of a place? She couldn't help but think that Beth had chosen this place deliberately. Punishing Danni, and, by extension, Mia. She could have sent them to the next town over, not made them sleep in this shit hole.

There was no food in the room, so Danni and Mia caught a taxi to the supermarket where they purchased some essentials and then a taxi back to the motel again. Danni refused to call it home. Home had burnt down to the ground. They arrived back at the motel and Danni had just finished putting the food away in the tiny bar fridge and the dry food on the dresser when there was a knock at the door.

Surprised, Danni opened it cautiously, the chain still firmly anchoring the door to the door frame.

'Excuse me, Miss Brooks?' asked the front desk clerk.

'It's Mrs,' she whispered, pain flooding her body. Was she still a Mrs when she had no husband?

'Sorry. Mrs Brooks?'

'Yes?' she said, already weary of the conversation.

'Well... someone left some stuff for you at the front desk, thought you might need it straight away. Been waiting for you to come back.' He nodded down at the two garbage bags at his feet.

'What's in the bags?' she asked suspiciously.

'Feels like clothing, Mrs Brooks. I guess the people round here found out where you were staying. Not that it was hard, only motel in town and all.' He laughed nervously, like he expected her to laugh with him.

Would she ever laugh again?

'Can I bring the bags in?' he asked, gesturing to them again.

'Sure,' Danni said softly as she slowly slid the chain along the length of its casing and gently let it go. It swung, knocking against the door frame with a hollow tap. She opened the door wider so he could pass through the bags. She didn't want him in there for long. It may have been a shit hole, but it was their shit hole.

'Thank you,' she said as he receded, and she closed the door and put the chain on again. You could never be too careful, could you?

Once she heard the young man's footsteps walking away, she turned to Mia. 'Looks like someone is watching over us,' she said to her silent daughter.

Danni put the bags on the bed, opened them, then upended them. There was a heap of clothes in there, clothes that she folded neatly into piles, patting them gently. Toiletries that she hadn't even thought about when she was at the supermarket, and surprisingly, a prepaid phone with a note attached to it.

Thought you might need this. I put one hundred dollars credit on it. Call if you need anything, Susan Patrick. She had included her phone number and email address. Danni added her phone number to her contacts in the new phone. She never knew when she might need help.

Danni held the note in one hand and the phone in the other. She was touched by Susan's generosity and thoughtfulness doing such a lovely thing for her and Mia. Danni figured that she should at least text her thanks to Susan, even if she wasn't up to an actual phone call. Susan Patrick and Danni knew each other through the fundraising committee at the high school. They'd had dealings a few times but they were by no means close. Danni looked over at Mia, curled up, on the other single bed, facing the wall, silent, unmoving. Mia was so still, she might as well have stopped breathing. Danni resisted the urge to go over to her and touch her, just to make sure she was alive. Instead, she turned away from Mia, unable to look at her any longer. Danni was incapable of crying but when she looked at her daughter, the pain etched into her face, the stiffness of her shoulders, her eyes brimmed with unshed tears keeping her emotions to herself. She couldn't fall apart, she had to mother Mia, to get her talking again. She couldn't heal if she couldn't talk about the... fire. Could she?

Danni cleared her throat and began to tap out a text message to Susan. She needed to say thank you. She needed... she needed so much that she couldn't say.

Dear Susan, she wrote, then deleted. It sounded too formal. But what was right in this instance?

Hey Susan sounded too casual.

She settled for:

Hi Susan. It's Danni. I wanted to thank you for the generous donations.

She couldn't write any more. Just writing that had taken its toll on her and as soon as she hit send, she collapsed on the bed, knocking over the pile of neatly folded clothes. She didn't even care, she just needed to sleep for a decade.

Danni was woken by a funny noise itching at the back of her mind. She thought it was Pooch, but then she remembered that Ryan had taken him back to his farm. Then the rest of it came back to her in pieces, like a kaleidoscope from hell. The burning house, the golden yellows and oranges of the flames licking up the back of her house, the ash that fell upon her head like dirty snow, the sound of popping and hissing, Mia's screams. As soon as she thought of Mia, she bolted upright, for a moment not knowing where the hell she was. Then she remembered. A motel. A horribly depressing motel.

It was dark, she had been asleep for hours. Danni fumbled for the light in between the two single beds. Finally, she found the switch and turned it on, worried that Mia might have run away while she'd been sleeping, but she was still curled up on her side. She had been sleeping even longer than Danni. She guessed shock would do that to you. She heard the noise again, which, upon waking, sounded nothing like Pooch. It was more of a chirp. Danni figured out that it was a text message and went searching for the phone on the crowded bed.

Eventually she found it under a stack of fallen clothes. Not wanting to wake Mia, Danni put the phone on silent and read the message.

Hi Danni, thanks for your message, I understand that this is a time of incredible grief and I am happy to help. If you need anything else, just text or call.

Danni looked at the time at the top of the phone. It was after seven in the evening. Time for her and Mia to eat some food, although she wasn't hungry and she guessed Mia wouldn't be either, but they had to eat to keep their energy levels up for the coming emotional days. She stood and turned on the main light. Mia stirred slightly, as if roused by the sudden explosion of light, even though the bulb was dim and covered in a thick layer of dust. She wanted to clean it. In fact, she wanted to disinfect the whole room.

Danni walked over to the second bed and gently touched her daughter on the shoulder. Mia made a mewling noise in her half asleep state.

'Mia honey, time to wake up. You need to eat and change your clothes.'

Danni went about making Vegemite and cheese sandwiches for them while Mia woke up slowly, as if coming back to the real world was the most difficult and exhausting thing she had ever done. Danni wondered if, in her dreams, her family was still alive. She balanced the plates in her hands and sat down on the end of the bed where it dipped alarmingly.

'Mia, come on love, just a few bites,' she coaxed.

Mia uncurled herself from her balled up position and turned her body to face her mum, crossing her long legs. She looked at the sandwich that Danni offered her.

'All I could manage was Vegemite and cheese, but I know you won't mind. You've never been fussy, not like...' her voice trailed off, as she was going to say Noah. Danni swallowed the lump in her throat. 'I'm sorry,' she said, watching the tears fill Mia's eyes.

Shit. She was trying to take care of her, not make her cry. Then Mia started to cry in earnest. She sobbed quietly and started rocking back and forth. This made the lump in Danni's throat grow even larger. How could she have been so careless? Angrily, she ripped off a bit of the corner of the sandwich, which stuck in her throat, before standing up and taking the two plates back to the top of the bar fridge where she had prepared them. Mia wasn't going to eat them now. She knew better than to try to reach out to comfort Mia physically.

Fuck!

She couldn't push Mia to eat. Maybe she'd try again later. Danni looked over at Mia, who was back to being a curled up ball. She stood next to the bed, looking down at the girl, who had her eyes closed, but Danni knew she wasn't asleep. She just didn't want to talk to her mother.

'Mia honey, I...' How did she begin? 'I want to hug you, but I want to respect your boundaries. I want you to know that when you're ready to talk, I'm here.' Danni bit her lip, hoping that she had said the right thing. She wanted Mia to be able to open up to her when she was ready. She didn't push her. How was Mia going to handle their funerals?

The funerals.

How was *Danni* going to survive them? Saying goodbye to her family? While Danni volunteered at both the primary and the high school, she didn't really have any close friends. Most of the time she felt isolated, she knew that she did this to herself, not wanting to get close to anyone in case they hurt her. She thought it was a hang-up over the way Beth had treated her, she just didn't trust people. Danni thought a lot of people might come to the funerals, as Joe was a popular figure around town and her two younger kids had lots of friends. Mia was reserved, like Danni was. Danni didn't know if she could organise the funerals, let alone face going to see all those people. The idea was daunting.

She sighed, the thought making her tired and agitated. She paced the small living space. She felt like she was in another place as she stared at the blank wall and thought about her family. How much she missed them. About her other children, Alexandra and Noah. She let out a strangled half-sob but swallowed it down, lest Mia heard it.

Then the thought came to her.

She would text Susan, her kind fairy godmother. Surely she would help. Danni picked up the phone and started typing a message to Susan, then she erased it, then started again, then erased it. Susan had offered to help, and Danni was in such a state that she was willing to reach out and ask for it even if it hurt her pride.

Just ask.

Fine then, she would. Danni tried again.

Hi Susan. I'm sorry to be asking this, I need help with the...

She mentally stumbled writing the words.

... the funerals.

Before she could change her mind, she hit send. What would be, would be.

Almost immediately, the phone chirped. She would have to change that text tone, it reminded her of the chirping cicadas outside her house in the summer. She couldn't handle that, and bit back a cry, remembering Alexandra and Noah playing under the sprinkler in the back yard to the sounds of the bush. They would play for hours under the spinning sprinkler, coating their backs with the silvery water, splashing each other and squealing with glee. Danni felt her throat constrict as a hand gripped her heart and wouldn't let go. She went to the bathroom, filling the small glass beside the basin with water, taking a small sip. She looked in the mirror, startled by her reflection. She had aged so much in just a couple of short, pain-filled days.

Biting back the tears, Danni looked at the phone in her hand with trepidation.

Of course, I'd be happy to help. I'll get started tomorrow. Danni, I can't even begin to imagine how difficult this must be for you, to plan the funerals for your family. I'm so sorry and of course I'll help wherever I can. I'll organise everything. They are in good hands.

Danni drew in a deep breath, then let it out slowly. She didn't know if she should be happy that the funerals would be planned for her or not. The thought of picking coffins and hearing people talk about her family as if they knew them made her break out into a cold sweat. But she and Mia had to go to the funerals, they just had to. She felt immense guilt that she had asked Susan to plan the funerals, but she knew it was beyond her and her focus had to be on her remaining child.

She knew she had to message Susan back, but her fingers didn't want to cooperate. Eventually, after sitting in the half gloom of the room for God knows how long, she tapped the phone.

I don't know when I'll get them back.

As she wrote it, she choked on her breath. Was that the right thing to write? She didn't know. She looked over at Mia, eyes closed, frowning even in her sleep. She began to twitch, so Danni walked over to her. Her eyes were shifting rapidly under her eyelids, her hands clenching and unclenching. Danni reached out and gently rubbed her arm, trying to soothe her daughter, but even in her sleep she jerked away from her, wanting to be alone.

'I'm sorry,' whispered Danni, moving back to her own bed. She wasn't sure what she was apologising for. The fact that she wasn't inside and didn't die with her family? She sat on the edge of her bed and thought about her babies, her husband. She had no idea how long she had been sitting there, but when she became aware of her surroundings again the sun was just coming up. Danni moved aside the dirty curtain and looked at the colours streaking across the sky. The blush of dawn captivated her for a moment. Her body protested at the movement, her joints popping from what must have been hours of sitting.

Danni thought back to hugging Mia after she'd escaped and kissing the top of her head. She'd smelt petrol; she was almost sure of it. Did that mean that the fire was deliberately lit? Had someone tried to wipe out the entire Brooks family? Who would do that and why? The police would determine if the fire was deliberately set. But surely no one would want to do such a horrendous thing.

* * *

While Danni watched Mia struggle against her own demons in her sleep, she thought about the problems that Mia had been having at school lately. Mia hadn't told her and Joe about them, it was only when another student told her mother, who then told Danni, that they knew anything was happening to their daughter at all. Mia was just seventeen, shy, like Danni had been, and smart. She didn't date, although her friend Jane was boy crazy. Mia just didn't seem to have any interest in that. She was all about her friends and school.

Danni smiled as she remembered overhearing a whispered conversation between Mia and Jane, in Mia's bedroom. She had been walking past and heard Jane say, 'He likes you.'

'How do you know?' Mia had whispered back, her voice sounding higher than usual.

'I just heard it around. Why don't you ask him out, Mia?'

There was a long pause before Mia answered. 'You know why, Jane. I just can't. Can we talk about something else?' Her voice had changed, she sounded almost scared.

Danni had been curious, wanting to know why Mia wasn't interested in dating, but she felt that it wasn't her place to ask her about it. Besides, then Mia would know that she'd listened in on a private conversation and there'd be hell to pay. Danni could already feel Mia pulling away the last couple of months, she didn't need to give her more of a reason to freeze her out. One minute she was fine but then the next minute she was sad, moments away from crying, and she couldn't or wouldn't reach out to her mother. Danni had no idea how to breach the wall she'd erected around herself. Danni felt out of sorts as well, losing time and finding it hard to concentrate. Once she even noticed that the petrol gauge on the car had gone down and wondered if Mia had taken the car out without a licence.

A few days after that, Danni had been in the store, stocking up on chips and popcorn for the family's Friday night movie marathon; they were planning on watching all of the *Back to the Future* movies, when someone had stopped Danni with a hand on her arm. The arm that was full of junk food, just barely managing to carry it all.

'Hi Danni, how are you?'

'Oh, Addy, sorry I didn't see you there, I have too much stuff in my hands. Should have grabbed a basket!' she said, laughing, juggling her items.

Addy quickly crossed the floor and picked up a blue basket from the top of the pile, handing it to Danni who gratefully put her goodies into it. It was then that Danni noticed the look on Addy's face. She looked... worried, upset, and Danni wondered if she'd done something to offend her. 'Addy, are you alright?'

Addy looked around the small store, as if she didn't want anyone to hear the information she was about to impart. There was no one near them. Even so, Addy took a step closer to Danni. Danni set her basket down on the ground, waiting.

'What's wrong?'

Addy was the parent of a girl who went to Mia's school. Not quite a friend, more of a classmate, but the mothers knew each other from school fund raising meetings.

'Addy?' Danni prompted again.

Addy looked uncomfortable. 'Look, I'd want to know if it was my kid.' She paused for a beat too long and Danni wanted to shake her so the words would drop from her lips. 'I've heard that Mia is being... harassed, stalked even, by a boy in her class. His name is Oliver Marks, he's new apparently.'

The colour drained from Danni's face and she felt her heart skip a beat. 'Stalked? Someone in Mia's class is stalking her? Why? How long?' she demanded.

'I don't know,' sighed Addy. 'I was going to call you but then I saw you. It was fate.' She looked around the store, her eyes darting from Danni's like *she* had done something wrong. 'I'd suggest talking to Mia, then going down to the school. Maybe they can do something about it. I'm sorry, I have to go. Good luck.' She turned and walked out of the store without buying anything.

Danni paid for her purchases in a daze, forgetting momentarily how to use her credit card. She tapped the wrong spot twice before eventually being told where to hold her card. She hopped into the car after putting her bags in the boot and drove home on autopilot. They lived out the other side of town. Their house would have been very grand in its glory days and slowly she and Joe were restoring it. Right now, it was the perfect house for their young family. All three of their kids loved being outdoors and playing in the bush behind the inside yard. Noah especially loved helping his dad with anything tool related and was his little shadow when he was home, which was less and less often, but Danni didn't have the brain capacity to dissect their relationship right now. She was thinking of Mia and how to broach the subject of this Oliver Marks and what was going on with Mia at school.

Danni drove down the long dirt driveway with no recollection of how she got home. She knew that wasn't good, but she had been thinking hard about things. Did Mia ever plan on telling them? Or was she going to keep this huge problem all to herself? She and Joe could help.

In a cloud of dust, Danni pushed open the car door and Pooch jumped into her lap. She gave him a scratch behind the ears before setting him back on the ground, his rear end making a puff of dirt waft around him. Danni smiled a small smile. Pooch was a funny dog and could always make her laugh, more than once she had found solace in his warm little body, his soft fur. But today she had something else to do. Grabbing the bags, she went inside through the front of the house, the wooden door snapping closed behind her and locking automatically. She added it to the ever growing list of things for Joe to fix. One day someone was going to lock themselves out of the house without a key, and knowing her luck, it would be her.

'Joe?' she called as she walked into the kitchen, putting the bags on the bench with a deep sigh. He didn't answer her, so she looked through the kitchen window and saw him playing under the sprinkler with the two younger kids. They were all dripping wet, laughing under the burning sun. Danni absently wondered if Joe had remembered to put sunscreen on their faces. She guessed it was too late now. Danni wondered where Mia was, but when she stood at the foot of the stairs, she could hear music blasting from her room. Probably studying, as usual. She was a great student, always bringing home good marks in all of her classes, although Danni had noticed that her grades had been slipping a little bit lately and she was picking arguments with Danni over nothing. Was she just being a teenager, or was it down to being harassed at school? It would certainly explain the change in her behaviour and mood.

Danni put the dips in the fridge and the chips away in the cupboard before walking out onto the back veranda and waiting for Joe to notice her. He didn't, he was too busy chasing Noah around and lifting both kids up under each arm, spinning them around so fast that even Danni felt sick just watching them.

'Joe!' she yelled as she walked onto the half dead grass to the edge of the sprinkler's reach. He turned at the sound of her voice and put both the kids down when he saw the look on her face.

'Uh oh, looks like Daddy's in trouble!' he sang to the kids as they squealed with laughter and pointed at him. 'Be back soon, kiddos.' He grabbed a towel from the deck chair and walked over to Danni.

'What did I do now?' he asked. Danni's hands were on her hips and her lips in a thin line.

Danni could read Joe like a book. She knew right now that he was running through his behaviour the past few days, seeing if he could identify where he'd fucked up. Maybe not coming home right after work? Maybe the distance he'd put not only between him and her but the kids as well? This was the first time he'd played with them in well over a week. It was nice to see and she wanted to comment but she knew it would come out accusatory.

'You didn't do anything wrong, Joe.'

He heaved a sigh of relief. 'Thought I was in trouble,' he mumbled.

'What's wrong? You look worried. Is it the kids?' Now *he* looked worried. He turned around and looked at Alexandra and Noah.

'Yes,' Danni said quietly. She grasped Joe around the arm and pulled him to the other side of the house away from Mia's room so she didn't accidentally overhear them if she came downstairs. 'It's Mia.'

Joe looked confused. 'What about her?'

'I was just stopped by Addy Jensen, you know Addy, she's Jessica's mum, you met her at the last school fundraiser.'

'Vaguely. Why, what's happened?' he demanded, all business.

'Addy mentioned that Mia was being harassed, stalked, by some boy in her class. A kid named Oliver Marks.'

'I'll kill him,' Joe immediately said, anger burning deep in his eyes at the mention of someone hurting his baby girl.

'Calm down, Joe, I think we need to take a moment, then go and discuss this with Mia. This is her life, but we do need to know what's going on in it.' Danni was so upset with the thought that Mia had been having a hard time and had been keeping it to herself, trying to deal with it on her own. It just wasn't right, yet she softened her face and suggested to Joe that he do the same and not go in there guns blazing, demanding answers. Sensitivity was better in this instance.

Danni could hear the younger two still squealing under the sprinkler. They'd be there until Danni turned off the water and another half hour or so wouldn't hurt them.

Danni and Joe went up the stairs, Joe stepping on the third top stair which put Danni's teeth on edge when it squeaked. Danni knocked on Mia's door then pushed it open. Mia was lying on her bed doing home-work and didn't hear the knock over her music.

'Mia!' bellowed Joe too loudly, it almost sounded like an accusation.

Mia looked over her shoulder, the look of fright lighting on her face for a brief moment, and Danni wondered why she'd be frightened of her father. Mia threw Joe a look that Danni couldn't decipher as he walked into the room to turn the music down.

'I was listening to that,' she said, calm and matter of fact, at odds with her look of fear moments ago.

'Honey,' Danni began, sitting on the end of her bed, 'we need to talk to you about something.'

Mia sat up properly and crossed her legs. 'I'm listening.' She sounded so grown up. Danni looked at her beautiful daughter who was fast becoming a woman. She could pass for a younger version of Danni. She even had a similar cadence to her voice and they shared the same sense of humour. Danni guessed that was why she was hurt that Mia hadn't confided in her about this boy, about her problems. Danni had found it hard to talk about the stuff with Beth too.

Softly and as delicately as she could, she said, 'Tell us about this boy, Oliver Marks.'

Danni watched as Mia's tanned face was leached of colour, leaving her wan. Her fingers began to twist around and around each other, her leg started to jig up and down, then she managed to pull apart her fingers, only for her to reach for a chunk of hair and put it in her mouth, chewing on the ends. She hadn't done that since she was a little girl, at least not that Danni had noticed.

Mia looked up at her father, arms crossed, towering over her. 'I'm sorry, Daddy,' she whispered. Danni didn't know what she was apologising for and why she called him Daddy, something she also hadn't done for years. She seemed on the verge of bolting from the room. There was tension in the air, but Danni had no idea why. It was as if father and daughter were at war, a silent war waged that didn't include her.

'Sweetheart, who is Oliver?' Danni asked.

She watched as Mia shrank in on herself even more. 'Nobody,' she said in such a quiet voice that Danni had to lean forward to catch what she said.

Danni tucked a strand of Mia's hair behind her ear and tried again. 'I ran into Addy Jensen today, Jessica's mum, she was told and then told me that a boy in your class named Oliver Marks was stalking you, harassing you. Is that true, love? We can't help you unless we know what's going on.' Danni reached out a hand to touch Mia, but she shunned her, pulled away then stared up at her imposing father who, thus far, had remained silent on the matter.

'He... he... I guess he's been bothering me a bit,' Mia stuttered.

Relieved that she had got her talking, Danni didn't want her to stop, she wanted Mia to open up to her. 'What things does he do to you?' Danni was almost scared to ask, who knew what went on in schools any more, even mid-sized ones like Mia's. The teachers knew most of the kids and some of their immediate families. The Brooks family were known to the teachers for all the help and time that Danni and, on occasion, Joe donated to the school.

'He just creeps me out,' Mia said, looking up at her father again, so that Danni was left wondering what was going on there. Yet another thing to ask Joe when she got a moment alone with him.

'How, baby? Be specific.'

'I can't. He said he'd hurt me if I told.'

This time Joe did say something, it was mumbled under his breath, but Danni heard it and probably Mia too.

'You need to tell us so we can help you. Make it better,' Danni said.

'He sits behind me in class and plays with my hair. He sniffs it. I hate that. We can sit where we like but, he's always behind me. I can feel him staring at me. He takes my photo all the time, even when I'm looking straight at him. He doesn't even try to hide it. My picture is all over the inside of his locker. He takes photos for the school newsletter, I'm always in it. Sometimes, he rides the bus home with me, sitting a few rows back, but I know he's there, I've seen him, he doesn't hide, he sits there, just staring at me. He doesn't even live out this way. Mum, he knows where we live. I'm worried he's going to show up here one day and hurt me. We're isolated and Dad's not here most of the time.' She saw Joe swallow, no doubt feeling the weight of his absence. The added stress it had put on his daughter.

Mia stopped to catch her breath and swipe away the tears that had started to form in her eyes. Danni reached out to her again.

'If you touch me, Mum, I'm going to lose it. Just don't touch me. Please.'

Not comforting her crying daughter was the hardest thing she had ever had to do, and that included fighting for her life whenever Beth attacked her. But she had to do as Mia had asked.

'He follows me from class to class and asks me to let him kiss me. He says one day he'll just take his kiss... and more.'

Danni could feel her blood pressure rising, fast. She wanted to find this tormentor of their daughter's, knock him to the ground, and put her boot on his neck, pushing down until she heard the sharp snap. She was shocked at herself that she could even think of such a terrible punishment for a child.

'You're scared of him, aren't you, Mia?' Danni asked.

She nodded weakly.

'I'll sort him out,' Joe said evenly.

'No. This has to be done through the school, no point scaring the kid, you'll just get into trouble. I'll make an appointment to see the principal as soon as I can. We'll get him transferred out of your classes, maybe banned from photography for the newsletter. There are things we can do, honey.'

'That'll just make him mad, Mum, he might do something even worse than just following me and scaring me. And I'm already scared of him. What if he touches me?'

'Then I'll put him through a wall, diplomacy can get fucked,' said Joe, face red with rage.

'How about we try it my way first, okay guys?' Danni suggested, trying to calm the situation, despite fuming inside.

They both nodded, Joe angry, Mia apprehensive.

* * *

He craved her. He couldn't wait to leave work early to go and see her. Joe worked as a bricklayer, currently on a job in the next town over, a huge house on the outskirts of town. It was going to be bloody magnificent when they were finished with it. Like something out of a magazine. Pity the owner was such a pain in the ass. He rocked up every morning throwing his weight around, asking questions and basically wasting Joe's time. Despite this, Joe loved his job, it was his escape, his way into another life that he loved living.

As Joe worked, laying brick after brick, he wondered why he felt the need to have these two realities. If he was being honest with himself, he had been drifting away from Danni for a long time. Somewhere deep inside him, he still loved her, but he thought maybe that was habit, not love. He wasn't sure and he didn't want to explore any further in case he opened up a box that he couldn't close again. He'd been with her since she was a teenager, things change, people grow apart, right?

He loved his kids, little Noah, his beautiful girl Alexandra and his baby girl Mia. Could he ever leave them? Because leaving Danni meant leaving his kids as well. But he had to be happy too, right? Didn't he deserve that? Didn't he deserve the life that he thought he should be living? Joe had spent a lot of time while laying bricks thinking about his life, his past and his future. He'd always been protective of Danni, he had been drawn to her vulnerability from the beginning, but was he expected to take care of her his whole life?

Being apart from his kids would kill him but sometimes pain in the short term is gain in the long run. He had a special connection with each of his children but Mia especially had always been his little girl. However, lately they had been drifting apart. It was his fault. He knew it. As he thought about the deteriorating relationship that he had with his eldest daughter, he gripped the steering wheel tighter. Thinking of Mia always made his blood pressure rise, his teeth clench and his heart stutter. He resented the fact that she was pulling away from him, but he and Danni were powerless to stop it. There had been something wrong with her for a while. She thought he didn't notice, that he was oblivious, but he did see and he did care. Now it all made sense.

Joe swiped a hand across his sweaty and dusty face, he didn't want to think about Danni and the kids right now, he had other, more pleasant things on his mind. *His woman.* He was headed back to town to see her. To wash the filth of the day from his face, to be loved, to be somewhere where he was wanted, needed, desired as more than just a father. The window was down, the air rushing across his face, drying the sweat from his manual labour.

His girlfriend (he loved calling her that in his head and couldn't wait to be able to say it out loud to everyone) was pretty much the only person he could be himself with. That person used to be Danni, but no more. His woman was sweet to him, caring and loved him for who he was. There'd been other women in the past, which he wasn't proud of. He hadn't been able to stay faithful to Danni and he wondered if it was due to the fact that he simply wasn't in love with her any more. He didn't want to break her heart, but he figured it was inevitable at some stage.

He pulled up outside her house, a smile already on his face, anticipating the warm welcome he knew he'd get, the stress-free existence of being with her. He pulled the key out of the ignition and grabbed the bunch of slightly wilted flowers from the passenger seat. He checked the street before getting out of his pick-up. There was no one around, so he hopped out and walked up the path, overgrown with weeds.

He knocked on the door and waited for her to open it. When she did, he smiled broadly. 'Hello, my love.'

14

The day after they'd first broached the subject of Oliver, Mia was very subdued when she came downstairs for breakfast. Danni had been awake half the night, pacing downstairs so she didn't wake everyone else up. She was trying to work out how to fix Mia's problem without making it worse, and avoid pushing Mia further away from her. Every plan she came up with ran the risk that Oliver would retaliate, but there was nothing else they could do, they could not let bullying and stalking stand. Their Mia was slipping away right before their eyes. She was upset or snappy, crying and moody all the time, and her schoolwork had suffered.

Danni offered to drive Mia to school since she was going there anyway, but Mia refused, presumably because she didn't want to be seen getting out of the car with her mum. Danni remembered her high school experience, well, until Joe had come along and changed everything. For a moment, she paused in the car and thought about how differently her life might have turned out had she not started dating Joe, had she not fallen pregnant with Mia. She would have left the town she grew up in and might not even have had kids at all. She could have lived in the city in some nice apartment. But she loved her life. Her life was here, her family was here, and she wouldn't change it.

Danni saw the school bus pull up outside the school and watched as Mia stepped off it. She slung her bag on her back and began to walk into school. Danni's heart swelled with love and pride. Mia was being victimised, yet still came to school every day, doing her best to ignore Oliver and keep up with her studies. Now she knew why Mia didn't date. It would be hard to trust boys after this. Danni was sad for her but remembered how she didn't trust Joe at first either. Sometimes she still didn't trust him. The thought flitted through her mind before she even had a chance to stop it, or to analyse it. *Sometimes she didn't trust her husband.*

Danni patted her hair and marched across the expanse of dead grass heading towards the principal's office. She didn't have an appointment, but she didn't care. She'd wait in the waiting room all day if that's what it took to see him and report this bullying behaviour.

And that's exactly what happened. First he was in a staff meeting, then a budget meeting, then back to back interviews with other parents who had appointments. The secretary who sat behind the desk gave her a mournful look every now and then and mumbled, 'He shouldn't be too much longer.' But he was always longer. Danni had waited patiently and was now waiting impatiently for her turn. Finally, he shook the last hand and ushered out the last lot of parents.

'Mrs Brooks, I understand that despite not having an appointment, you want to talk to me?' he said in a snappy voice, a frown on his haggard face. He was clearly miffed that she dared arrive without prior arrangement. She didn't much care.

'If you have time.' She knew it came out sarcastically but she was too tired to worry about it. She was annoyed. He had failed her daughter; therefore, he was part of the problem. Question is, would he also be part of the solution?

He motioned for Danni to sit down on one of the two plush chairs provided. She chose to stand, hands gripping the back of the chair so tightly that her knuckles were white with indignation.

He inclined his head slightly. 'What can I do for you today, Mrs Brooks?' he asked in a polite yet patronising way. His voice was confident and calm yet imposing, designed to make students shit themselves and parents to calm down. But Danni would not be calmed. She was pissed and she hoped it showed.

'Well, you can start by telling me why my daughter Mia is being harassed and what punishment the boy, Oliver Marks, is receiving.'

He steeped his fingers under his chin like a stereotypical bad guy. 'I'm not sure I know what you are referring to, Mrs Brooks. How about I call for Ms Jane Appleby, the guidance counsellor for Mia's year, and see if she can shed some light on the situation?'

Already he was distancing himself from the issues, putting it on someone else's shoulders. Principal Peterson picked up the phone and asked to see Ms Appleby. A moment later Danni heard the command over the loudspeaker. Command, not request.

'Won't you take a seat while we wait, Mrs Brooks?' He looked slightly uncomfortable at having a woman standing over him.

'No, I don't think I will, thank you, Principal Peterson.' She liked seeing his discomfort. It gave her power over him. Danni turned at the muted sound of high heels click-clacking over the tired lino floor. There was a light knock at the door.

'Come in,' said the principal with palpable relief. Danni's anger was taking over the room. 'Ms Appleby, please take a seat,' he said in a neutral tone, fingers steeped under his chin yet again. *It must be his power move,* Danni thought. Wouldn't help him here though.

'Ms Appleby, I'd like you to meet Danni Brooks, Mia Brooks' mother. I believe she is one of your students?'

'Yes, she is.'

Danni was not surprised by her breathy Marilyn Monroe voice. She was dressed in a dove grey pencil skirt, a tight white singlet, low-cut, and red lipstick. Danni wondered how appropriate her outfit was for a teacher but didn't say anything. She was here to fight for Mia and her right to walk around school and not be scared by some creep with a fixation on her.

'And Oliver Marks? Is he a student of yours too?' Principal Peterson asked.

Ms Appleby dropped her golden head, eyes lowered, then looked back up at him demurely. 'I know what this is about, and I have to say that in my professional opinion, this has been blown way out of proportion.' She smiled gently at Danni, as if Danni was a parent who'd be taken in by her excuses. Or her looks. Obviously she'd never come up against a mama bear like Danni before.

'And what exactly is your understanding of this situation?' Danni asked calmly. She waited for the guidance counsellor to speak.

Ms Appleby turned to face the principal. 'It's not what you think,' she began, leaning her hands on the desk, giving him an eyeful of her ample cleavage.

'Hey!' said Danni, folding her arms. 'How about you talk to me?'

'Oliver Marks is not the problem here.'

Danni was struck speechless for a moment before exploding, 'Are you trying to blame the victim of stalking and harassment here, Ms Appleby? Because that would be great as a headline on the news: *local high school protects bully.*'

'Now, now, Mrs Brooks, I don't think we need to go that far. I'm sure Ms Appleby didn't mean to imply that Mia had any part in this behaviour or encouraged it in any way. Did you, Ms Appleby?'

There was a pregnant pause and Danni swore she saw the principal's face fall.

'I want answers. Now,' Danni said, staring down at the woman who sat there, hands now folded neatly in her lap.

'All right, if you insist. Oliver Marks recently moved here, a couple of months ago, with his parents. He confided in me that his father is an alcoholic and there's abuse in his house. Mia showed him around the school when he first arrived. She was nice to him. Unfortunately, due to his lack of stable relationships, he... fixated on Mia and has been trying to have some sort of relationship with her ever since. She has rebuffed his advances.' The way she said it implied that Mia was a cold-hearted bitch for not accepting him into her life. There would be none of that.

'So, you're telling me that because he's had a shitty childhood, that he is allowed to take photos of my daughter without her permission, and follow her inside and outside school and frighten her to the point of not wanting to come to school? Did you know he followed her, caught her bus home and now knows where she lives? He's stalking her and you seem to think it's a harmless crush that hasn't been returned. Why is that?'

Ms Appleby stared at her for a moment. 'Well, if Mia would simply give him a chance.'

'Are you fucking kidding me?' Danni yelled, drawing the attention of the assistant on the other side of the glass. She glared at the principal. 'You endorse this kind of behaviour, from your students and your staff? Have Mia give him a chance? Are you fucking kidding me?' she repeated. Danni's blood was rushing around her body like a tsunami. Her face was flushed with rage and she didn't know how much longer she could share the room with the snotty Ms Appleby and her fucked up ideas. Principal Peterson now looked very uncomfortable.

'Now, now Mrs Brooks. Why don't I speak with Ms Appleby by myself, we'll work out what's going on and I'll call you?'

'He really does want to be friends. He told me so and I believe him,' the guidance counsellor said, making the situation that much worse.

Danni looked at her in disgust then glared at the principal. 'Fix this. Now.' Danni stalked out of the office, slamming the door behind her so hard that she was sure she'd put a crack in the glass. If he didn't call her with news that Oliver Marks had been punished in some way and her daughter protected, she would be royally pissed off.

Danni slammed the car door, her anger still not abated. She had more rage than she knew what to do with. She drove home, seemingly on wings, because she made it back to the farm in record time. Actually, she didn't really remember the drive home, so deep was her concentration on the problem. Her ability to lose time worried her sometimes, but she couldn't be self-absorbed right now, she had Mia to think about.

She needed to tell Joe what had been happening at the school. She unlocked the front door, putting her keys on the small table by the front door, handbag on the floor in front of the table.

The house was silent, no kids, no husband. She headed towards the back door. She saw Joe was on the phone, shoulders hunched while he spoke, his free hand was wildly gesticulating.

'Joe?'

He whirled around, an indecipherable look on his face. It took her a second to place it. *Guilt.* Like he had been caught doing something that he shouldn't. But what?

'You almost done? I've just got back from...' she said quickly, trying not to dwell on it. One problem at a time.

She was interrupted by Joe sliding an arm around her waist loosely, something he hadn't done in a very long time. It made Danni feel even more intensely that he was hiding something from her.

'What was that call about?' she asked, after she had decided that she wasn't going to ask. Yet the words came tumbling out of their own accord. She licked her slightly cracked lips and pulled her shirt around her, ruffling it up at her stomach even though it was still taut due to the work she did on the farm. Joe had changed over the years, too. His stomach rounder than it had ever been, yet she still found him attractive. She wasn't sure he could say the same.

'Nothing. Just a work deal that isn't going to go through. I guess I was just pissed off and letting them have it. Should have kept my cool, I think, alienating clients isn't a good idea.' Joe was the foreman where he worked, he ran the job site and she knew that this one had been particularly hard with the owner arriving almost every day to check on the progress and offer suggestions that were neither needed nor wanted.

Danni wasn't convinced, but she had other things to discuss and only a limited amount of time before the kids arrived home.

'We have to talk about Mia.'

'About the thing that you told me yesterday? The boy?'

She frowned. Had he cast it so easily from his mind already? 'Oliver Marks. Yes. I went into the school this morning, saw the principal.'

'God, Danni. How bad did it get?' he sighed. He was used to her passionate nature. Passionate or fiery, depending on the day, but she'd do anything for her kids.

Danni huffed out a breath. 'Are you saying that I have made things worse?' He looked away, but she grabbed his arm. 'Is that what you're saying?'

'No, of course not, I'm just saying that sometimes you can get overzealous about... important things.'

'The guidance counsellor said our daughter was asking for it and that she should just be friends with him, to give him a chance. Have a relationship with him.'

'What?'

'Still think I'm overreacting?'

'A teacher said that? What were they thinking?' Joe asked in disbelief. 'How can they say that? Do they protect bullies, too?'

'That's what I asked. Seemed like the guidance counsellor was on his side. I mean, who says that? Be friends with your stalker? Yeah, that'll fix the problem right up. Poor Mia, going through this all alone. No wonder she's been changing.' Joe's glance slid from her eyes to a point over her shoulder. He looked guilty again. What the hell was his problem?

This was the most in-depth conversation they'd had in months that didn't revolve around inane everyday things such as who used the last of the milk and put the empty bottle back in the fridge. Some days she felt like she was losing him, like a house losing its foundation, brick by broken brick.

'We'll talk to Mia tonight Danni, okay?' he said, dismissing her. He dropped an unexpected kiss on her forehead before heading back outside to resume his conversation. Danni listened at the back door to the much more subdued conversation. He was so quiet that she couldn't catch a word of what he was saying and he had moved further away. Probably for the best for now, she had too much on her mind to think about him and their marriage. Mia had to come first. The children always came first.

15

Since she had decided to embrace what they thought of her, she decided if she was going to do it, then by God, she was going to do it well.

The party was in full swing by the time she arrived, the bass crashing through the ribs in her chest, making her heart thump in time to the beat. She tugged on her low-cut top, showing much more cleavage than was necessary. It was held together by two pieces of black cord that criss-crossed her breasts tightly. Her jeans, so tight they looked sprayed on, worn down low on her hips, her pierced belly on show. She swung her hips seductively as she walked into the party. Everyone stared at her. The crowd parted for her. It always did. She saw people talking about her, not even bothering to hide behind their hands, no doubt wondering how she had the guts to show her face again after the last party. She did a loop of the room, grabbing a shot of vodka as she went, sipping slowly. She would get down to serious drinking after she'd found her mark. She stood in the corner, admiring and jealous glances being cast in her direction. She was used to it now, and it didn't bother her any more what people thought of her.

Taking a small sip of her drink, she saw a boy who was staring at her intently. He was in the same year as her but, for obvious reasons, they didn't travel in the same circles. There was lust written across his face, desire in his eyes. Eyes that slid from her glossy hair, down to her breasts, and over the swell of her hips and back up again to meet her eyes. She dropped him a wink and his eyes slid to the girl sitting beside him. His girlfriend, no doubt. Hmm, maybe he wouldn't be the one tonight.

She walked to her left out of the side door and into the yard, throwing him a backward glance. It was just as crowded outside as inside. They were talking about her out there too. She could feel their stares. It seemed that all the guys at the party were paired up. She slept with taken boys, whoever took her fancy. That would teach the girls to call her a whore. She was a product of their making. They were reaping what they sowed.

He followed her outside, just like she knew he would. They always did. They were so predictable, so easy to trap and manipulate, these boys. She walked to the edge of the garden, just out of reach of the blazing back garden lights. Some saw her go over there, shaking their heads, probably wondering if it was their boyfriend she was going to steal for half an hour of fucking. She waited and he came.

He walked in under the bush that overhung the archway. As far as spots went, it was secluded enough for what she was going to do.

'What's your name, handsome?' she asked, knowing full well what it was. Might as well give him the full experience.

His voice cracked a little as he said his name. 'Matt,' he croaked out.

'So... Matt,' she said running her fingers down his lightly stubbled cheek, 'Are you up for it? Do you want me?' She leaned forward and nibbled his ear, whispering, drawing out her words.

'Yeah,' was all he could manage to get out and even that was said in a broken voice. He cleared his throat.

'Okay then.' She kissed him deeply on the lips, her small teeth catching his bottom lip, pulling gently. He moaned into her mouth, his breathing shallow. He grabbed her hips and pushed her against the tree, fumbling with his pants.

'Don't tell anyone about this,' he whispered, like she was some dirty little secret, but he had yet to realise that people had seen him go into the secret garden with her. It was no secret now. The girl he was with would eventually come looking for him and find out that he was getting his knob polished by her. She'd be called a whore and he'd get away with being a stud for fucking her. Such was life.

She helped him unzip his pants, pulling down his boxers as she went. He stood before her, half-naked. He grabbed her hair and pushed her face towards his cock. On her knees, she began to suck, he groaned loudly, leaning forward, putting his hand on the tree, steadying himself as her head bobbed up and down, hand gripping the base of his cock, the other playing with his balls.

She could tell that he'd never had a blow job like this before. She couldn't imagine his prissy girlfriend on her knees in the dirt, cock stuffed all the way into her mouth. She may have been on her knees, but she had all the power. His balls tightened in her hand and she knew he was close. She pulled back.

'Where you going, sweetheart?' he whispered hoarsely, cock still standing proudly at full mast. She turned around and stuck out her ass, pulling down her tight jeans and her G-string, giving him the best view.

'Oh yeah!' he whispered, moulding his body to hers, hands cupping her breasts, his fingers pulling at her nipples through her lace-up top. He undid the laces, her breasts spilling out into his hands. 'Oh God,' he whispered into her neck. 'I shouldn't,' he said. But he did anyway. They always did.

She reached for his cock, guiding it to her tight centre, inserting the head of his cock into her wet pussy. He groaned as she backed up onto him. He moaned and seemed powerless to stop her. When he was balls deep in her, he started to thrust inside her. In and out. She had never felt so powerful. She could stop this at any time, but she didn't. She was enjoying herself too much. She forgot about the audience outside, waiting. She moaned loudly and he clapped a hand across her mouth, cutting off her noises of pleasure. She met each one of his thrusts with her own, knowing he was getting close again. She could see the feet of the people outside, no doubt ready to vilify her and do what they always did, call her a whore.

She didn't care, it felt good to have his hand in her hair, arching her back towards him. Suddenly, he pulled her hair tighter, pulled out, shuddered and came. She smiled. Her end goal was complete. His girlfriend had tried to shame her, now she had her revenge, and boy wasn't it sweet?

He wiped his cock on her ass. *Classy.*

'Don't tell anyone about this, okay?'

'No problem,' she said, knowing that there was a crowd of people outside who would have heard everything. She pulled up her jeans, retied her top and went out first, to a quiet audience.

'Whore,' someone mumbled in the crowd. Who the fuck cared anyway? She owned it, their words could no longer hurt her, no matter what they said.

'What's going on?' the girlfriend demanded, pushing through the crowd. She looked around.

'Where's Matt?' she asked, glaring at her, already knowing the answer.

'Zipping up his trousers, I suspect,' she said, smiling. 'He's good, yeah?' She smiled and walked through the crowd that parted for her again as she deliberately adjusted her top. She left the party; she'd done what she had set out to do. She had now humiliated them both.

16

'Don't look now, but your stalker is on the bus with us again today. Oh wait, he has his camera out. Taking candid shots of the object of his affection. Again. How romantic,' teased Jane. She turned back to Mia. 'What a loser.'

Mia turned to stare Oliver directly in the eyes. He didn't look away, so she did. There was no way she could confront him again. She would just have to put up with the creepiness.

'Why don't you just tell your parents? They can deal with it.'

'They know,' she said, looking out the window.

'They know? Your mum must have pitched a fit,' Jane said.

'She did.'

'Anyway, this is like the third time this week he's followed you home. He loves you,' she teased again. 'Just let it go for today and come over later.'

'Fine, but when they find my mutilated corpse dressed up in a wedding dress, I'm gonna say I told you so,' Mia half joked.

'You'll be dead, stupid.' Jane winked at her.

'Then I'll come back and haunt you. I'll make sure you never have a love life!'

'Okay, okay, I'll stop giving you a hard time.'

'Yeah, yeah. This is me,' Mia said, walked down the centre aisle, trying to ignore the click and whir she heard coming from the back of the bus. She was looking forward to going home where she could forget about Oliver Marks and just be herself, not be on guard all the time. His constant watchful gaze freaked her out. Some said that she should 'be flattered he is taking an interest in you', but she hated it. Hated him. He didn't approach her that much these days, just followed her and took pictures from afar and sometimes left letters or photos in her locker. Jane said he probably used the photos for his spank bank. Mia shuddered at the thought.

She got off the bus, saying goodbye to Jane who had one more stop to go, and turned to stare directly at Oliver. She wanted him to know she wasn't afraid of him. As she stared, he raised his camera to his eye, and took a series of photos. She gave him the finger, hoping he'd catch that, then she jumped off the bottom step and began walking down their long dirt driveway towards her sanctuary.

Why did this have to happen to her? What had she done to encourage this little freak?

Mia used her key to get in the front door. Her mum was kind of weird about security and doors being locked. They had bars on the ground floor windows, for goodness sake. You'd think they lived in a bad neighbourhood where people would rob you for your shoes, not the edge of a sleepy town. Sighing, she put her key back into her bag and began to unpack the myriad of shit that had accumulated in there, numerous and heavy textbooks, a squashed sandwich, pens without their lids and a random piece of paper that she didn't remember putting in there. She put down her bag with a thump and turned the paper over.

I will never leave you alone. You are mine. Tell anyone and I'll hurt you.

It was typed, but she knew who it was from.

'What the actual fuck?' she whispered to herself. How the hell had he got that into her bag when it had been inside her locker all day?

'Mia? Is that you?'

Who else would it be?

'Yeah Mum,' she sighed, 'it's me.'

'Can you please come into the kitchen?'

Uh oh, what had she done now? Mia folded up the note and stuffed it into her dress pocket. It wouldn't do for her mum to find it. She'd hide it upstairs when she went up to her room. She headed towards the kitchen but was suddenly attacked by two very wet, lycra-clad ninjas who appeared out of nowhere, attaching themselves to her body.

'Eww! You're all wet and cold!' She laughed at Alexandra and Noah. She loved these two little goofballs more than anything. Hugging them both to her so tightly that they complained, she released them back into the wild where they scattered, heading for the back door, which slammed in their wake. Smiling, she walked into the kitchen.

She stopped cold when she saw her father was standing there, arms crossed, watching her. *Shit!* What had she done now? As she was rewinding the tape in her head from the last few days, her mum spoke.

'Have a seat, honey.'

Mia didn't like where this was going. Her dad sat next to her, which made her a little uncomfortable and she was already feeling thrown off balance. 'What's going on?' she asked nervously, tugging on a piece of long dark hair, wiping it across her lips in fear. Mia glanced sideways at her father, a look that didn't go unnoticed by her mother. She was going to have to sort that out too one day.

'First things first, you're not in any trouble, okay? We love you.'

Well, that was never a good way to start a conversation.

Mia stared at her mother, tears welling in her dark eyes already. She glanced at her father, but he offered no such comforting words, merely stared at her. She looked back at her mother. 'Is this about Oliver? What did you do, Mum?' She felt the panic rising within, the fear and uncertainty making her fingers drum the tabletop, a move that didn't go unnoticed by her mum.

'Well...'

Mia narrowed her eyes. 'What did you do this morning when you went to school?' she demanded in a shrill voice. 'Mum, what did you do?'

'Don't speak to your mother like that,' growled her father. 'She's trying to protect you.'

Mia tried again in a more neutral voice. 'What happened?' she asked, hands clutching each other tensely.

'I went down to the school and demanded answers. Demanded to know why they hadn't done anything about the stalking and harassment, then I find out that your guidance counsellor knew all along and didn't report him, because he was having a hard time at home. Like that excuses his bad behaviour. Principal Peterson is talking with Ms Appleby and, in all likelihood, Oliver will be suspended for his actions against you. At least, I hope that'll be the outcome.'

'Suspended?' Mia said in disbelief. 'Do you know how much worse you have made this?' Her eyes were wide, fearful, glittering with tears and anger.

Her mother looked dumbfounded. 'Well, excuse me if I care about what happens to you. How has it made it worse?'

'Because he left a note in my locker that said if I speak to anyone else about this, he'd hurt me. Now he'll know that I told and I'll be in trouble, he thinks he has some weird sort of claim over me.' Mia put her head in her hands and refused to look at her mother.

'Mia,' Danni said, grabbing her hand, 'I'm sorry, but this has to be dealt with at a higher level. He won't be able to hurt you because he won't be at school, he'll be suspended.'

'And what happens when he comes back? He knows where I live, you know. Why couldn't you have just left it alone?'

'Then we'll make a complaint to the police.'

'Jesus, Mum! You just don't get it! I was handling it my way.' Mia pushed back her chair and stormed from the room.

* * *

Danni looked after her daughter, long gone now, then turned to face Joe, finding that he was already staring at her.

'Don't tell me you're going to give me a hard time too? I was doing what I thought was best.'

Joe scratched his whiskers, shot through with grey. He needed to shave and Danni longed to tell him so, but it would just end in another argument.

'Maybe we should have let Mia handle the situation her way, like she said. We – you – stepped in, and now it may be a bigger mess.' He stared her down until Danni looked away, tears dotting the corner of her eyes.

'I can't believe you'd say that to me,' she said, getting up and pushing down the tab on the side of the kettle until the blue light winked on. Danni stood by the sink, looking out of the window at her two youngest, waiting for the kettle to boil. She'd do anything for her kids, anything she felt was right, Mia was no exception. The school must suspend or expel this boy.

'Danni?' She turned at the sound of her name. 'No more, okay? Just leave it be now. I mean it.'

Joe pushed his chair back, making a scraping noise on the floor-boards. He was a big man so she thought he would have left gouge marks in the sanded and polished boards. She had tried to put a rug down but Joe had asked what the point of sanding the floor was if they were just going to cover it up. She saw his point, but the patch of floor under his chair was getting ruined. Danni walked over to the table, squatted down and looked at the floorboards. Sure enough, there were fresh gouge marks there. She bent and traced them with her finger. They were rough and she felt a small prick, a splinter, stick into the pad of her finger. She removed it then put her finger in her mouth, sucking on it gently.

Danni heard a squeal and walked back over to the bench to make her cup of tea. She watched Alexandra and Noah playing under the sprinkler again, beads of water clinging to their skin, catching the light so she was momentarily blinded. Once, they'd talked about getting a pool for the kids, but pools cost money to install and maintain. Watching the kids under the sprinkler made her think again it was a great idea. She couldn't talk to Joe about it, he was stressed about money as it was. Adding yet another big-ticket item to the list would surely push him over the edge.

While Danni was pondering the benefits versus the costs of a pool, she heard Mia's music turn on. It was so loud it reverberated down the stairs, all the way into the kitchen, breaking the happy screams of the kids. The walls shook with the bass and Danni sighed.

'God damn it!' she whispered angrily to herself, before stomping up the stairs, missing the third one from the top, out of habit. No one would hear it with Mia's racket. She had no idea where Joe had gone to, probably out to the shed to tinker with his pet project, a Holden Statesman, electric blue, or to make furtive calls on his mobile. Danni threw open Mia's door and stormed over to the docking station where her phone rested. She pulled it out and set it down none too gently on the dresser.

'Do you think you could use your headphones? I can hear that all the way downstairs.'

'What does it matter what I want, you're just going to do what you want to anyway,' Mia said sullenly, rolling over to glare at her mother.

So this was what it was going to be like from now on? Combative? Well, Danni could do that if it kept her children safe.

'For the last time,' Danni said, holding in her pent-up annoyance, 'if you'd just told us about this... problem in the beginning, perhaps we could have worked out a solution together.'

'That's it, blame me, Mum. I'm the victim here, you know.'

This time Danni did show her annoyance. 'I know that,' she snapped, instantly regretting it. 'But what's done is done. I expect him to be suspended any day now.' Danni whirled around and headed back down the stairs, skipping stair three. As she reached the bottom, the music blared from the open doorway of Mia's room. Bloody hell, this parenting gig was hard.

Danni went outside to check on the kids since Joe was still a no show. 'Having fun, my babies?' she asked, smiling at them.

'I'm not a baby!' shouted Noah, indignantly. 'I'm five!'

'Of course you are, honey. But you're always going to be my baby, right?'

Noah stopped running and pondered her question, a small crease forming between his brows. 'I guess so,' he replied cautiously.

'Well then, you're my baby.' Danni laughed then dashed under the sprinkler to chase him. He laughed and ran after Alexandra. Danni caught up to him easily, arms outstretched, moaning like a zombie. She picked him up with ease and snuggled her nose into his neck. He smelt of sunshine and clean little boy smell. She rained down kisses on him then set him back down on the ground. He laughed then ran away.

'What about you, Alexandra? Want to play chasey?'

'Mum,' she drew out the word. 'I'm too old for chasey.' Danni backed out of the sprinkler's range, now completely soaked.

'Fine, you're a big girl now, I'll leave you and your brother to it.' Danni went back inside, closing the back door gently. The screen door had a tendency to slam behind you if you didn't close it slowly using the heel of your foot. She walked back up the stairs. Halfway up, she saw Joe come out of Mia's room. He saw her standing on the stairs.

'Hey babe, what's for dinner?' he asked casually, before making his way over the squeaking stair, paying no attention to it.

She had thought he was outside. Was he talking to Mia about her behind her back? She walked into Mia's room and found her sitting on the edge of her bed, crying.

She immediately felt guilty. 'Sweetheart! I'm so sorry I did what I did. I won't do it again. Okay? There's no need to cry. I was just trying to help.' She tried to touch Mia, but she shrugged her hand off and threw herself onto the bed dramatically.

'You don't understand, you'll never understand. Just get out.'

Danni didn't know what to say, so she left Mia's room for the second time, heading across the landing to hers and Joe's room to get changed out of her soggy clothes. Mia slammed the door shut. The sound was final. There would be no more talking to her today. Danni had just finished changing when her mobile phone rang. It was sitting on the dresser where she'd left it after coming home.

'Hello, this is Danni Brooks.'

'Mrs Brooks,' came a familiar slick tone. 'This is Principal Peterson. Is now a good time to talk?'

'Not really, but it'll have to do,' Danni replied, feeling angry at him all over again, at herself just as much.

'I was calling to follow up on your complaint earlier today.'

'Yes?' she prompted when he stopped talking.

'I've made the decision not to suspend Oliver Marks.'

Danni was livid. The heat rushed to her face, and her previously chilled body was hot and itchy all over. 'And why not?' she demanded, her voice dangerously quiet.

'Well, we conducted an investigation, and due to lack of evidence and Ms Appleby's glowing recommendation, we have decided that suspending such a promising student was not in the student's or the school's best interests.'

'I see. And what about the safety of my daughter? Who's liable when he follows her home and stabs her one day? Are you going to be there, watching every move that he makes? If you're not going to suspend her, then I want assurance that Mia will no longer be harassed.' Danni was fuming, her pulse pounding in her wrists and neck. She could feel it in her ankles, such was her anger. A light sheen of sweat covered her face as she argued with the principal.

'I can understand that you are disappointed with the outcome, but so far, as far as we know, Oliver has not made any direct threats against Mia, nor has he hurt her in any way.'

'She is bloody well scared of him!' Danni yelled into her phone. Joe walked in, catching the tail end of her outburst. He turned and walked back out again. So much for counting on his support.

'Of course, we will monitor the situation closely.'

Danni hung up the phone in a blind rage. She wanted to scream. She had upset her daughter for what? Nothing. That's what. They didn't give a shit about Mia, all because some wannabe guidance counsellor had said he was a good boy, troubled, but that he'd never hurt anyone. Danni knew deep within that Mia was right, he'd hurt her, and she had to be there to protect her when he tried, but how? What could she do?

17

The bar was full of people, so packed she had to rub her breasts against both men and women to get to the counter. She wasn't eighteen but a good fake ID could do wonders. That and a great pair of tits. She'd sauntered to the front of the line, knowing that there were people from her class in there too. They had been organising an event for an eighteenth birthday, but she had conveniently been left off the guest list, so she'd just invited herself. The birthday boy was Thomas, the boy she had lost her virginity to. The boy who had put her on this path of so-called whoreism. She expected there were many whores there tonight, woman taking back their sexuality, but only she'd be vilified, as usual, and she knew it. She didn't care as she had a plan, one she was looking forward to enacting.

She waited, watching him. They couldn't see her, so crowded was the place. By her count, he'd had four rum and cokes, he'd be getting loose by now. When it was his turn to go to the bar, she sauntered her way over to him. She ordered a syrupy concoction that had a cherry on top which she popped into her mouth, crunching down on it, juice flooding her mouth. She'd taste delicious now, sweet.

Thomas stumbled up to the bar. 'Four rum and cokes,' he slurred slightly.

She bumped into him on purpose. 'Thomas!' she said in surprise.

He turned and saw who it was, recognition lighting up his face. 'Hey, how's this that I'm running into you tonight of all nights?'

'Yeah, what a coincidence. I heard it was your birthday and I wanted to give you a birthday present,' she said seductively into his ear, her breath tickling the hairs on his neck.

'Oh yeah?' he said, and she knew she had him hooked.

There was no hidden agenda here, no girlfriend who had wronged her, she just wanted to do her first, see how much had changed. She had certainly changed from their first tryst on the bank of the river. She remembered that day, and what followed, of course, but she had become what they said to and about her. Many of the bullies had paid the price, when she took and fucked their boyfriends. Some of them knew, some of them didn't, but it was all the same to her. Her work here was almost done. She'd be graduating school soon, she just had one more person to punch her card, then she'd be done with high school. Finally, she would get out into the real world, maybe even be someone else, meet someone decent. Was that even possible?

'What are you doing here?' he slurred into her ear.

'I'm here to give you your present. Don't you want your present?'

'Only if it's a fuck,' he laughed, joking around, running his fingers down her arm.

'Well, you're in luck then,' she smiled slowly.

His eyes went wide, as if he couldn't believe what she said.

'Are you serious?'

'How about you follow me outside?'

'But what about my friends?' he said.

'I'm not doing them, if that's what you mean. This present is for you only. You good with that?'

'Oh yeah, I'm good with that,' he said, winking at her. He turned, saw his friends were busy talking and left the drinks on the bar.

She grabbed his hand and drew him through the crowd, pushing through the people. Nothing was going to stop her now. She was going to have her seconds if it killed her. Once outside, the cold wind hit her square in the face. She had on her jacket now, Thomas dressed and ready to go.

'Do you live around here?' he asked.

'Nope.' She pulled him into the alleyway, threw him against the wall and started to kiss him.

'Oh, you filthy whore,' he whispered between kisses. There it was.

She undid his pants with practiced ease and lifted up her skirt. She wore no underwear, aware of what this night would entail. He pressed her against the brick wall and, without any foreplay, thrust his cock into her. She wrapped her arms around him, drawing him close, waiting for the ecstasy to envelop her.

She had had many partners since Thomas and knew how this would go. A fuck, then he would walk away, never to speak to her again and that was fine with her. Thomas thrust into her three or four times then suddenly went still and groaned.

What? He'd come already? That wasn't in the plan. That wasn't how a good fuck was supposed to be.

'You're amazing,' he said, kissing her on the side of the neck

She turned around and looked him dead in the eye. 'And you're not. Haven't you learned anything?' Disappointed, she pulled her skirt down in disgust and walked out of the mouth of the alley. She had the whole thing laid out in her mind, so why did he disappoint her? She was supposed to go out of high school with a bang, not a whimper. She wondered if she should have a palette cleanser before she went home. She looked down the line up of men waiting to get into the bar. Should she pick up one of them and have a couple of hours of fun? But what if it turned out to be another dud? She didn't think she could handle that again. She wondered how, in the years since they'd first slept together, he had not got any better? Learned any new tricks? Same old, same old.

In the end she decided to go home, alone.

18

Mia was nervous. Her hands were clammy, so she rubbed them down the sides of her dress, drying them. She didn't know why she was so nervous; she saw him every day. So why was she almost fearful of what was going to happen, even though it was innocent?

She found her way to the café, her textbook and a notebook tucked under her arm, searching for him. Where would he sit? What would he be wearing? Would he look different outside of school?

'Mia!' called a deep voice as she stood still, looking around for the man who the voice belonged to. Then Mia caught sight of him through the crowd, standing up, waving his hand above his head to get her attention. She saw women noticing him. The broad shoulders, the lightly stubbled and chiselled jawline, the tight jeans and the promise of what was underneath. She blushed at the thought.

Weaving her way through the crowd, Mia finally arrived at his booth. Comfortable and plush, it was the perfect, if not a fancy, place to meet.

'Can I order you a coffee or hot chocolate, Mia?' he asked attentively.

'No thanks, Mr Simmonds, I'm perfect.'

He motioned for her to sit and she took up a position opposite him.

'Well, that's not going to work, Mia. How am I supposed to show you the work with you sitting across the other side of the table? Come around this side.' He patted the spot right next to him and suddenly Mia's mouth went dry. She swallowed but all she could hear was a clicking sound. As soon as she sat down next to him, she poured herself a large glass of water from the jug in the centre of the table, draining half of it immediately before her thirst was quenched. Mr Simmonds looked on in amusement.

'Haven't been here before?' he asked, a cheeky, slightly lopsided smile on his face which left her wondering what he meant. Had she been to this café before or had she been in this situation before? Who knew? She distracted herself by rearranging her books on the table.

He took a sip of his coffee. 'You sure you don't want something to eat or drink?'

Mia said no, but her stomach decided right at that moment to grumble loudly. She had been so nervous this morning that there had been no appetite for toast.

Mr Simmonds smiled at her. 'We'll have a bowl of wedges with sour cream and sweet chilli on the side,' he told the waitress who had walked up to their table

'Thank you, Mr Simmonds,' she managed to get out.

'Mia, when we're not at school, I'd like you to call me David.'

Blushing deeply, she said, 'David.' It felt weird, wrong somehow, like she had stepped across an invisible barrier she hadn't meant to and maybe could never come back from.

She was sure David could feel her tension, as he began telling her a story about his early teaching career, one that was designed to make her laugh and relax her a bit. It worked. She laughed at the appropriate parts and did feel herself begin to calm down. *Just breathe.* She sat back into the chair, making herself more comfortable, sitting slightly closer to David.

Mia was feeling so grown up that she wished they could share a bottle of wine together. Shocked at herself, she tried to keep in mind why she was really there, but the heady scent of his aftershave, and the fact that he too had moved closer somewhere along the way so that his thigh now touched hers, had her caught up in the moment.

The waitress arrived with their food and put it on the table in front of them. She had also brought more water for Mia, who gratefully poured herself another drink.

'You know, when you mother first approached me about giving you extra tutoring, I was a little surprised. I thought she'd get some university student to tutor you. I'm a little bit more expensive normally but I agreed to give her a generous discount because you're my favourite student.'

'I am?' she asked, taken completely by surprise. Her eyebrows knitted together, even as her eyes screwed up, her mouth wide open. 'No, I'm not,' she teased, still not getting it.

'Actually, you are. You're a hard worker, you're polite to everyone, and you're easy on the eyes.' He looked at her directly as he said the last part.

Mia blushed deeply, the warmth spreading from her toes to her face. Surely he didn't just say that. Mia had had a crush on Mr Simmonds, David, since the start of the school year. She daydreamed about him, fantasised what it would be like to kiss those full lips, but she never imagined in a million years that he might have felt the same way. He was only ten years older than her, and that was nothing. She conveniently pushed away the thought that she was his student, and nothing could ever happen between them, but a harmless flirtation made her feel grown up. After all the nastiness with Oliver, someone desiring her in a good way would be nice, and even better that she liked him back.

All these thoughts ran through her mind with lightning speed as she was wondering what to do with the compliment. David took a sip of his coffee, watching her intently.

'Are you all right? Was that too forward?'

'No... I just... I just didn't think you felt like... that.'

'Why don't we change the subject for now?' he said, and she breathed a sigh of relief, her heartbeat settling back into its normal rhythm.

'So, why are you failing maths?' It was such a direct question that Mia found herself wishing they were talking about their mutual attraction again.

'It's not as easy as just failing maths. I feel like I'm failing at life.' She had never said that out loud before. She had thought it plenty of times, but never said it to another soul.

'Why on earth would you be failing at life? I looked over your academic scores and report cards before meeting you today. You seem to be a model student who is always willing to help out others, but then something happened, teachers noticed changes in your behaviour. You've become withdrawn, antisocial even. Do you want to tell me why? What's going on? Is there something happening at home?'

Tears began to fill her eyes. 'Yes,' she whispered. 'I think my parents are going to get a divorce. I think my dad is cheating on Mum, he's not nice to her, I know he loves us, but he is distancing himself, like he's getting ready to go somewhere.' Mia couldn't believe how much she was sharing.

'Have you talked to either one of your parents about this?' His concern was palpable, his eyes soft and probing.

'My mum lives in a dream state half the time. She's either loving and caring or all up in my face yelling at me. It's like she has a switch that is regularly flipped. I don't know how to talk to her any more.'

'And your dad?' he asked, crossing his legs, his jeans pulling tight across his crotch. She couldn't help but wonder if he had done that deliberately.

'Can't talk to him either, he's rarely home. Makes excuses to work late, comes home and I've caught a whiff of perfume on him before. That's why I think he's cheating.'

David reached over and covered her hand with his for a moment that was so fleeting she wasn't even sure it had happened. 'And school? Is your home life the only thing affecting your schoolwork?'

She looked at his beautiful face, imagining what it would feel like to touch the stubble on his cheeks, to run her fingertip gently along his full bottom lip, to inhale the woodsy scent at the hollow of his neck.

He watched her staring at him before giving her a lazy smile.

'Like what you see?' he asked, and she felt the heat building again, but this time it was between both of them. The heat of longing, of passion, of doing something forbidden.

'Yes,' she whispered, before clearing her throat and looking down, playing with the saltshaker. This couldn't happen, no matter how much she wanted it, and it was clear he wanted it too.

'There's this boy,' she began.

'Oh yes. A boyfriend, perhaps?' He was teasing her, mock jealously in his voice.

'No, the opposite. I gave him a tour of the school on his first day, and he hasn't left me alone since. He's been... he's harassing me.'

'How do you mean?' David, all business, sat forward, staring at her intently, waiting to listen to her tale.

'He follows me everywhere. I see him down the street, at the movies, on the bus going to my house. He's always taking photos of me.' She found once she opened up, she couldn't stop, it just poured from her. 'I'm... scared of him. He's grabbed me before, shoved me into the girl's toilets, I got past him, but I don't know what he would have done to me had I not got out.' This time the tears did come. She had been so stressed about Oliver and his stalking that she hadn't realised how much it had been affecting her until she talked about it. How stressed it was making her. Her hair was falling out, for goodness sake.

'We'll go see the principal on Monday morning,' David said immediately.

'My mum has already been there and done that. It made no difference.' She began to cry again and this time David gathered her up in his arms and drew her to him. Immediately her tears turn to soft sobs then stopped altogether, yet still she didn't move away and he didn't move away either. She liked being held by him. Safe, warm, enveloped. She felt safe. He rubbed her back, low down, over her shirt and she put her hands inside his jacket, reaching around his waist, emboldened by his touch. She never wanted to let go, and when he moved one hand, slightly raising the back of her top so his hand touched her bare skin, it was like a fire had been set alight in her soul.

Mia jumped, his hand falling away from her back. 'We shouldn't do this,' she said, leaping up from the table and walking fast from the crowded café, weaving her way in between tables and people. How she thought she could be with a teacher was beyond her.

19

Danni remembered that day so vividly, right down to the smell of chicken nuggets on her fingers, a snack for Alexandra and Noah after they had played outside, a favourite pastime of theirs in summer, in the sprinklers and exploring beyond the back yard, sun beating down on their heads so they came inside with burning scalps. She was going to make them wait for dinner, but it was still an hour away and she could see them staring longingly at the fridge. She had just hung up on Principal Peterson, incensed by his ruling on Oliver Marks. How dare he put her daughter in danger?

Danni looked over at Mia, still curled up on the bed in the motel. Danni knew she was awake, the change in her breathing giving her away, but she stayed still, turned away from her, staring at the ugly painted concrete wall. This truly was a depressing place, she had to get Mia out of here as soon as she could.

The knock on the door startled her. Danni didn't want to answer it. It was probably the motel clerk again, but honestly, she didn't want to see anyone. They knocked again.

'Mrs Brooks? It's Detective Shaun Jacobs. I need to talk to you. Please open the door.'

Danni had nowhere to run to. She was in a room with one way out and he knew she was in there. Slowly, Danni slid the chain across and opened the door a crack.

'ID, please,' she said, protecting her and her daughter. He could be a reporter, anyone, in fact. She couldn't just let him in, not when she suspected the fire had been deliberately lit. Their lives could still be in danger. The man showed her his ID and she stepped back, opening the door for him. His gaze was firmly on her. He looked past the unkempt hair, grey pallor and dark circles under her eyes. Her voice was croaky from disuse. It had been a week now since she had lost her loved ones and her home.

'Mrs Brooks.' He paused. 'May I call you Danni?' he asked politely.

She pondered this question for a long while before eventually nodding.

'Okay, Danni then. I have been assigned to your case and, in coordination with the arson squad, we have come to the conclusion that the fire at your house was suspicious.' He looked her directly in the eye.

'What does that mean?' she asked, clearing her throat so the words would get past the lump in her throat.

'It means that we are certain someone deliberately set the fire. There was an accelerant used. Petrol.'

Danni remembered the smell of singed hair and what she identified as petrol on Mia. She had suspected as much, and she was quite sure she knew who had done it too. It was all she had been thinking about.

'They tried to kill us,' Mia whispered from the other side of the room. She was lying down, facing the wall. Her usual position.

Detective Jacobs stared at Danni, not hearing Mia. 'Is there anyone that you can think of that held a grudge against you or your family? Someone who might want to hurt any of you?' He was intense, still staring at her, his gaze unwavering, waiting for her to crack, to give him a name.

She felt like she was being led to the slaughter, that she would get a bolt between the eyes at any moment. 'No. We didn't have enemies, Detective Jacobs. I don't know who did this. Is it possible that it was random?' She hoped he would say yes.

'There is a chance that it was a crime of opportunity. Do you remember anything out of the ordinary that night?'

'Well, I locked myself out of the house early the morning of the fire. I couldn't get back inside. Our dog, Pooch, was barking and howling, so I went out to see what he was going off at.' She was sure she had told him this before.

Detective Jacobs pulled out a small notebook from his jacket pocket. 'Did you see anything or anyone suspicious?'

'Honestly, no. It was dark and windy, anyone could have been there and I wouldn't have seen or heard them,' she apologised, feeling sweat beginning to pop out under her arms. She hoped he couldn't smell her fear, her lies.

'Based on the timing of the fire, early morning, we believe that the arsonist was intending on capturing you all in the fire. Also, the medical pathologist has come back with her findings.' She waited for his big reveal. 'Your children succumbed to smoke inhalation before the fire took hold.' She let out a pent-up breath of relief. 'But I'm afraid your husband did not,' he said quietly, respectfully.

'Thank you for letting me know,' she said woodenly, staring back at him with wet eyes, willing him to just leave them alone. 'I'm tired and I have things to take care of,' she said looking over her shoulder towards Mia.

He looked at her. 'Of course, Danni. I'll keep you up to date on the case.'

'Thanks. You do that,' she said, ushering him out the door. Once he had gone, she reengaged the chain. Not that it would stop someone determined to get in, but it gave her some measure of peace. She could at least sleep – well, try to, anyway. Every time she closed her eyes, she saw her home burning, her family, dying. *Smoke inhalation.* At least her children hadn't burnt to death. She felt the tears form behind her eyes but refused to give in to them. There would be time for tears after she found Oliver Marks. Once she had taken care of what needed to be done. Her family, their justice. Danni sat down on the bed and stared again at the wall, painted an ugly shade of grey.

She had no idea how long she had been staring vacantly at the wall, but when the phone chirped beside her she woke from her reverie. She had been finding that she was losing time more and more frequently these days, not knowing what she had said or done. All she knew was that things were difficult at the moment and she was suffering mentally. She tried to comfort herself, she had Mia at least, and Mia had her.

She checked the message. It was from Susan.

Please rest your mind, I have arranged the funerals for Tuesday, two days from now.

She gave the name of the funeral parlour and the address of the cemetery and the details of the service afterward. They would all share a service, together in death as they were in life. Danni was desperately close to tears. The thought of putting her family in the ground was more than she could bear. They would all be going into the same grave as there wasn't much to bury after... after what had happened.

I can't thank you enough. I appreciate all that you've done for us.

Danni dropped the phone on the bed and walked over to Mia's bed.

'Mia? Mia, you have to eat.' Mia rolled over onto her back, the tears sliding down each side of her face, wetting her cheeks. 'Oh, honey,' Danni said, reaching out a hand to wipe the tears from her vacant face. Mia grabbed her hand and pushed it away from her. 'How long are you going to punish me? What, because I didn't die like the others?' she demanded bitterly. 'How was I supposed to know that I should have died that night? I think I lived for you. To take care of you, so let me take care of you, Mia.'

She stared at her daughter, who merely rolled over again, her thin shoulders hitching as she cried. How was Danni going to get through to her when she didn't even know what she was hating her for? Did her mind go to Oliver as well? Was that what it was? She believed he set the fire too and was blaming Danni for her part in this whole mess? Didn't she blame herself enough?

* * *

Danni hadn't slept well. Actually, she hadn't slept at all. Today, she was going to bury her family. When the sun streaked across the sky, Danni watched from behind the grimy window. At ten o'clock, a car was coming to take them to the cemetery where there would be a graveyard service for the Brooks family. Danni could hardly comprehend how they'd come to this. After hearing what Detective Jacobs had told her, she knew with absolute certainty who had set fire to her house, destroyed her family. She was going to try to pay a little visit to Oliver Marks and find out why he did what he did. She just had to find out where he lived first.

Danni turned and looked at the lump in the other bed. It would take her a while to get Mia ready, so she'd better start now. She began by making toast and sitting on the edge of the bed, gently shaking Mia's shoulder. She opened her eyes immediately, a vacant stare, a flash of... recognition, maybe?

'We have to get ready, love. We're... there's... well, the funerals are today,' Danni choked out. She didn't know if she would be able to get Mia to the funeral. She was hard pressed to get her out of bed, to eat something, let alone attend the funerals of her siblings and dad. Danni gave Mia a small smile, but Mia did not return it. Slowly, Mia pushed back the covers and lowered her feet to the worn, harsh industrial carpet, the most Danni had seen her do of her own accord since that night.

Danni's heart was full of pain, she could barely stop herself from screaming with the unfairness of it all. But what good would that do? She couldn't lose it in front of Mia, not today of all days. No, today she must be strong, be present. Her girl needed her. Danni looked over at Mia as she nibbled the smallest bite possible of toast.

Small victories, she thought.

Danni wondered how Mia was going to manage the funeral. Would she cope? Or would her heart break into a million pieces like Danni's had? Mia still hadn't let Danni in, so Danni didn't know what she was thinking. Danni wondered if Mia would ever find her voice again, ever forgive her. She missed her, she even missed her snarky teenage moodiness and would take it all right now, as long as she would speak to her. Danni wondered if she would be able to give a eulogy for those she loved. A million times she had tried writing it in her head and a million times she had failed to capture the essence of what made them... them. They were all such beautiful and unique people, something she couldn't put into words, even though she should have been able to. All she had to do was talk about them honestly.

Noah, with his cheeky grin and tiny dimples in each of his cheeks. Joe called Noah their 'whoopsy baby' as he had been a very happy accident. He was a loving and empathetic child. Smart as a whip, easy going and above all else, a Mumma's boy.

Alexandra, beautiful, graceful, a wonderful sister to Mia and especially to Noah. She was almost like a second mother to him, taking care of him when Danni was otherwise occupied. She was a wonderful daughter with an old soul.

So why was she frightened to say these things out loud? Why, when she opened her mouth to practise, did all of those things just fall away, the words refusing to leave her lips? The boulder in her throat would grow bigger, allowing almost no air to be drawn in. Danni panted, hand to her throat, afraid she was going to suffocate, all because she wasn't in the house that night. It played in a loop over and over in her mind. Pooch barking, being locked outside, seeing her house on fire.

Danni turned away from Mia in frustration, determined not to let her worries show. She had made a decision, though; she would not be speaking about her family at their funeral. She did not want to share these memories of her family with anyone. They were hers and Mia's memories. No one else need know them. Danni stood still, staring into the mirror, not even aware of how long she looked at her damaged reflection.

For a brief moment she wondered if Beth would be at the funeral. Danni didn't want to see her sister and she was sure the feeling would be mutual. No, she wouldn't be there, she didn't care enough.

Mia stood and looked at the outfit Danni had laid out for her with a blank look. Danni moved closer to her.

'Can I help you get dressed?' Mia didn't answer but picked up the top. 'Good girl, baby. That's my girl.' Danni went to move a piece of hair from over Mia's eye, but she shrank back, an indecipherable look on her face. Danni grabbed her own clean clothes and went into the bathroom, only closing the door halfway. She still wanted to be able to hear Mia if she needed her, or if she spoke. Danni longed for just one word from her. Just one.

Danni lathered up her hair and scrubbed her body as hard as she could, the stinging skin punishment for being alive when they weren't. She showered until the boiling hot water cascading down her body ran out, turning lukewarm then cold. Then she viciously rubbed herself with the thin, hard towel that smelt strongly of mothballs and bleach. She really had to get Mia out of this place, it was doing neither one of them any good. Danni heard the phone chirp and quickly pulled on her cobbled together outfit.

She checked the phone.

It was Susan.

The car will be there in twenty minutes. I'll see you soon. It will be good to see you again.

Susan's words, while innocuous, worried her. Danni didn't want to see Susan again, or anyone else for that matter. She didn't want sympathy; she didn't want a bunch of people staring at her. Judging her for crying too much, or not enough, and exactly what would they think of Mia? The girl who'd lost her voice and couldn't mourn properly for her family?

She stuffed her feet into high heels a size too small. Why did people feel the need, the pressure to get dressed up to go to a funeral? To honour the dead? The dead were dead, they wouldn't care what you were wearing. Besides, her family knew her best in her favourite jeans and a coloured top, not some outdated dress and too-small heels. These conventions felt constraining to her, suffocating. Looking down at herself, Danni tore through the pile of clothes still neatly folded on the dresser. She found a pair of light blue jeans in her size, then a sunshine yellow t-shirt. This outfit seemed more appropriate than this depressing black on black outfit. Her family would have appreciated her looking like herself, and that's all she cared about.

As soon as she'd changed, there was a knock at the door. Chain still firmly on, she opened the door a crack.

'Yes?'

'Mrs Brooks?'

'Yes.'

'I've come to pick you up to take you to the... your destination.' The driver seemed embarrassed to say the word funeral.

Danni could understand his hesitation at using the word. She didn't want to use it either. Some people thought of funerals as celebrations of life, but that seemed wrong. She didn't want to celebrate them, she wanted them with her, with Mia, together. Even if they were all huddled together in this dingy motel room, she wouldn't care.

'Mrs Brooks?'

She must have been standing there, not saying anything. 'Okay, let's go,' she said, turning back to make sure Mia was following her.

She opened the door wide and watched as the man backed up. Danni and Mia both sat in the back. The seats were fake leather, pleather, she thought it was called, and even this early in the morning felt sweaty underneath her hands. Lucky she didn't wear that dress after all, the backs of her legs would have stuck to the seat. She looked down at her outfit, colourful and cheerful. Noah would like to see her looking normal. She wasn't wearing a scrap of makeup either. What was the point? She needed to say a final goodbye, but she knew it shouldn't be at some impersonal cemetery.

Looking over at Mia, she moved to hold her hand, but once again, Mia pulled away from her mother. Danni longed to touch her. She needed Mia to speak so she could get some answers. The detective had told Danni that the children had died in their sleep, but Joe... did Mia hear any of that, she wondered.

The air conditioning was blowing at full blast into the back seat as it was a hot day outside. Danni's hair would go frizzy at the sides, as would Mia's. It made Danni smile to think of something so mundane, the normalcy of it all. The driver drove at a sedate speed, almost too slow for Danni, it felt like they were driving to their doom, but finally they arrived at the service road to the cemetery. Danni could see, in the distance, people already milling about, the coffin, roses, friends. She wasn't ready for this, not by a long shot. She wasn't even sure she could make her legs work to get out of the car.

When the car slowly stopped, Danni took a steadying breath and grasped the door handle and went to open it. Then she felt someone grab her wrist. She looked down, to discover Mia's small hand clutching hers. Mia had touched her! After weeks of Danni trying, Mia had finally responded and reached out to her. She had hoped that if she persevered, Mia would eventually come back to her. Maybe it was finally happening.

'Sweetheart, it's okay. We'll get through this together. I promise,' she said gently.

Mia's mouth opened and closed as if she was trying to speak, but it had been so long that Danni wondered if she had lost the ability.

Mia swallowed hard; Danni could see she was still trying to say something. She waited, outwardly patient and calm, but inside, she wanted to shake the words out of her daughter.

Mia looked her mother deep in her eyes, and Danni felt as if they were connected by something deeper than just a stare. They were connecting souls.

'Don't,' Mia finally croaked.

'Don't? Don't what, honey?' she said, putting her hand over Mia's hand.

'Don't,' she said again, this time stronger, louder yet still so very weak. She tightened her grip on her mum's wrist and finally Danni got the message.

She whispered, not wanting the driver to hear their conversation. 'You don't want to go to the funeral? Is that it, Mia?' Danni had to admit that she had mixed feelings about the whole thing as it was. The people, what remained of her family. A shudder ran through her, from the inside out. Mia looked pained, her face screwed up in fear.

'Don't.' She looked at the driver. 'Turn around,' Mia whispered.

'You want to turn around?' Danni asked quietly, pushing a piece of hair from her eyes. Mia nodded her head. Obviously the thought of saying goodbye to her family was too much for Mia to bear. Danni understood completely, it was hard enough for her, let alone a teenager. If she was honest with herself, Danni was relieved that Mia didn't want to go, it gave her a way out as well. Danni took one final look at the scene. The people waiting on them to begin, the pastor that Susan had arranged, the flowers, roses and the sea of black. No, black was not the colour of the day, not today.

'Excuse me,' she asked, tapping the driver on the shoulder.

'Yes, Mrs Brooks?' he said, turning slightly to look at her.

'Can you please take us somewhere else?' She glanced over at Mia but she was staring intently out the other side window, ignoring the scene completely.

'Somewhere else?' he repeated, seemingly confused. 'Where else do you want to go?'

'I'd like you to take me to my home.' She gave him the address, which he put into his GPS, then he smoothly pulled away from the kerb. Danni didn't bother looking back. There was nothing there for her any more. Susan would wonder where she was going and would likely stall for as long as possible, but there were always more funerals to do. Her family would be buried today and tears would be shed, but it wouldn't be by them, not there, anyway. That would be left to the friends who wouldn't watch them grieve. She'd rather do that in private, away from prying eyes.

The scenery slipped by them outside the window. Dark golden stubble in some fields, lazy, fluffy sheep standing perfectly still in the next, guarded by a lone alpaca. She knew that, the further they got from town, animals like kangaroos would come out to frolic once the baking heat of the day had passed. Then their letterbox came into view. Danni's heart slowed then skipped a beat entirely. She used to be able to see the top storey of the house from the bitumen road that connected to their dirt driveway. Now Danni could only see a great expanse of nothing where the house used to be. Taking in a deep breath, she watched as the charred remains of their house grew closer. When it came into view, Danni let out an involuntary sharp intake of breath, her eyes immediately welling with tears, her heart feeling like it was going to burst with the pain. She had to look away for a moment, wipe the tears from her eyes.

The car stopped short of the front yard, which was full of dirt and burnt leaves. She opened the car door and was blasted by the hot sandy air. Eddies of dirt kicked up by the wind throwing grit into her eyes. She wiped at them, blaming the dirt for her wet and sore eyes. Danni was so transfixed she forgot Mia was still in the car. The driver sat behind the wheel, staring down at his lap, probably on his phone giving her privacy as Danni walked towards the ruins of her family home. So many years, so many memories, each child bringing more than just memories: love, happiness and togetherness as a family.

Now that was all shattered. Alexandra and Noah, gone. Their happy voices and laughter echoed in her mind, taunting her with the memories of better times. Then Danni thought about Joe. Complicated Joe. Where once Danni had thought him simple and easy to understand, she quickly realised that, despite loving her, he could never be fully trusted. She thought back to the cruel taunts that her sister had said to her when they were in high school, laughing in her face about how she had had him. Before Joe had told her the truth, she could blow it off as mere jealously, but once she asked him point blank and he'd told the truth, something inside of her had faded away that day. How could he have broken her trust and her heart like that?

It wasn't the first time, either. She had heard the rumours of girls before Beth. But after? After they were married? It was a small town. It was full of people who liked to gossip. Be seen with someone of the opposite sex and suddenly you were cheating on your spouse, breaking up someone else's family. Danni might have tried to ignore the rumours, the whispered conversations that she heard behind her back, but some of them seemed to find traction within her mind.

Joe was dead now. She could never confront him. Never ask him if he had strayed outside of their marriage. Danni had felt a disconnect between her and Joe for some time before that night. It felt like they had been drifting further away from each other with each passing day. Their once strong bond, slowly disintegrating, disappearing like puffs of cloud on a strong breeze. Danni had noticed it but had been powerless to stop it. It was like watching an accident she couldn't look away from and was unable to stop.

It was around the time of the second round of gossip, this time about a mystery woman, although Danni never did get a name, that Danni decided to seek help. She began seeing a psychologist at first, one who listened to her talk, but the more she talked, the sillier she felt, her problems seeming inconsequential compared to what other people were going through. She sat across from the doctor that one time, unloading her innermost thoughts and feelings onto someone who she didn't know. It felt indulgent. Even though she'd been Mrs Brooks for nearly eighteen years, she still felt like her old self on the inside, like a fraud posing as a woman who seemed to have it all together, when really she was just as insecure and lonely as she always had been.

The realisation, pulled from within her by the doctor after just one visit, shocked her. Danni thought she had it all together. Wife and mother, two things she excelled at. But it seemed as if her mind had other ideas. She was not as put together as she thought she was.

Danni glanced back at the car, she couldn't see Mia inside, but she knew that she would be sitting, facing forward, hands clasped neatly in her lap, face as if made of stone. Danni didn't blame Mia for not wanting to come out, but it was the only place that Danni could think of to go to say goodbye. The place where her kids had roamed free, happy and loved.

The day was hot, burning hot. The wind dried her face, making it feel like her skin was stretched too tightly over her bones, dried like parchment. The small of her back felt slick with sweat. She wished she had remembered sunglasses.

Danni sat down on the ground in front of the pile of burnt-out rubble. She felt sure that the air was still tainted by the acrid smell of burnt wood and paint. Everything she owned had gone up in the fire. Everything. The clothes on her back didn't even belong to her. She was relying on charity. Her mind wandered, back to her children's laughter and the kind words that Joe would say to her. He would tell her that he loved her, cherished her, desired her, but that was a long time ago. So long ago, she couldn't believe a thing that he had said towards the end. By the time of Joe's tragic death, he hadn't made love to her in well over a year and Danni realised that she didn't even care. Not after what she knew now.

The last time she'd heard about another one of Joe's affairs was when she was in the video store selecting ten DVDs for ten dollars for the week. One of the last holdouts against online streaming; Danni still had a thing for the old ways. Picking out movies to cater to her family's tastes was a way she showed her love. Noah liked westerns, Alexandra liked Miley Cyrus, Mia liked horrors and Joe liked action movies.

Danni had also discovered recently that Joe had liked movies of a different kind. She had been clearing up in their bedroom, putting away the clean, folded laundry that always ended up in a pile at the foot of the bed, never quite making it to the drawers or wardrobe where they belonged. While she was doing that, she had accidentally bumped the mouse beside the open laptop on the dresser. Danni had never been one to snoop, despite all the rumours, or possibly because of them. If she was honest, she really didn't want to know if they were true. If Joe was with other women – women that didn't look like her, that didn't have mum bodies from bearing and birthing his three children – well, Danni didn't think she could handle that. But this time? This time, it must have been fate.

Seeing the screen burst into life, Danni put the pile of clothing on the floor and cautiously walked around to stand in front of the laptop. She looked at the doorway, expecting to see Joe standing there, fists clenched in anger, but he wasn't there. No one was. The login screen popped up. Danni had no idea what Joe's password was or where to start guessing. Her fingers itched to type the only obvious password she could think of, but it couldn't be that easy, could it? Taking another look at the door and angling the laptop away from the door, she typed the word 'password' and held her breath.

Well, fuck, it worked!

Danni smiled for a brief second, marvelling at either Joe's stupidity or the trust he had in her, before the smile fell from her lips. There was a website open, not even hidden or bothered to be closed. For a second, Danni didn't know what she was looking at. She wasn't innocent, nor was she boring in bed, they used to enjoy a great sex life until... well, it looked like until Joe had found something else to entertain him.

The girl on the screen was tied spread-eagled to the bed, naked, red welts covering her breasts, a gag stuffed in her mouth and a man ejaculating onto her face. She looked at the camera. Her eyes were red and swollen from crying, her face haunted and distressed. Danni slapped her hand over her mouth to keep from crying out. *This* is what Joe liked? *This* is what her husband of nearly twenty years liked to watch? He got off on the pain of women? How could she not have known this or seen any evidence of this in the years they had been together? The worst part was that the woman on the bed wasn't a woman, she looked to be barely older than Mia.

Danni slammed down the lid of the laptop in disgust, quickly repositioning it to where it had been so Joe wouldn't know she had been snooping. Suddenly her mouth filled with blistering bile and she ran to the toilet, just making it before she vomited, over and over, emptying out her stomach till only the churning remained. Oh God, how could this be happening? Who was the man downstairs playing with their children? How could he do this to her? To them? To all those women, *girls*? Toxic fluid pushed itself into her mouth again as she leaned her head into the toilet, retching until she was left a shivering, quivering mess, holding onto the sides of the toilet bowl for dear life. How she'd ever leave the bathroom she wasn't sure. How she'd ever look at him again she wasn't sure. She had to confront him about this, didn't she? But when?

It was times like this that Danni wished she had a close girlfriend. Someone to confide in. But even if she did have a best friend, how would you even bring that up into conversation? No, she was on her own here.

Danni stood up slowly on shaky legs that barely took her weight. Thrusting out her hands to support her, she turned on the tap, rinsing her mouth with handfuls of lukewarm water. She rinsed and spat over and over, then repeated the process with mouth wash. Over and over, cleansing herself, washing away the filth. She retched again as she thought of her loving husband, a man who she was in love with, looked up to, watching that shit and jacking off to it. A fucking teenager! She was so angry, so betrayed, so full of hate.

Staring at herself in the mirror, Danni wondered what the hell was wrong with her that he felt the need, the fucking *desire* to go and look at shit like that.

She couldn't confront him tonight. The kids were here and she was just too damn distraught to even think straight. Her insides were hot and cold, her stomach roiling like she was going to vomit again at any second, her face ashen and covered with a layer of nervous sweat. She put her fingers to her heart, it was beating dangerously fast. Was it possible to have a heart attack from what she had just witnessed? Maybe, but she wouldn't die and leave her babies with a fucking monster like him.

* * *

Two days went by. Two agonising and pain-filled days without her speaking to Joe about what she'd seen. She had come down from the bedroom, sure that her face was saying everything that her lips couldn't, but as she walked into the lounge no one even turned to look at her. Since she wasn't noticed, she took the opportunity to observe her husband. He was playing Monopoly with Noah and Alexandra, Mia sitting on one of the armchairs, long legs dangling over the side, reading a book, ignoring them all, in her own little world.

Joe laughed with the two youngest kids, rolling the dice to come up with two sixes, much to the loud noises of disgust coming from Noah and Alexandra. The three of them laughed as he moved his piece and landed on 'go to jail'. She almost laughed at the irony of it but knew that if she started laughing, that she wouldn't stop and it wouldn't be the good kind of laughter. Her children would stare at her and they would know that something wasn't right. No, she couldn't start laughing.

When she confronted Joe, she needed to have a clear head and a game plan. After all, she'd be demanding a divorce and full custody of the kids.

Danni hadn't consulted a divorce lawyer, nor had she told anyone her plan to kick Joe out of the house. When she realised that no one was even aware she was in the room, she sneaked back upstairs, accessed his laptop using his idiotic password and took photos of the picture on the screen, the web address and a picture of the browser history. Clearly he was cocky. She closed the laptop and went back downstairs. He would have to agree to her demand for divorce or people would be seeing him in a whole new light. So, when Danni had overheard two women that she knew talking about Joe and his new lover, she just didn't care. She was done with him. But for now, she had to bide her time and play it clever.

She had no money, except from her temp job. She'd only had that job for a few months. She hadn't finished high school, so she wasn't qualified for much. She had started once Noah began school, and the small wage went straight into the mortgage. There was nothing left over for her and the kids to live on.

Danni had enjoyed getting into the workforce, making money, being independent from her family. Joe had been initially resistant, but after Danni had explained that it was nice to sometimes leave the house for something other than grocery shopping and school runs, he said he understood.

He was probably lying about that, too. Just like everything else. Danni wondered how old his new girlfriend was, if she did those things for him. She wasn't shocked by much now. One night, Danni had fallen asleep on the couch after working most of the day, picking the kids up from school and taking Noah to karate and Alexandra to swimming. She was exhausted. She awoke, still on the couch, to find the house was quiet and her stomach was rumbling. She checked the time; it was nearly midnight. No wonder the house was so silent, only the cicadas outside making their unique chirping sounds. She had been sleeping for hours. Joe must have reheated some leftovers for the kids so as to not disturb her. Normally she would have been grateful that Joe had done anything for the kids without being asked, but she just didn't have the energy to care what he had done these days.

Letting out a low groan as she swung her legs off the couch and onto the floor, Danni stretched her arms into the air, bending from side to side, working out the kinks in her back. What she needed was a hot bath and a long massage. While Danni was deliberating whether she should eat or go back to sleep she heard a small noise, a quiet click, and looked up the stairs. Standing in the darkened lounge, she wasn't seen, but she knew what she saw.

Joe coming out of Mia's room, after midnight.

Danni slapped a hand over her mouth to keep from verbalising her shock. What was he doing in there so late? Perhaps telling her to turn down her music, but she didn't hear anything, or maybe he was telling her to turn out the light and go to sleep? Or maybe he was doing what her mind had immediately gone to. All she could see was the teenage girl tied to the bed, gag in her mouth. Surely he wouldn't. Danni resisted the urge to barge into Mia's room and demand answers. She would talk to her, she just had to get it straight in her head first. She didn't want to say the wrong thing and alienate her even further. Now that she thought about it, Mia had been different with Joe for months now. Talking back, then ignoring him. Snapping and rolling her eyes, and generally disrespecting him. Surely he couldn't be hurting her.

With her mind churning the way it was with accusations, there was no way she could go back to sleep. It was two in the morning when she went upstairs, knowing that Joe would be asleep by now. She stood at the foot of the bed, shrouded in darkness, staring at his body lying in the bed they shared. Eventually she went back downstairs and sat on the couch, staring into nothing until dawn spread across the sky. When she stood up and started her day, blinking the grit from her eyes, she felt devoid of any emotion except rage. A week later he was dead.

20

Danni sat in the dirt, staring at the charred remains of her house, remembering that night. She was angry and felt cheated that she had never had a chance to confront Joe about the videos, about seeing him come out of Mia's room. She would never have a clear understanding of what he was doing in there. What he had done. It would forever remain a mystery. Unless she could get Mia to talk. So far, Mia wasn't saying much of anything and Danni didn't want to push her further. She wanted her daughter back and if she had to wait for answers, then so be it.

The wind picked up, throwing her hair around her face and into her eyes. She grabbed at the dancing streamers of hair and tucked them behind her ears. She had sat here long enough, mourned her dead long enough and was now ready to go and take care of the living. *Fuck Joe.*

Danni stood up, brushed the dirt and ash from her jeans and made her way slowly back to the car, dragging her feet. She knew this would probably be the last time she came out to the husk of her home, so she stopped, turned and soaked up the landscape for a little while. Burnt fields beyond the half dead grass of the interior yard stood out starkly against the vivid green weeds surrounding the fence line. Some were long, waving in the breeze, others were burnt to little nubs in the ground. It broke Danni's heart to see what had become of their home. It looked so much worse now that the fire department had been through it. *Total loss*, they had said. Nothing to recover except the bodies. The accelerant had burned so hot that even her stove had melted.

A fly landed on her cheek and she raised her hand to lazily swipe it away, but it took flight as soon as her palm got near it. The wind kicked up eddies of dirt in the backyard, swirling around her ankles. Noah had giggled at the feeling, watching the dust swirl into the air. Danni would give anything to hear him laugh again.

Danni slowly walked back to the car and told the driver they could leave. She reached out to touch Mia, but pulled her hand back before she did.

Once they returned to the motel, Danni held the door open for her silent daughter. The day had been hard on them both. Running away from the funeral had seemed like an act of madness at the time but, as soon as they had driven off, Danni knew that Mia was right and Danni's idea of going to the house to say goodbye had been more fitting. She pulled her phone out of her bag before throwing the bag onto the bench. There were missed calls from Susan on there. Four of them. No one else had her new number, otherwise she was sure there would have been more calls.

Mourning for her family had consumed her thoughts for the day but now her mind wandered to other things. Like confronting the person who had murdered her family. The person who needed punishment. Oliver Marks. She had no idea where to start. She didn't even know what this boy looked like or where he lived. She would have to get her information from someone she trusted, and she knew just who to ask.

Another sleepless night followed, but in the morning she had a solid plan about what she was going to do. Danni told Mia she was going out for a while but received no response, not that she had expected one. Danni got into the beat-up car that her sister had loaned her, or given her, she wasn't sure, which was rusty enough to give her tetanus while still being just about roadworthy. But a car was a car at this point, she wasn't going to say no. It had shown up in front of her room, the key shoved under the door one night, and she had assumed it was from Beth. The car let out a belch of foul-smelling smoke with a burp, then puttered down the road. Danni was heading for the high school. She parked, then walked up the stairs, hoping that these were the doors the kids used. Otherwise, she'd have to come back another day.

She waited ten minutes until the bell rang and the teenagers came pouring out of the door. Then Danni saw her, beautiful and surrounded by friends. Were they Mia's friends as well?

'Jane!' she called out. The girl turned at the sound of her name being called, made her excuses then hurried over to Danni.

'Mrs Brooks, what are you doing here?' she asked, a slight frown on her pretty face.

'Danni, please. We've known each other for years, Jane, you're old enough now to call me Danni.'

'Is everything okay, Danni?' She realised her mistake. 'I mean... it's not... I'm sorry...' she said quietly. 'I mean it, I'm really sorry. For everything that's happened.'

'It's okay Jane. I just need your help.'

'Help? What could I possibly help you with?'

Someone called out a goodbye to Jane and she turned to wave. Would Mia ever be carefree like that again?

'I need to know about Oliver Marks. I want to talk to him.'

Jane turned. 'Are you sure that's a good idea?' she asked, her delicate brows pinching together.

'I am. I need to ask him some questions. The problem is I don't know what he looks like. Where he lives. I want to know. Can you help me?'

Jane looked at Danni with desperate eyes, the set of her mouth, the clench of her jaw. It was clear she was weighing up the information given and was trying to decide whether to help her or not.

'Follow me,' Jane said eventually, heading back into the school.

'Where are we going?'

'The library. You wanted to see a photo of him, right? Want to know what he looks like?' Danni followed Jane as she hurried along the long hallways, walking past rows and rows of lockers and empty classrooms. There were a few kids wandering around but most of them had left with the bell. Jane stalked into the library, heading towards the back of the building, bypassing shelf after shelf of colourful spines of books. Danni followed her, trying to look inconspicuous. Jane turned and began trailing her delicate fingertips across the spines until she came to the one she wanted and pulled it out.

'Aha! Here it is,' she said triumphantly, pulling out the yearbook for the current year. She took it over to the nearest table and set it down, sitting and motioning for Danni to do the same. Flipping through the pages, Jane came to the one she was looking for. It was of a good looking young man with neatly combed hair and a camera around his neck. The caption said: *Oliver Marks, photographer.*

That was him. Danni coughed and ripped out the page, folding it quickly and stuffing it into her handbag. Jane stood. 'Is that all?' Jane asked politely.

'Can I have your phone number, please? My phone burned up... in the... fire,' she finished lamely.

'Of course.' Jane said. She ripped a piece of paper from her notebook and scribbled her number on the back, passing it to Danni.

After thanking her, Danni folded the precious piece of paper and put it in her bag along with the photo of Oliver Marks. 'I don't suppose you know where he lives too, do you?'

Jane stared at Danni then her eyes slid away. 'No, I don't,' she said quietly.

Danni remembered all the times Jane had been to their home. All the times she had seen her and Mia playing dolls together, running under the sprinkler, sitting across the table from her for breakfast, then, as they got older, whispering and gossiping when no one was looking. Danni knew when Jane was lying, and she was lying right now.

'Thanks,' Danni said and followed her out of the school grounds. She watched as Mia's best friend jumped on the late bus.

Danni drove into the drive-through of the local burger store, grabbing two meals for her and Mia. She drove back to the motel thinking about Oliver Marks, finalising her plan in her head. She felt a rage build deep inside her, clawing to get out to be let loose on the world but Danni swallowed it back down. For now. Sitting outside the room in the car, unable to go in yet, she pulled out the torn photo as the young man smiled at her. Chiselled jaw, neatly combed hair, deep blue eyes. She could imagine many a girl falling in love with him, just not her girl. Her girl had been harassed by this apparently fine, upstanding young man who had teachers vouching for him. But who was vouching for Mia? Angrily, she stuffed the photo back inside her bag just as her phone chirped. Fishing around in her bag, she found the phone. She didn't really want to check it, but it chirped again, reminding her she had a message waiting.

It was Susan.

I understand why you couldn't come to the funerals.

The funerals. She hadn't even thought about them for hours. She shook her head, dislodging the guilty thoughts and kept reading. But they were over now and she had said goodbye to her family.

It must have been so hard on you, too hard to bear and I hope I didn't contribute to the stress of the day. I saw you pull up, then drive away. Please call if you want to talk. I'm here for you.

Breathing shallowly, Danni made her fingers type a response.

I just... couldn't. It was overwhelming. All those people. They would have stared at me, judging me for not being in the house, for not protecting my family...

She couldn't finish. She pressed send before she could change her mind. She threw the phone back into the cheap black patent leather handbag. She was done with Susan.

Unlocking the door was... difficult. Not that the lock was difficult to navigate, she just found it difficult to walk into the room, to face Mia. She knew what she'd see. Mia curled up on the edge of the bed, facing the wall, and that's exactly what she found. Danni put a smile on her face, holding up the crinkled brown paper bag, hoping her cheerfulness would catch on.

'I went and got us some hamburgers, love. One with the lot for me and a cheeseburger for you. Let's dig in.'

Mia ignored her.

'Mia, you have to eat something, you're going to starve to death.' Exasperated, Danni slammed the food down on the bench. She unpacked her hamburger and sat on the bed, stuffing her face full of juicy meat. She had a mouthful of lettuce, meat and egg when Mia rolled over and looked at her.

'What?' Danni said, mouth full. 'You all right?'

All she received was blank look from her daughter, with what looked like a hint of hatred. What had Danni done to deserve hate? She wanted to ask but she was sure she'd get no answer, and what if she did get an answer, one that she couldn't handle? She swallowed her mouthful. She tried anyway. 'Baby, what's wrong?'

Mia turned away from her yet again and Danni took another huge bite of her hamburger. It tasted like ash in her mouth, but she kept eating because she needed to fuel up for what she was going to do. That and she was trying to set an example for Mia.

Later that night, lying on the lumpy mattress, Danni tossed and turned, trying to get comfortable but failing. Between her body and her brain, there was no sleep to be had. She watched as the night sky receded, the moon fading to a pale crescent of itself. Dressing in the relative paleness of the room, and after checking Mia was still sleeping, she gently picked up the car keys, holding the key away from the key chain so it made little noise. Danni left the motel and drove to the high school where she staked out a spot near the bike rack. It was time to do a little stalking of her own. Jane had told her that Oliver rode his bike to school and put his bike in the rack out the front.

* * *

She watched as the car park slowly began to fill up, cars arriving as the time to sound the bell drew nearer. She dug out the photo of Oliver for one last look. She needed to concentrate on his face, find him in the crowd. Looking around, seeking him out, she scanned over the bike racks.

It was him. *Oliver Marks.*

It was all she could do not to race from the car and shake him until she heard his teeth rattle, shake the living shit out of him. But now was not the time and definitely not the place. She had to wait until they were alone. Just him and her. No witnesses.

She went back to the motel to stay with Mia, trying to feed her a toasted sandwich. When she went back half an hour before school finished, her eyes were fixed on the bike rack, making sure she didn't miss him when he came out. Her eyes drooped occasionally, startled awake by the screech of a bird or her own nervousness. Eventually the bell rang, the chiming reaching her ears even though the window was up.

Show time.

She watched the bikes intently, the car park dotted with cars bearing a P plate on them. She didn't stand out in the sea of shitty first-time cars so that was something. She waited for Oliver Marks to begin his ride home. As he swung his leg over the seat of his bike and hooked it into the peddle, she pushed down gently on the accelerator, a distance away so he didn't get spooked or spot her. She didn't want to be seen just yet. Not until she could safely do what she had to do. After following him for a few blocks, she realised he was headed out the other side of town. She couldn't believe her luck. Soon, he would be cycling down an empty road in the middle of nowhere. She looked down at the crowbar resting on the seat beside her. She didn't want to use it, but she was fully prepared to, to get the answers she sought. The thought made her palms sweat against the steering wheel.

The bitumen road turned into gravel and then dirt. Oliver must live a fair way out of town as they'd already been travelling for fifteen minutes, him on his bike, her in her car making sure that she pulled over to let other cars past, but not letting him get out of her sight as he turned corners. As soon as he turned off the bitumen road and onto the graded dirt and rock road, Danni inched the car forward so she sat right behind him, almost touching his back wheel, then she backed off again, dropping back a few metres behind him. Then she surged forward again, almost nudging him, then backing off. He turned, sensing her, a look of pure fear on his face. Oliver began to pedal with wild abandon, raising his ass off the seat so he could power through with his legs. She didn't know where he thought he was going to; she'd just follow him anyway.

She decided to go all in, he'd seen her face anyway. It had never occurred to her to cover herself up. Oh well, too late now.

She pushed forward one last time, the bumper kissing the back tyre of the bike, causing it to veer off the road into the dirt that was peppered with gravel, which then pitched him into the long weeds by the side of the road. Oliver somersaulted over the handlebars, landing heavily on the ground. His bag flew through the air, landing a couple of metres from where he was.

Danni stopped the car with a screech of tyres, dust kicking up around the vehicle. She opened the door, stepped out with the crow bar and put it on the bonnet before walking over to the prone boy. She hoped she hadn't knocked him unconscious, but she was prepared for that, she had duct tape in her boot. She squatted down beside him and noticed he was breathing shakily, his breath going in and out, ragged with distress.

He watched as she stared at him, naked fear in his wide eyes. His legs were all scraped up, blood running down his knees and pooling into his grey socks. His head must have made contact with the road at some point as there was blood and dirt and bits of fine gravel stuck to his forehead. He lay panting on the ground, looking up at her. His fear was palpable and, for a brief moment, she wondered if what she was doing was right. But if she thought too hard about that, she'd lose her nerve.

'Sit up,' she commanded. She was done playing.

Groaning, he pulled himself up into an awkward seated position, looking at the damage to his knees.

'Do you know who I am?' she asked, her intense eyes glittering coldly.

'N... n... no,' he stuttered, looking at her fearfully.

'I'm Mia Brooks' mother.'

This time recognition settled in his eyes. 'Shit,' he said shakily. 'What do you want?' he asked in a squeaky voice, all manliness and bravado deserting him.

Danni had thought about this moment for weeks. 'I want you to feel the terror you made my daughter feel. Having someone follow you, having someone scare you so badly you think you're going to die.' She paused to let the words sink in. 'Do you think you're going to die, Oliver?'

He looked completely shocked at the question, as if he couldn't comprehend someone even asking him that. He squeezed his eyes shut tightly, then he opened them, a lone tear cutting through the grime on his face.

'Please don't hurt me,' he begged. His words tugged at her, then she remembered her daughter. She hardened her heart.

'You mean like you hurt my daughter?' she hissed.

'I never touched her!'

'Maybe not, but you threatened to, didn't you? You followed her home, took her photo when she didn't want you to, made a nuisance of yourself. You hurt her, Oliver, you said you'd take a kiss and more from her. You made her sick. You make *me* sick!'

'I'm sorry,' he said, blubbering, covering his mouth as if to stifle the sound. If she hadn't been so angry with him, she might have smiled at his fear.

'I'm not going to hurt you, Oliver, not right now, anyway, but I am going to teach you a valuable lesson. One that clearly no one has taught you before. The meaning of the word *no*. You won't forget this one.' She pulled the crowbar from the bonnet of the car, where she'd placed it as she'd got out of the driver's seat.

His eyes latched onto it and widened, rounded and full of expectation and terror.

Danni felt the rage building up inside of her again, the memories of Mia's fear flittering through her mind. The anger grew and grew as she stared down at this boy, ready to strike him with the metal bar that she gripped tightly in her hands.

He began to cry in earnest, seeing the resolve on her face, seeing the pain that lived there now.

Do it!

It was almost more than she could handle. Her head hurt, throbbing in pain, throbbing in time with the blood rushing through her veins. Sweat popped out on her forehead, everything in an instant, but for Danni, it stretched out in front of her like a blacktop ribbon that never ended.

Without any more warning she brought the crowbar down, hard. Oliver yelled, covering his face from the blow that never came.

Danni had screamed when she had brought the crowbar down, striking the ground so hard that her face was showered with sharp slivers of rock and dirt.

'How many girls, Oliver?' she panted. 'How many girls have you harassed? Be honest and I'll go easy on you.'

'Th… three,' he said, stumbling over the words. 'Please don't hurt me.'

'Three girls should mean three swings of this crowbar, don't you think?' She should break his kneecaps, make him hurt, feel pain unimaginable. Part of her wanted to do it. She began to feel herself fade in and out.

Instead of Oliver, she took her anger out on his bike, luckily for him. If she hadn't, she would have ended up killing him. She knew this. She smashed his bike over and over, paint chips throwing up, scratching her hands with their jagged little edges. After attacking the bike, she turned her attentions to the boy who whimpered in front of her.

He flinched from her, afraid of what she might do. She knew what she wanted to do. But she needed the truth.

'Oliver, I'm going to ask you a question and you need to tell me the truth.'

He nodded, tears gathering in the corner of his eyes. 'What is it?' he asked, his voice high-pitched.

'Why the fuck did you murder my family?' She felt the rage building again. Her children…

'What?' he asked, appearing shocked.

'You set the fire that killed them. You couldn't have Mia, so you lit a fire that killed them. Don't deny it. I know you did it.'

'I didn't!' he whispered, a look of naked fear crossing his face. 'I didn't, I swear. It wasn't me. I didn't, I would never, I loved her. Maybe you should ask Mia's boyfriend. Maybe he did it.'

Danni stopped cold. 'You're lying! Mia didn't have a boyfriend.' Memories of Mia flitted through her mind, Mia moody, Mia elated, Mia whispering behind closed doors on her phone. Maybe she did have a boyfriend that she never told her mum about. There seemed to be so many secrets that her family were keeping from her. Danni stood still. 'How do you know?' she demanded, her eyes darkening.

'I'll show you,' Oliver said nervously, aware of the weapon still in her hand. 'Pass me my bag and I'll show you, but please, put down the crowbar. Please.'

Danni looked around her and saw his bag lying in the weeds. Retrieving it, she threw it towards Oliver, who winced at his precious camera being treated that way. He fumbled with the zipper, seeming to forget how to use it. Finally, he unzipped the bag and pulled out a Nikon camera with all the trimmings.

'Before I show you, you have to promise not to hurt me. I took photos but I would never have hurt her. I loved her.'

'So you said.'

'Do I have your word that you won't hurt me?'

Danni wanted to throttle him, to wrap her hands around his neck until he couldn't breathe. She wasn't shocked by these thoughts any more. In fact, her rage fuelled her, kept her going without unravelling as she struggled to uncover whoever set the fire that killed her family. Oliver had seemed as good a place to start as any, but what if it was this secret boyfriend? What if, like Oliver, Mia had pissed him off and he did the unthinkable?

He stared up at her expectantly, waiting for her agreement.

'Fine,' she said through gritted teeth. She dropped the iron bar to the dirt where it rang out with a dull clang.

Oliver began clicking through a series of photos until he found the ones he was looking for. He passed the camera over, and she shivered in revulsion when their fingers touched briefly. She looked at the photos, clicking through, seeing her beautiful daughter in a series of stills, dark hair covering her face. She had to admit, if Oliver weren't a stalker, she'd have admired his photography skills. Mia's long glossy hair picked up by the wind, Mia smiling, then a male came into the frame, at distance so she couldn't see who he was. She turned to Oliver.

'Keep scrolling,' he said.

Mia reaching out her hand only to be in the man's arms in the next photo. Wild abandon as she kissed him full on the lips, him bending down, her standing on her tiptoes to meet for a passionate exchange. The next photo, Oliver's curiosity had obviously got the better of him as they were close up shots. The man's hand on the swell of her breast. His white teeth flashing, stubble on his cheeks visible.

Betrayal shot Danni through the heart as she recognised the man's face.

'Is this for real?' she asked, steel in her voice.

'It's real all right. They've been dating for a month or so, maybe longer. I only found out 'cos I followed her, them.' He looked apologetic but didn't say he was sorry. His previously combed hair was now mussed up, falling over one side of his face in disarray.

Danni could barely comprehend what she was seeing. Mia had a boyfriend, he was older than she was, there was photographic evidence out there, proof that she was with him. Why hadn't she confided in her? She had never felt the distance between them more than now.

'You see,' Oliver said somewhat triumphantly. 'I wasn't the bad guy in her life, I was just a guy.'

Fire.

'Get out of here, Oliver, before I hurt you.' Danni's quiet voice could barely be heard over the bush noises, birds, insects, the breeze blowing leaves across the dirt road.

Oliver stared at her, not sure what to do.

'Fuck off, Oliver!' she screamed, the birds taking flight at the sudden noise, startling Oliver so much that he too took flight, grabbing his bag, throwing his camera inside and picking up his ruined bike, rolling it as quickly down the road as he could before Danni changed her mind. He looked back at her as if afraid that he would see her car bearing down on him, but she wasn't following him, she was rooted to the spot, unable to take a step. After a while, she didn't know how long, she fell backwards onto the warm bonnet of the car. She needed answers. Oliver denied that he set the fire and strangely enough, after looking into his eyes, she believed him. She needed to take a closer look at David Simmonds, Mia's maths teacher and apparently her lover. She needed to talk to Mia, find out what the hell was going on. Why would her daughter start a relationship with a teacher? It was so out of character, but then, lately, she hadn't been herself.

It was all Danni could do not to speed down the road, take the corners on two wheels. As it was, she lost her concentration, not understanding how she made it back alive to the motel. These episodes of losing time were beginning to worry her, and she would have to do something about them eventually. If she was being honest, it had been going on a lot longer than a few months and she was worried she needed medical help, but Mia with her issues came first and an affair with a teacher definitely qualified as a fucking issue.

Pulling into the car park in front of the room, she sat in the idling car for a while, wondering how on earth she was going to get Mia to talk to her about Mr Simmonds and what was going on. Suddenly angry, she flung herself out of the car and pushed the key in the lock. Mia sat facing the door, as if waiting on her mother to come back.

'What the fuck, Mia?' Danni demanded, her brain deciding on anger rather than any other emotion. She couldn't get her anger under control and she didn't want to. 'Your teacher? Your fucking teacher? How stupid *are* you?' she yelled, incensed beyond all reason.

In the face of her rage, Mia stayed resolutely silent.

Danni yelled at Mia for God knows how long, walking around the room, picking things up and slamming them down again, telegraphing her anger to her daughter when she didn't need to, her voice was getting the message across just fine. Mia's eyes tracked her mother as she whirled around the room, then glazed over again when she started to yell at her after a moment's pause to catch her breath.

'I just can't even begin to fathom why you would do such a thing. Your father and I... we...' Danni swallowed hard. 'Your father and I trusted you. We trusted Mr Simmonds, too. What do you have to say for yourself?'

Stony eyed and ignoring her mother, Mia stared over her shoulder. Unable to stand her daughter's silence any longer, Danni marched over to her and grabbed her by the shoulders and shook her roughly.

'Why did you do this?' she screamed. 'Why?' She drew her arm back and slapped Mia across the face so hard that she left an angry red imprint on Mia's cheek. Danni stood above her, panting hard.

'Oh, baby. Oh Mia. Mummy's sorry. I didn't mean to do that. I didn't mean to slap you.' Danni was mortified by what she'd done. How could she have hit her child? What kind of rage would possess her to attack Mia?

Mia's eyes focused on her for a second. 'And you wonder why I found love elsewhere,' she said quietly.

It was the first proper sentence that Mia had uttered in weeks, then she was gone again, drawn back into her own little universe, one where Danni couldn't reach her. It had broken Danni's heart to hear those words. Love had never been the problem.

21

It was hard for Danni to settle into her new life with the Johnsons. She didn't trust easily and she supposed, other than Joe, she might never trust anyone again. Her first night in their home, in a foreign bed, the third in as many weeks, she thought about her family. Beth in particular. What was she doing right now? Was she plotting her revenge against Danni for breaking up the family? What she needed was Joe, not thoughts of Beth. She sat down, feeling the firmness of the mattress and wondering how many kids had slept here before her.

She opened up her bag and pulled out her brush. Since her hair had grown long again after Beth had cut it years ago, she had taken good care of it. Danni stood up and walked over to the dressing table, sitting down in front of the mirror, and began to brush her long glossy hair. She had counted to twenty-six, her routine was one hundred, when she heard a voice say, 'Want me to do that for you?'

She whirled around, immediately raising the hairbrush as a weapon. It was second nature. Her vision wavered as she looked at the figure. Tall, sandy brown hair, and fourteen. Andrew.

She hadn't even heard the door open. She was letting her guard down too much now that she thought she was safe.

'What do you want, Andrew?'

'Just to get to know you better, that's all.' It sounded creepy coming from his mouth and Danni wondered if this was the place for her after all. She was almost eighteen now, so she wouldn't be here much longer. Surely she could tough it out, she'd been through worse. Much worse. At least she was out of the group home.

'We can get to know each other, but we have to respect boundaries. You can't just open my door and watch me, okay?'

'Okay,' he said, dropping a wink at her before he turned and left.

This could turn out to be a problem if she didn't nip it in the bud right now. She closed her door again and did something she hadn't done in a while; she wedged the chair under the door handle so no one could get in.

Soon after, Michelle called out to her that dinner was ready. She moved the chair back into its rightful position and walked down the hallway into the kitchen.

'Can I help with anything?'

'Oh, you're so sweet, but no thank you, everything's already done. Just go and sit down, honey, I'll dish in a second.'

Danni went and sat down. She assumed Michelle sat at the other end of the table from her husband so she sat to the left of Michael, opposite Andrew. Andrew was staring at her intently, and she could still feel his stare as she dipped her head and looked at the meal that Michelle was dishing up.

'This smells delicious Michelle, thank you.' It was the best meal she'd had in a while, months even, possibly years. Her mother wasn't big on cooking and Beth sure as shit wasn't going to cook for her.

During dinner she answered the questions that Michael and Michelle asked her. They seemed to be going out of the way to make her feel at ease. Halfway through the meal, she felt a foot touch her ankle, sliding its way up her leg. She looked directly at Andrew for the first time. He was smiling.

She stood up and he frowned. 'I hope you don't mind if I don't finish my dinner, I'm suddenly not feeling so well.' Without waiting for a reply from either one of them, she quickly walked down to her room, shut the door gently and placed the chair under the knob. She did actually feel unwell. How dare this boy act like that toward her. In that moment, she felt like feeding his balls to him. She was not going to stand for another abusive house, yet another person that made her feel small, scared and alone.

She managed some sleep early in the morning, most of the night spent with one eye open to vigilantly check the door. It was a familiar feeling. When she went into the kitchen the next morning after getting into her school uniform, Michelle was making pancakes and toast. 'Which would you prefer?' she asked.

'Do you have any coffee?' Danni asked.

'Coffee?' asked Michelle as if it were a foreign concept to her. 'Well, I guess there's no harm in it.' She grabbed a cup and poured coffee into it. She put it to her lips, and it tasted bitter, like her life. She couldn't wait to get to school to see Joe. Everything would be fine once she saw him, talked to him, felt his arms around her. She'd be safe.

Danni grabbed her bag after finishing her coffee. Luckily for her, Andrew caught the bus to another school, a fancier school where they all wore blazers. Michael and Michelle were so proud that he went to that school. They couldn't see that he was a spoiled twat. Danni didn't see the big deal. It was like throwing away perfectly good money.

'Oh, Danni, before you go, I needed to tell you something. I've booked you an appointment with the psychologist.'

'What? Why?' she said, alarmed. She didn't need to see a psychologist. She was fine.

'The department suggested that it would be a good idea to follow up with one. Okay?' Michelle smiled reassuringly at her.

Danni, stunned, just nodded. She walked out the door as fast as she could, some long-forgotten memory tugging at her, just out of reach, but instinctively she knew she didn't want someone poking around in her head. Was it really just a case of her needing help due to her background? Or did Michelle do this to make sure they weren't sharing a house with a psychopath? The latter seemed more likely to Danni.

* * *

She smiled as she walked through the gates of the school, desperate to see Joe. She went to the courtyard where she and Joe normally hung out. He was there... but so was Beth. Hanging on his every word, her laughter carried on the breeze to reach her ears. How could Joe even sit near her? He knew what Danni had gone through at her hands. Instead of going to stake her claim, she went to the toilets to do something she'd been meaning to do for a week, she'd just been waiting to be somewhere safe and private.

Three minutes after entering the toilet, she got her answer. She was pregnant. She didn't know whether to laugh or cry. How could this have happened? They always used a condom. Neither of them wanted a baby, yet here it was, growing inside of her. She lifted up her dress, bunched it around her waist and slid her hand over her flat belly. One day soon it would be swollen with Joe's baby. *Joe.* How the hell was she going to tell Joe? She didn't think he'd be happy, in fact, he'd be furious. She thought about Beth and wondered if they'd picked up where they'd left off again? But she believed Joe when he said it was over. She resolved to tell him that afternoon when he drove her home. But he didn't appear at their usual pick up spot. Was he with her sister?

Danni went straight back to the house and used the phone to call Joe's mobile. He picked up after the third ring.

'Hey,' she said when he picked up. 'I missed you this afternoon. Was I late?'

'Nah, had some other things to do.' She heard the tittering of a female in the background as he shushed her quiet.

'Joe, I really need to talk to you. Today. Could you please come over?'

'It'll be dark soon,' he said, as if that was an excuse. She was silent and he exhaled noisily. 'Okay, I'll be there in twenty.'

She brushed her hair and changed out of her uniform, waiting anxiously for Joe to come around. When he did, he beeped the horn and she went out to his car, getting in the front seat.

'Hey, babe,' he said as he leaned over and kissed her. She kissed him back, wondering if it was going to be the last time their lips ever touched.

'I came looking for you this morning and saw you with Beth, you two looked cosy.'

'Jesus, Danni, not everything is about you.'

'You're right,' she said calmly, 'this is about us. Joe,' she said, taking in a big gulp of air. 'We're pregnant.'

He sat there looking at her for a long moment, frozen.

'Joe, did you hear me? I said...'

'I know what you fucking well said, Danni!' he spat. 'How did you let this happen?'

'How did I? You were there too, weren't you?' she asked angrily.

He hit the steering wheel in frustration, banging it hard repeatedly. Danni had never seen him violent, so she knew he was really angry at her, or at the situation, she couldn't tell which.

'Well, what are you going to do about it?'

'You mean what are *we* going to do about it?'

'Danni, how am I ever supposed to get out of this town saddled with a kid? A wife even? I had planned on going by myself.'

'You little piece of chicken shit. How dare you say that to me. This is happening to us both. I had plans as well, you know. I turn eighteen in two months and I was going to leave too, with you, I had hoped. Are you going to do the right thing or what?'

'What? Stay in town, get married and raise a family?' he asked sarcastically.

'Yes,' she said simply. 'We'll stay in town. We don't know anyone in the city and we'll have a baby. It makes sense to stay where we know.'

Joe was silent for a good five minutes, obviously running through his options. While she waited, Danni played with a thread on her jeans, pulling at it until it came away in her fingers.

'Okay.'

'Okay what?'

'We'll have this baby and get married when you're eighteen. Till then, shit has to stay a secret, okay? No one can know, they might separate you from me.'

'Cross my heart. But you have to do one thing for me.'

'What?'

'Stop hanging around Beth.'

For a moment she thought he was going to say no, but then he smiled and suddenly all her worries faded away as he nodded.

'I trust you,' she whispered. Finally, she felt happy.

It didn't last long. Within two days Beth came for her. She had just finished sport, wondering how much longer she would be able to play soccer, knowing that she only had a couple of months until she turned eighteen. She was so caught up in her musings that she didn't realise everyone had left but her.

She had her back to the door and didn't hear anyone enter the locker room until she was pushed violently against the wall. The person spun her around and Danni saw immediately that it was Beth, but she didn't look like Beth. Danni had never seen her like this, so angry; her face was red, livid with rage. She punched the wall, hard, right beside Danni's head. Danni flinched from the blow. Beth looked ready to kill her and Danni was seriously frightened for her life.

'How could you?' Beth said in a low dangerous voice.

Danni felt the hairs on her arms stand up. 'How did you find out?' she asked weakly.

'You think he didn't tell me? How you trapped him. He's devastated, broken. You did that to him,' she spat.

'Beth... I never meant for this to happen, I was going to go away, leave this place but it all went... wrong.'

'If I ever see you again, I'm going to kill you, do you understand Danni?'

22

Mia couldn't stop thinking about the meeting at the café with David. The way he had looked at her, what he'd said to her, how she felt safe in his presence. There were no warring parents, and no Oliver stalking her and trying to scare her. She knew it was wrong, that she shouldn't have let him hug her to his side and she should definitely not have let him put a hand up her shirt. She had touched him back, wasn't she leading him on? Then again, no one had seemed to see her in a long time, seen within her soul. Not ever actually. David *got* her.

Walking into the classroom for first period maths with Jane sitting beside her and Oliver behind her as usual, for once Mia was able to ignore Oliver. It was only after Mia looked in her bag that she realised that she didn't have her textbook and notebook. Where the hell had she left them? It was then that she remembered that she had left them at the café when she had run out on David.

'Mia?' She looked up. 'I'd like a moment of your time outside in the hallway if you don't mind.'

Mia scraped her chair as she stood, her classmates making noises at her. She looked over at Jane who gave her a look as if to say, *what did you do?*

Mia walked out into the hallway. David kicked the door shut with his foot.. 'You ran out of the café before you could take your books, so I thought I'd be a gentleman and return them to you.' He handed over the books to Mia who took them from him, their hands touching briefly.

'Meet me after school, Mia, near the shed on the edge of the oval. Please. I want to help you with your problems, and I can't do that if you won't talk to me.' He touched her on the shoulder, gripping her gently. 'Let me help you.'

'Okay,' she whispered before opening the door, holding her books and going inside.

She saw both Jane and Oliver staring at her. Jane raised her eyebrows, a questioning look on her face. Oliver looked angry.

The day went slowly. Mia kept glancing at the clock in each class-room, watching the minute hand go round and round, inching ever closer to the three o'clock bell. Should she meet David after school? She still wasn't sure, even when the bell rang, yet she found her feet walking towards the oval. As the shed came into view, David stepped out from the doorway. His arms were stretched up, hands gripping the top of the door frame. It was hot and his t-shirt was pulled tight across his chest and his arms. Mia found her breath increase in speed, her heart beating faster and faster.

'Hey Mia,' said David in his gravelly voice.

'David, hi. I'm not sure... not sure why I'm here. This is weird. I don't know.'

'There's nothing wrong with meeting up, Mia, we can work on your maths, just like we planned to the other day if you want. We don't have to do anything you don't want to do.' He put down his arms, placing his hands on both of Mia's shoulders. 'What do you want to do?' he asked, his voice husky with desire.

As if she had a choice. Mia dropped her bag to the ground and stepped into David's arms. He gently wrapped her against his chest where she felt his heartbeat. It was a nice, steady beat. Comforting, solid. Some-thing real she could cling to. She pulled back, staring up into David's eyes. He looked down at her, as if he was staring into her soul. She felt the electricity crackle between them. He stood closer to Mia, breathing her in, then he gently bent down and kissed her on the lips.

Mia's whole body was on fire with desire. She knew it was wrong, but as he slipped his tongue into her mouth, she didn't give a damn. David pulled her closer, crushing him to her, then backed away.

'I'm sorry, Mia, I just can't help myself.'

Mia stood up on tip toes, the wind blowing her hair over her face as she turned to check no one was watching. 'I can't either,' she whispered, as she leaned in for another kiss. This time she felt David's hand gently cup the curve of her buttocks, pulling her to him, melding their bodies together. It felt right, like they belonged together. She never wanted this to end, but eventually, they heard laughter and were forewarned that students were nearby. Mia left first, picking up her bag where she had carelessly dropped it to the ground. David followed her out a few minutes later.

Neither of them were aware that their romantic tryst had been caught on camera. Oliver had seen, and recorded, everything.

* * *

At first Danni didn't know what to do with this information. She couldn't deny that Mia was seeing her teacher and tutor. Oliver, Mia's stalker, had photographic proof. She couldn't explain it away as innocent because it wasn't. They had been in the pictures in all their glory, kissing in the doorway of the shed. *How romantic.*

She felt so many emotions flying around her head. Trust was her biggest issue right now. She couldn't trust her daughter to tell her the truth and she had trusted David Simmonds to be a role model for Mia and teach her maths, not how to have an affair with her teacher. How did they even get to this stage? They had only had two lessons to her knowledge. Did they even study? Thoughts of naked limbs entangled pushed their way into her already full and jumbled mind. She struggled to get them out. She wanted to wring his neck for what he had done and slap Mia again for being so... well... stupid.

Danni knew that she should have taken snaps on her phone of the photos that Oliver had taken in case he erased them down the track. The thought made her mad all over again. He'd probably never agree to meet her again now, especially not alone. She had thought Oliver the one responsible for starting the fire, but now she wasn't sure. She found herself believing him. David, on the other hand, he had a lot of explaining to do.

* * *

Oliver Marks pushed his damaged bike the rest of the way home, paint missing from where Danni Brooks had taken a crowbar to it. It was ruined beyond repair and he was not only pissed, but scared. He had to hide the bike before his father saw it. He headed toward the shed, but then he heard swearing coming from within. Oliver could hear things being thrown around, smashed against the walls. Oliver knew that he couldn't hide it in the shed, so he wheeled his bike around the side of the house to push it against the wall under his window. It would have to do.

Oliver went into the kitchen slowly, quietly closing the door so he didn't startle his mother.

'Oh, hi, how are you?'

'Good thanks, Mum. I'm just going to my room,' he said, too quickly.

His mum looked at him strangely, but she had learned to keep her mouth shut. He went down to his bedroom, pulling out the camera from his bag. He had plans for these photos. He downloaded the images quickly, copying them to two thumb drives. He tucked one into his pocket and put the other one in his hidey hole.

'Oliver!' called his mother.

'Coming, Mum,' Oliver responded. He headed down toward the kitchen, knowing that his mother would never have yelled like that if his father had been in the house. He must still be outside.

'How has school been?' she asked, flour dusting the end of her nose.

'Fine,' he said, swiping the flour from her nose. As he set the table, he could still hear things being broken in the shed. 'Dad having a bad day again?' he asked, knowing the answer.

'Your dad lost his job today. He was laid off,' she whispered. His mother had such a terrified look on her face that Oliver felt sorry for her. He knew she was going to cop it later, and he knew that, as usual, he'd step between them. He had never successfully managed to really hurt the big, burly man, but it didn't stop him from trying. He'd had black eyes on more than one occasion. The only person he had confided in was Ms Appleby, the guidance counsellor at school.

He sat down to dinner, as did his mother, waiting on his father to come inside. Finally he did, slamming the door, not taking his boots off, tracking mud and dirt across the lino. Just another thing his mum would have to clean up after him. His dad sat down, dropping his weight into the chair which groaned alarmingly.

'How was school today?' he asked in a quiet voice.

'Fine thanks, Dad,' Oliver said.

'That all you got to say, boy?' his father said, spoiling for a fight.

Oliver looked at his mother, her eyes pleading with him to just leave it alone, just for one night.

He nodded slightly, he wouldn't make his mum's life harder than it already was.

After dinner, Oliver went to his bedroom and checked that the thumb drive was in his bag, ready to use. Since he didn't have his newer bike, he would have to ride his old one, smaller and with a slightly wonky wheel. It would have to do. The next morning he rode all the way to school, leaving early and wondering how his mother was going to cope with his father home all day. She'd get nothing done, she'd be scared to. He would have stayed home today to help her, but he had something important to do.

He parked his bike and chained up the piece of shit that no one in their right mind would steal. Oliver headed straight for the maths class-room and found Mr Simmonds sitting at his desk, alone.

'Oliver,' he said as he looked up. 'How are you this morning?'

'Fine thanks, David.' Mr Simmonds frowned at the use of his first name. 'I just have something I want to show you. Some photos that I took.'

'Okay, show me what you've got,' Mr Simmonds said, smiling tenta-tively at Oliver. When Oliver starting flicking through the photos, the smile disappeared from the teacher's face.

'Why did you take these?' David asked, breathing so heavily that Oliver could hear him.

'Because I love her, and you were taking advantage of her.'

'But...'

'I took them, and you're going to pay to have them erased,' said Oliver calmly. If he got enough money he could take his mother away from all of this.

'I... I... I'm going to what?'

'Pay me, David, you're going to pay me.' Oliver had never been so bold, not even with Mia.

'How much?'

'I guess I have to wonder how much your career is worth. Possibly even your freedom, I mean, she's underage, right?'

Mr Simmonds put his head in his hands and for a moment Oliver thought he was going to cry. He felt a pang of regret. 'I can pay four thousand dollars, but that's all I have.'

Oliver was ecstatic. He had no idea he would get that much money. He could definitely get his mother away from his father now.

'Go get it.'

'What, now? What about my classes?'

'Well, you could go get the money or I could put these photos up on the internet. Which do you want me to do?'

'No. It'll just take me a couple of days to get it together. I'll have to go into the bank, I don't have that kind of cash just lying around.' David picked up his bag and quickly left the room.

Oliver was shocked. He couldn't believe this was actually going to work.

A few days later, Mr Simmonds found Oliver, grabbed him by the arm and thrust him into an empty classroom.

'I want those photos gone now, for good. Erase them now, in front of me.'

Oliver held out his hand for the money and took the bag Mr Simmonds gave to him. He opened it up and flicked through the most money he'd ever seen.

Oliver made a big show of standing beside Mr Simmonds as he wiped the card clean. No more incriminating photos were left on the camera. Although Mr Simmonds didn't know about the thumb drive. Oliver would be keeping that information to himself. He couldn't believe Mr Simmonds hadn't asked if there was another copy.

'Thanks, David, your secret has now been erased forever. No one will ever connect you with Mia Brooks.' Oliver gave the stunned maths teacher a broad grin before taking off and heading around the corner.

* * *

Danni finally decided what to do, something she should have done with Joe. She decided to confront Mr Simmonds and find out exactly what was going on and why. She didn't want to wait, but she had no idea where he lived. She was angry, at him, at Mia, at herself. Mia ignored her and Danni didn't even want to talk to her. Danni was afraid. Afraid of what she might do, might hear, might say.

She was staring out of the window when the sun finally started to stretch across the sky. She looked at her phone again, three hours until she could confront him. The time passed quickly as Danni repeated in her head the speech she had prepared. Succinct, yet accusatory, but in a calm, reasonable manner. She was going to keep her cool. Finally, she left for the high school. Danni pulled up against the railing that edged the parking lot and killed the engine. She knew who else she'd like to kill.

David Simmonds.

She had a thumping headache forming behind her eyes that made her see double for a moment or so, but it quickly passed. Danni knew she couldn't just walk into the school, but she knew that the gym door was always propped open, totally against school policy, which she had found out when she was on the fundraising committee and some of the parents had gone out for a cigarette. Walking with purpose, like she belonged, she strode down the hallways, looking into the small windows and checking the number on the doors.

Finally she found the room she was looking for and pulled open the heavy door. She tried to calm her mind but as soon as she saw the handsome man she had hired to tutor her daughter, all reasoning and calmness went out the window. He was talking to the class, facing the teenagers, and explaining something that Danni didn't understand.

David Simmonds heard the door open and turned to stare at her, a look of recognition and panic crossing his attractive face in quick succession.

'Mrs Brooks, let's step into the hallway for a chat,' he said quickly.

She stood her ground, staring him down, aware of the whispers of the class.

'Please, Danni, let's go outside,' he said quietly.

She turned on her heel and strode out the door, Mr Simmonds following her quickly, pulling the door closed firmly behind him.

'Danni...' he begun.

'Don't even!' she hissed.

'Danni...'

'How long, David?' she yelled. 'How long have you been fucking my daughter?'

'I never, Danni, I never slept with Mia. We were just friends. I was helping her through a tough time. She wasn't coping at home.'

'What do you mean?' Danni demanded. 'Are you blaming me for what you did?'

'No, there's no blame to be had. I'm just saying she was lonely and confused.'

'That's no excuse to take advantage of a seventeen-year-old girl!' She was livid, so angry, her blood was boiling. How dare he set the blame at her feet, tell her that he was just helping. Helping!

Danni saw the window crowded with faces and suddenly smiled slyly. 'I have proof that you and Danni were together and I'm going to march down to the principal's office and then the superintendent's office and show them what I have.'

He swallowed, his Adam's apple bobbing up and down nervously. 'And what do you have, Danni?' he asked quietly.

Danni smiled again at him and she folded, then unfolded her arms. This was her nuclear option. It could destroy Mia as well. Did she really want to risk that?

She pushed past Mr Simmonds and flung open the door.

'Oliver!' she yelled. The boy looked up with a startled expression on his face at being called. 'Come here and bring your bag,' she demanded. He did as he was told, grabbed his bag and walked into the hallway. He looked scared, nervousness written all over his face when he looked at his teacher, who stared down at him.

'I take it you heard what was said out here?' Mr Simmonds asked.

'Yes, sir.'

'Very well, do you have anything to add? Like why Mrs Brooks would pull you out of class to participate in this conversation?'

Oliver looked down at his feet, scuffing on toe against the floor. 'No, sir.'

'Bullshit, Oliver! What about what you showed me yesterday?' she argued, glaring at the boy. He shook his head.

'Fine, I'll get them myself.' She spun Oliver around and reached into his backpack, pulling out the camera.

'You can't just take someone's private property, Danni. I'm going to have to call another teacher to remove you if you don't leave right now.'

'You think no one but me knows about the disgusting affair you've been having with my underage daughter, but there is someone else. Oliver here.'

Oliver looked like a rabbit caught in the headlights of an oncoming car. Startled, eyes wide, mouth popped open.

Danni turned on the camera and began flipping through copious amounts of shots of Mia, but not the ones she saw of Mia and her tutor just yesterday. 'Where are they, Oliver?'

'Where are what, Mrs Brooks?'

'The photos you showed me yesterday. The ones of Mia and Mr Simmonds kissing.'

'I don't know what you're talking about. I never showed you any photos yesterday. This is the first time I've ever spoken to you.'

Danni looked frantically at Mr Simmonds, then at Oliver. 'What did you say to him?' Danni demanded of Mr Simmonds. 'I saw those photos with my own eyes, now where are they, you little shit?'

'That's it, I'm calling a teacher to come and remove you.' David disappeared back into his classroom, ignoring the stares of his class, and requested two teachers to come and remove Mrs Brooks from the premises.

Danni was desperately pleading with Oliver, asking him what had happened to the photos, and saying that if he really wanted to help Mia like he said he did, he'd help her now. But Oliver was adamant that there were no other photos and Danni knew she couldn't prove that she had seen him yesterday without admitting what she had done to him. He would still have his bike as proof that she attacked him. She would have to get rid of that crowbar as soon as she could. There'd be paint flecks that police could connect to the damage to the bike. But why was he lying now?

Danni turned as she heard heavy footsteps barrelling down the hallway. Two teachers dressed almost identically in black pants and checked shirts were coming towards her.

'It's time for you to leave now, Danni,' Mr Simmonds said, after coming back outside.

'This isn't over.'

'Yes, it is.' Danni saw David touch Oliver on the shoulder and guide him towards the classroom.

Before the teachers escorted her from school property she yelled, 'Why did you set fire to my house?' She saw the shocked look on his face. She wanted to question him further, but the men crowded in beside her without actually touching her and hustled her out of the building. Danni had started the engine when she heard someone calling out her name.

She looked to the left and saw Jane running across the cracked asphalt. Jane made it to the car, and went to open the door, missing the handle the first time then catching it the second time. She threw herself in the car.

'Didn't think I'd catch you,' she said, breathing heavily. She must have run all the way from maths class to the car park.

'What are you doing here, Jane?'

'I wanted – needed – to talk to you.'

'What is it?' Danni asked wearily, all the fight gone from her.

'It's about Mia. There's something you should know.'

'What is going on? I feel like we're going around in circles.'

'I'm guessing she didn't tell you what happened, then?'

'What happened?' demanded Danni, brushing her fingers through her hair in exasperation. She was running out of patience, fast.

'Well, you know about Oliver.'

'You know I know about that little fuck. What is it you want to tell me?'

'Okay, well he was following her everywhere. Wherever she was, there he'd be, watching, just being creepy in general. She started to get really paranoid.'

'Jane, I know all of this.'

'You don't know this.'

'Jane!' Danni yelled, her voice rocking around the beat-up car with the peeling interior. The girl flinched back from Danni, her eyes wide.

Danni immediately wanted to take her words and her anger back, but it was too late. She had scared the young girl.

'I'm so sorry, I didn't mean to...' she trailed off. 'What did you want to tell me?' she asked quietly and calmly. She hoped Jane would trust her again.

'As I was saying,' she said, 'Oliver had been stalking Mia. He knew where she was every second of the day. He followed her everywhere, making her really uncomfortable. We went to a party one night, I had to convince her to come. I said we were staying home watching movies, but we snuck out. She had two beers about an hour apart but she seemed... drunk, out of it. I asked the guy pouring the drinks what she'd had. He said what I'd thought, that Mia had just had two beers. I looked for her, but she was gone. I asked around but not many people seemed to know her so I started asking about Oliver instead. Some guy had seen him helping some wasted girl upstairs. I panicked. I ran up the stairs two at a time. I banged on the first door, but they weren't in there, I did the same for the three other rooms, then I barged into the last room. You know what I was expecting to see. Oliver and Mia, maybe him on top of her... you know. But he wasn't there. She was, though,' Jane said, looking down into her lap.

'What happened then?' prompted Danni, wanting the girl to keep on speaking.

'I found her in the bathroom, her head half in the toilet, hair hanging over her face, passed out. I yelled her name, shook her shoulder, but she didn't wake up. I saw a bottle of pills next to her. It was empty. I did the only thing I could think of; I stuck my fingers down her throat until she puked them all up. She was okay but groggy. I dragged her to the bed where I kept her awake for the rest of the night. Come morning, she was back to her old self but didn't want to talk about it.' Jane stared at Danni as if trying to read what she understood. Danni was silent, uncomprehending.

'Danni, don't you see? She tried to kill herself.'

'No! She would never do that! She never would. It was just a mistake, a terrible mistake,' Danni whispered, but something niggled at the back of her mind.

'This happened because of Oliver. He pushed her to the brink, then over. Mr Simmonds brought her back. He loves her.'

'He loves her? What kind of love is that?'

'I'm not sure, I just know that it's true. Mia felt it.' Jane put her hand on the door but was stilled by Danni.

'Thank you, Jane,' she said. Letting go of Jane's hand, Danni started thinking. Was it possible that David was trying to protect her daughter after all? She needed to speak with Oliver, but this time, there wouldn't be much talking.

23

Oliver spent the rest of the day in a happy haze. He passed the time alternating between looking at the scenery out of the window and the pretty girls inside his class. He wore a dopey grin on his face, his eyes unfocused. He almost looked like he was stoned. All he had to do now was get home and convince his mother to leave with him as soon as possible. He was counting on his father being at the pub so he could get his mother out of the house without his dad even knowing. He was sure that would be the easy part, especially when she saw the money. He could always blackmail David again if the four grand didn't go as far as he hoped.

Oliver rode his too-small bike with the wonky wheel home. It was rough going over the dirt road, the clods breaking under his wheel, causing his bike to veer off course. He frowned, at this rate, he was ever going to get home to his mother before his father arrived back. It wouldn't do Oliver any good to be found with that much money.

Finally, he arrived home, the breeze drying the sweat that had dotted his chest and his previously neatly combed hairline. He didn't care. A new school and a new life, just what he and his mother needed. He gently put the old bike around the side of the house under his window with the beat-up bike. No one ever came around this side of the house so no one would see the two bikes and ask questions.

His mother was in the kitchen as usual, making God knows what, but it smelt amazing. She was a great cook and an even better mother. She deserved everything he could give her.

'Hi Mum,' he said grinning broadly.

She smiled back at him. 'What's got you so cheerful today?'

'Well, I guess I've finally figured out a way to start a new life,' he said, excitement colouring his voice.

'A new life?' she asked, stopping what she was doing and tucking a piece of hair behind her ear. 'What are you talking about, Ollie? You're not making any sense.'

Oliver opened the bag so she could see the money inside. 'It's four grand, Mum. You and me, we could get the hell out of here and away from that sadistic fuck. Go pack your bag, now. Please,' he added when she didn't move immediately. 'We can run away together now, start a new life.'

'Just leave, Oliver? Your dad... I... love him.'

'So, you love being bashed about every night? You love hiding the bruised eyes do you? 'Cos I don't. It's a start, Mum, enough to get us going,' he begged.

'Get you going where?' a deep, husky voice asked as his father's bulk filled the doorway.

Oliver turned in horror, grabbed the bag and made a mad dash for the door that led into the hallway. His dad lunged at him and for a second, Oliver thought he was free and clear until he felt the iron grip of his father's fingers latch onto his wrist.

'Fuck!' Oliver yelled, his voice filled with frustration.

'Come back here, boy, and explain yourself. Where were you going?' He pulled Oliver back into the kitchen and threw him into a chair. His mum stared at him, petrified of what her husband might do to her son. At least she hadn't been packing a bag when her husband came home. She might be able to plead Oliver's case to him.

His dad looked at him with bushy lowered brows, his mouth sneering, one side curled up. 'What's going on?' he asked in that low tone of his that sounded reasonable but was anything but.

Oliver sighed. There was no point lying. 'I found some interesting photos of a teacher with a student and I gave that teacher a chance to buy their deletion.'

'So you blackmailed someone? To what end?' he demanded.

Oliver looked at his mum who had sat down and was now trembling in her seat.

His dad banged a meaty fist on the table. 'To what end?' he asked again.

'I – I was trying to convince Mum to come away with me, start again without you. Didn't work though, she refused to come,' he said, hopefully saving his mum a beating later.

'You need a fair amount of cash to run away. You got that?'

'Four grand.'

'Four grand?' He could see the greedy look in his father's eyes. The planning, the execution, the blackmail, all gone to waste. His dad would most definitely take it now. He grabbed at the bag and looked inside, whistling to himself. 'That's a lot of bets at the ponies with a chaser of beer.'

'Or you could put it on the mortgage,' Oliver said, trying to offer an actual solution for the money. He didn't see the punch coming until it hit him in his eye. Tears instantly streamed down his face, his mother screamed and his eye swelled shut.

'Don't tell me what I can and can't do with *my* money. Now, tell me this guy's name and where the copies of the photos are.'

'I made no copies, I deleted them in front of him.'

'Only an idiot would do that, and you're not an idiot, Oliver.'

'He's a schoolteacher, he doesn't have money, this was his life savings.'

'Give me the copies or I'll make your mother pay.' His eyes slid over to her. 'I'll do it.'

Oliver knew he would. He went into his bedroom and pulled the thumb drive from its hiding place. He felt so bad turning it over, but his mother's safety was at stake and he'd do anything for her. He put it on the table and slid it across to his father.

Sorry, David.

24

Going inside the motel room was like walking into hell. She had seen and heard so much recently that she wasn't even sure what to make of it all. Danni stifled a sob of pain as she opened the door to the room.

Mia wasn't there. She wasn't lying with her back turned to her. She was just gone.

'Mia!' screamed Danni, racing around the beds to check the bathroom. She flung open the door, which rebounded off the wall, and found her daughter sitting in the shower, freezing cold water cascading down her body.

She leant in and turned off the water, looming over Mia. 'What the actual fuck Mia? Are you trying to kill yourself? There are easier ways, I assure you.' Danni walked from the room and began to pace the small space. She had to get them out of this motel. It was doing things to her. Her temper, her rage, her pain. They were all getting out of control.

Marching back into the bathroom, she pulled a threadbare towel from the rack and threw it at Mia. 'Get dressed, we need to talk.' She turned from her daughter, Mia's face still dripping. Tears or water? Maybe both.

Finally, Mia made an appearance, her long dark hair leaving a wet patch on her pale grey t-shirt. She was skinny, almost painfully so, her collar bones showing through pale skin. How could Danni not have noticed how much weight Mia had lost? When was the last time she had really looked at her daughter? When she was yelling at her to keep her music down? When she was yelling at her for fighting with her dad? When she was yelling at her just because she was angry at the world? Or when she switched off? Lost track of time again? No wonder Mia had never come to her with the David Simmonds thing, or the apparent attempted suicide. Why would she? All she had was a mother who yelled at her constantly, or who wasn't present. Who would want that? Danni couldn't imagine what was going through Mia's head right now.

All these thoughts were running on a constant loop inside her brain and she had no clue how long she'd been standing there. Mia was standing in front of her, the wet patch on her top nearly dry.

Fuck!

'Um... Mia, I need to talk to you about something. Can you sit... please,' Danni said to the motionless girl. 'Mia, please.'

The girl went and sat down on the bed facing her mum. The look on her face was like a blank canvas until Danni started talking, then a look of fire lit behind Mia's eyes, making them flash and spark.

'Talk to me, Mia. Tell me why you're acting like this.'

Mia opened her mouth. Danni held her breath.

Mia glared at her. 'I hate you.' Her voice was throaty, like she'd been screaming for days. Maybe she had, and Danni was too messed up to notice.

She took two steps to her daughter and grabbed her hands tightly between her own chapped ones.

'Mia, you don't hate me, you can't hate me. I love you. No matter how many times you say it, I'll never believe it.' Danni stood up, still holding Mia's hands in hers.

'Let go of me!' Mia shouted, her voice ringing out. Danni flinched then let go of her hands.

'Honey, please calm down.'

'I am calm,' she said in a quiet voice, 'don't you see? You're the one who's not calm. I don't want to talk to you any more.' Mia walked to the other side of the small room. There was nowhere to get away from each other, to have space.

Danni wanted to scream. She wanted to rail against the unfairness of it all. Why did Mia hate her so much? What possible reason could she have? She was grieving right along with her, having lost the same people, the same loved ones, so why were they grieving so differently? She didn't understand.

'Mia. I don't care how much you hate me right now and whatever the reason is, but you will listen to me. I know what happened. Jane told me how you took those pills at that party.'

'What?' Mia let out a croak, a look of hurt crossing her face.

'I know about the overdose attempt. Why did you want to die, Mia?' she asked, trying to soften her voice.

'That's none of your business, *Mum*,' Mia said sarcastically.

'Don't talk to me like that, you ungrateful shit.' Danni wished she could take the words back as soon as she'd said them, but again, she had put her foot in her mouth. When would she ever learn that Mia kept count? She always had. But Danni had to try again, she had to.

'Why? You owe me that.'

'I owe you?' Mia hissed at her mother. 'I owe you shit. You couldn't even keep your family safe, you fucker.'

Danni was shocked by the venom that spewed from her daughter's lips. 'I tried to save them, I really did, but I was locked outside, I couldn't get in.'

'I'm not talking about that, Mum. You just never listen, do you? I'm not talking about the fire.' Mia was enraged with her, she wouldn't tell her what she meant or why she was so angry with her. There was no point trying to talk to her when she was like this. Danni walked over to her bed and did exactly what Mia always did. Lay down and turned her back, trying to suppress her sobs.

25

For once the house was quiet. Noah and Alexandra had gone into the bush beyond the borders of their property looking for rabbits. Mia loved it when the house was like this. No one around, whisper-quiet, all she could hear was the settling of the old bones of the house. Her mother was at her job, which she had recently started, and God knows where her dad was. Either sleeping one off or out in the paddocks. She was supposed to have gone with the littlies, but she needed some alone time, where people weren't always wanting things from her.

Mia felt like she had no time to breathe, to just... be. She looked out of her bedroom window, the sounds of the bush strong on the breeze. She heard the cockatoo in the tree near the edge of the back yard. He was a regular, coming to visit most days. Mia could distinguish him because he had a slightly crooked wing when he flew. He seemed to like their place, returning frequently. Mia wondered what it was about this place that kept drawing him back when she would do anything to get away.

Was it how Mum and Dad played happy families for the kids while fighting in private? Or her personal favourite, saying they were there for their kids then being nowhere to be seen when they actually needed them.

Mia needed her parents. She needed them to notice her, to notice that when they asked her if she was okay, that they should realise she *wasn't* okay, not by a long shot. Oliver Marks was making her life a living hell. He was always there taking his photos with his little fucking camera. But it wasn't even that – she was actually afraid of him. Of what he might do to her when he tired of taking photos. When he wanted to be closer to the object of his affection. In truth, Mia was petrified, living on the edge of sanity and insanity and not a damn family member had noticed.

She smiled and laughed, told jokes to keep her siblings amused, but inside, she was dying. No one noticed her smile slip just a bit, falter when asked if she had had a good day at school. No, they didn't notice, they never did. They were too wrapped up in their own things, Mum proving she could have a job and have kids and run a household without it all going to shit, and Dad, well Dad seemed to be slipping further and further away with each passing day. The sad thing was her mum didn't seem to notice that either, or if she did she was doing nothing about it. She loved him, Mia knew that, in fact, she loved them all, but her Dad, her Dad was *the one* for her mother. She would do anything for him.

Neither of them realised that Mia was depressed. No one knew that she struggled every day. For her, this depression was like a deep, dark hole, no light at the end, so inky she couldn't even see the sides. If she fell into that darkness, no one would ever be able to pull her out again. She would be stuck in the dark, forever. But no one saw that. Not even Jane, not until the night at the party. When the day had finally dawned, Jane had said in a raspy voice, 'Don't you ever do that to me again.'

She had the house to herself. Everyone gone. She looked at the tray of strong painkillers that she'd stolen from Jane's mum's bathroom. They ought to do the trick. There was a bottle of water in her bag. She felt around until she found it and held it up to the light. Sunlight reflected off the water within, throwing splashes of various hues of blues onto the walls. It was pretty and Mia moved the bottle this way and that, almost enjoying the respite. She uncapped the bottle, took a long swig then put it onto her dresser. Standing up, Mia popped the painkillers out of the tray one by one and put them next to the water bottle.

Ready or not, here I come.

The back door slammed. *God, couldn't she have a moment to herself?*

The first thing she heard was a raised voice, her father's. She knew he was angry not only because of his loud volume but because he was stomping around the house. She waited to hear the small tread of her mother's as she danced around him, trying to make it better. When she didn't hear that or hear her voice Mia concluded that her father was not arguing with her mother. So, who was he arguing with? He was in the lounge room and she just couldn't help herself. She crept down the stairs, for once skipping the third stair. She wanted to hear what her dad was talking about. Who was he yelling at?

He was seated on the couch, just around the corner, and she could clearly hear his now considerably quieter voice as he talked on the phone. She ruled out a work call by the way he was talking. He wasn't swearing or anything like that, besides, they weren't talking about concrete.

The cold seeds of doubt began to germinate inside Mia. *Say something that will put my mind at ease!* her mind screamed at him.

'It's not for much longer. We agreed I would wait until Noah was in school and she had a job. No, I haven't gone back on my word.'

Mia shook her head, unable to believe what she was hearing. Was her father cheating on her mother? Her dad may have put distance between his family, but he had to still love her mum, right? If he didn't, then her world just became that much worse. She needed her dad around. And by the sounds of it, this affair had been going on for some time. Mia felt sick, like she wanted to vomit but didn't want to draw attention to herself. She needed to listen to the rest of the conversation. Knowledge was power.

'I'm leaving. I promised you a life, and I'm gonna give that to you, you just have to be a little more patient, okay? My kids need me at the moment.' There was a pause. 'Oh, don't give me that crap! He's two years old and I see him as much as I can. But these kids need to be told first, they can't just come home one night and find out that their dad is gone for good. That I'm a liar. You need to give me more time.'

Mia had heard enough. Her two-timing father had been having a long running affair for at least three years as he had a two-year-old child. A son. Like Noah. On nimble feet, she ran back up the stairs, missing the third from the top. She was hyperventilating, her lungs feeling like they weren't getting enough air and her heart burning like it was on fire. She collapsed down onto the floor, staring up at the bottle of water, the white pills sitting there, waiting.

If she swallowed them, if she killed herself, she would be giving him an easy out. He'd just tell her mother that he wasn't coping with his grief and move out. Her mother, distraught, wouldn't have the strength to fight him. She'd let him go, hoping it was like that saying, set them free, blah, blah, blah. He would be gone and none of them would be able to get him back. Sure, for the first year or so, he'd be there for the milestone birthdays and holidays, and of course the anniversary of her death, then Alexandra and Noah would come home from his place and tell her mother that he has a new girlfriend and a baby boy who was two. She'd do the maths. She'd cry once the kids went to bed, she'd put on her wedding veil just to remind herself what it was like to be in love again. To be loved.

Then his visits would turn into 'sorry I missed it, sweetheart' calls, where he would hang up on his kids and Mum would be left to pick up the pieces.

No, she couldn't, wouldn't, do that to her family. She would *not* give him a way out. If he loved this other woman so much, let her come and tell their family together, like the grown-ups they were supposed to be.

Mia stood on shaky legs, opening her drawer and swiping the pills into it so they fell through the crack like lollies. She heard her dad clomping around on the downstairs flooring like a troll. Her mother had lovingly restored the floors, now here he was with his boots on inside, making a mess of her mother's nice, clean home. Disrespecting it the way he disrespected her.

Mia closed her door but the wind caught hold of it and slammed it closed harder than she had intended. She winced, what if he came to investigate? Mia quickly put her headphones on and threw herself onto the bed and rolled over on her stomach. She heard him coming. He reached the landing, then opened up her door. Her music was down low so she could hear everything. Yet she jumped slightly when a hand reached out and grabbed her round the ankle. Startled, she pulled off her headphones and turned to stare at her father.

'Jesus, Dad, you scared me,' she said, not lying. She was shitting herself.

'Uh... were you just downstairs?' he asked, his eyes wide and fearful. She longed to tell him that yes, she had heard every disgusting word he had said, but there was a time and a place for everything. 'No, why?'

'Where are your brother and sister?'

'Last time I saw them they were in the bush beyond the back fence line. Rabbit hunting or something. Why? Did you need something?' Mia asked innocently. It was all she could do to not spit at him. The fucker had one foot out the door, why hadn't he gone already? When would it be? A day? A week? A month?

How the hell would her mother cope? She had only just found her footing after going into to the workplace after a decade and a half of raising her children. There was no way she could do both jobs, which meant what? Mia was going to be stuck raising Alexandra and Noah? Finishing school and working in a dead-end job to help out her mum until Alex was old enough to take care of Noah? By then, Mia's dreams would have turned to ash, burnt beyond all recognition.

'Oh well, I guess I'll see you later then,' he said as he turned, dwarfing her doorway, and clomped back down the stairs.

Mia looked out the window and saw Alexandra and Noah running towards the back door. What would their life be like only seeing their father every other weekend? The knowledge that they had a half-brother out there and had done for some time. The more she thought about it, the angrier she got. While it was true that she and her mum had been drifting apart, she still cared.

But the questions remained firmly on her thin, fragile shoulders: should she tell her mother what she had overheard? She could implode their world on her own or wait until they were blindsided by her father.

Noah must have passed his father on the stairs because she heard him say, 'How's my little champ?'

Bastard.

Noah's little voice piped up as he talked to his father. Alexandra was next. 'Want to go for a bike ride, Daddy?'

'Not now, sweetheart, Daddy needs to rest.'

All that cheating, that keeping up a double life must be hard, tiring work.

Mia went to stand at the top of the stairs, passing Noah. 'Hey buddy, what's up?'

Alexandra stumbled up the stairs, her little pixie face shinning with innocence and love. 'Why don't *I* do something with you?' Mia said brightly.

'No thanks, I'll just be in my room.' She gave her big sister a smile which broke Mia's heart. She had to say something.

Mia marched down the stairs and saw her father lying on the couch, eyes closed, football on the TV, TV that he wasn't even watching. She walked over with purpose and flicked it off. Her dad sprung to life.

'What are you doing? I was watching that,' he said in his deep voice.

'No, you weren't. Besides, the question is, what are *you* doing?'

A shadow of unease crossed his face before his brows lowered and his lips pressed into a snarled line. 'Whatever you're going to say, I suggest you think about it long and hard before you open your mouth.'

Mia stood her ground, looking him dead in the eye. 'I—'

Her mother bustled through the door carrying two armfuls of shopping. She looked at the tense situation before her and probably assumed that they were having another bust up.

'Can someone come and help me?' she asked cheerfully, thereby diffusing the situation... for now.

Mia looked at her father, a promise in her eyes that this wasn't over. Not by a long shot.

26

Sitting on the single bed, reading the newspaper, Danni saw that her family had finally been knocked off from the cover of the local rag. She flipped through to see where they were and was relieved to find the story buried on page six. Just as Danni was about to flip to the next page, a headline screamed at her.

Local teacher takes own life.

Danni read through the article once quickly, then again, more slowly. Mia, asleep yet again, or at least pretending to be, made no noise when Danni clicked her tongue. Mia's maths teacher, tutor and lover, David Simmonds, had killed himself overnight. There was a suicide note and the police were not treating the death as suspicious. But Danni knew something wasn't right. Maybe he killed himself over his affair with Mia. Danni had gone at him pretty hard. Did the police know that? There was a funeral notice at the bottom of the articles page. Danni decided to attend the funeral. It was tomorrow and Danni wanted to see who turned up. Was he a popular teacher? Did he have many friends? Family? She had helped kill him, she should at least attend. It felt like the right thing to do.

Danni spent most of that night thinking about Mia and David, and whether he truly was helping her. Mia and Jane seemed to think so, that he had pulled her back from the brink of depression. Danni felt guilty that she hadn't noticed what was going on with her own child. She guessed she thought that Mia could take care of herself, but that wasn't the case, she'd been drowning and Danni hadn't been there for her.

It was another sleepless night for Danni, one more night of being ignored by Mia. It hurt her so much that Mia hated her. She knew she hadn't been the best mum to her but she was trying to make up for it now. She was the only child she had left; she loved her and needed to prove it to her.

The next morning, Danni kept an eye on the time. Half an hour before the funeral began, Danni sat on the end of Mia's bed. She was staring at the wall, blinking slowly. Danni wondered how she'd react if she knew David was dead. Would she blame her? Probably.

'Mia? Mia love, I'm going out for a bit. I'll be about an hour, okay?' Danni didn't expect an answer and she didn't get one.

Danni stuffed the article about David into her bag – it wouldn't do for Mia to read it. She quickly dressed and headed out the door. Turning the key in the ignition, Danni couldn't help but relive the hand she had played in David's death. Overcome with exhaustion, it was all she could do to drive to the cemetery where the graveside service was being held. Her question was answered on whether he had many family or friends. There was barely anyone there. It was sad and depressing. While Danni hadn't felt totally responsible yesterday, she had seeds of doubt inside her. Did her confrontation with him drive him over the edge? She would never know the truth of her role in David's death, or Mia's role either. She looked at the gravel, the small bouquet of flowers and a few people milling around wearing sombre expressions.

There was one face there she recognised. Oliver Marks. He put his camera up to his face and snapped a series of photos of her. She glared at him from across the fake grass until he put down his camera, which then hung loosely from his neck. He saw her looking at him and looked away. Danni recognised the principal. He nodded at her and she looked away. This was the principal who'd refused to do anything about Mia's stalker, who now stood not ten feet away from her. She glared at him again as she caught him watching her. At least Oliver wasn't taking photos of her any more. The service was short and to the point. No one hung around afterwards to say a personal goodbye, which Danni found sad, so she stood there, standing awkwardly until someone gently touched her on the shoulder.

'Mrs Brooks?' said Oliver tentatively.

She spun away from him, pulling away from his touch. 'What do you want?' she asked coldly.

'I just want... I want... I need to confess something.'

Danni stared at him. 'Confess what? I know what you did to Mia. And I know how you lied about everything, the photos, the affair.'

'No, not Mia, Mr Simmonds. David.'

'Mr Simmonds?' she said, surprised and confused. 'I'm not sure what you mean. Oliver, what did you do?'

Oliver looked down at his feet, shuffling them backwards and forwards in the dirt. 'I blackmailed Mr Simmonds. I showed him the photos I showed you and he gave me four thousand dollars to erase them.'

'You did what?' she whispered, incredulously.

'I wanted the money to get my mum out of... our house. But I downloaded the photos before I erased them. I put them on a thumb drive.'

'Oliver,' she breathed, shaking her head. 'How could you?'

He looked close to tears as he confessed, his hands clenched in front of him. 'My dad found the money, worked out what I was going to do with Mum. He has the photos. He was blackmailing Mr Simmonds after I did. He must have been asking for a lot more money.' He seemed relieved that he had finally got it off his chest. His father was the bad guy here, not him.

'Is that why he killed himself?' demanded Danni, knowing he couldn't possibly know the answer to that question.

Oliver began to cry. Danni felt nothing for him, no empathy, just... nothing.

'Is that why he killed himself?' she asked again, stepping towards him. 'You helped do this? Did you?'

'I don't know. I didn't want this to happen, he was a good guy. I just wish... my dad, he found out and I couldn't stop him.'

'So, you did to him what you did to my family? You destroy the innocent? Do you get off on that?' she demanded, thinking of Mia.

Oliver dropped his gaze from Danni's eyes. 'I didn't do that thing you accused me of. You know... the fire that killed your family.'

'I know which fire you're talking about, you arsehole!' she said, pushing him backwards, palm flat on his chest. The rage was building inside of her. He may not have set the fire, but she believed he set it in motion. Danni still wasn't sure if Mr Simmonds had set the fire. If he did, Oliver's actions had driven Mia into his arms.

'I didn't, Mrs Brooks. I didn't set that fire. I promise.'

'Admit it, you helped kill them!' The stinging slap she delivered to Oliver cracked loudly, throwing his head backwards. The electricity that coursed through her veins needed an outlet, and she found it in Oliver. She pulled back her hand to slap him again.

'Admit it!' she screamed at him.

Suddenly, the principal was there, grabbing her hand. 'Mrs Brooks, get a hold of yourself. What do you think you're doing? He's just a child. You can't slap a child,' he said, shocked and horrified.

Danni suddenly let go at his words, paused for a beat then began to laugh. Both of them looked at her like she was going insane.

'How do I know you didn't burn down my house for sure? You could be lying; I don't know you.'

'Because I didn't. I couldn't have. I was across town taking footage of... a girl... another girl. Her name is Felicity and her dad caught me. I was at the police station. You can call and check if you want.'

Danni looked deflated by this information. It was obvious now that it wasn't Oliver. He wouldn't lie about something that could be confirmed with one phone call. It must have been Mr Simmonds. Maybe she should call the detective and tell him of her suspicions, but how would that help now? He was dead, by his own hand. Was it just the blackmail or was it a guilty conscious? She'd never know now. Never know if and why he murdered her family.

27

The affair continued. Mia wondered if it could be called an affair when David wasn't yet married. He did have a girlfriend, though. Mandy. And damn if she wasn't lovely. Sometimes they would study at David's house, a quaint little cottage with two bedrooms and lots of stained-glass windows. Mandy had decorated it tastefully, each room housing carefully selected pieces that matched the theme of country chic. A small square whitewashed table sat in the middle of the dining room, where they'd set up their textbooks and notebooks, ready to study.

Yes, they'd start off studying, David teaching her about trigonometry and the like. Mia wondered if, with all their extracurricular activities, she'd ever pass the exams at the end of the term. David would have to change the answers to help her at this rate.

They sat at the table, Mia moving her chair close to David's, so close that her thigh touched his. He tried to concentrate on the work, bending forward to show her the best way to work out the answer. She ran her finger down his cheek, but he ignored her.

'Let's just concentrate on the work, Mia, you won't pass your test otherwise.'

'I don't give a shit,' she said. 'I just want you.' She slowly leant forward and grabbed his face with her hands. 'You're so beautiful,' Mia said playfully, kissing his lips with the softest of touches. Then they heard the key in the lock and they pulled apart before Mandy came bounding into the house.

'Mia! I didn't know you'd be here. How are you?'

It hurt that she genuinely liked Mandy. It hurt that she couldn't have David and it hurt that he wanted her and couldn't have her either.

'I'm great, thanks. Just hitting the books, trying to pass my maths test, the usual.' Mia noticed her lip gloss on David's lips and when Mandy had her back turned putting away groceries, she quickly swiped her finger across them.

'What was that?' demanded Mandy in a quiet voice.

'Oh, I'm sorry Mandy, David had food on his lips, I was just removing it.'

Mandy stared at them both for a long moment. 'How stupid do you think I am?'

'Babe, you're blowing this way out of proportion. There's nothing going on, Mia was literally just getting cookie crumbs off my face.'

'How many times, David? How many times are you going to do this to me?' Mandy cried angrily, her hands on her hips, leaning in towards them.

Mia looked at him with fire in her eyes. 'You've cheated on Mandy before?' she asked, now knowing that she was just another girl in a long line of girls. It stung – she thought they had a special connection.

'Of course not,' he said indignantly. 'All Mandy has are suspicions and paranoia.'

Mia stood, grabbed her books and bolted from the dining room door, David calling after her.

'Bye, Mia,' called Mandy sarcastically. Mia could understand her hostility. She deserved everything Mandy could dish out to her. She'd take it. She deserved it. How could she have thought that no one would get hurt by this?

Mia slammed the front door, hearing them begin to yell at each other. What a toxic relationship. How could she have been so blind? Thought she was so special? She loved him, why would he not tell her there were others? Why did Mandy stay if she suspected he cheated? She didn't realise she was crying until she was two blocks away from David's house. Luckily she knew her way back into town. She would call her dad to come and pick her up, no questions asked. And he did just that. Picked her up and stayed quiet the whole ride home. Didn't ask her why her eyes were filled with tears or her face splotchy from crying. She appreciated that but she also felt a little sad that it had been so long since anyone had said, 'Are you okay?'

They pulled up in a cloud of dust, stopping just shy of the house. Mia's dad got out and slammed the door of the truck, looking at his phone, frowning. She wondered what he was frowning at, then realised it probably had to do with his mistress. Whatever her name was. She had no desire to know who he was screwing. Maybe he was organising a rendezvous to escape from the shitty life he obviously thought he had. Thinking about her father's betrayal just set her off again.

Mia barrelled through the screen door, letting it slam behind her. She swiped at her eyes, the tears leaking down her pretty face again as she thought about David.

'Mia, is that you?' called out her mother.

'Yes,' she replied.

'You're home early,' she yelled from the kitchen. 'How'd the session go?'

'Fine,' she said, only capable of one-word answers.

She heard her mum bustling in the kitchen, making dinner for her family. Her mum came out of the kitchen suddenly and Mia looked away. She held her breath, waiting for her mother to say something, anything.

'Mia...' she began.

Mia stepped off the bottom stair and threw her arms around her mum's stomach. Her mother wrapped her arms around Mia and hugged her tightly to her, her hand patting her on the back, surprised.

'Tell me what's wrong, honey.'

At the sound of the term of endearment, Mia let loose. The floodgates opened and her tears washed down her face to splash on her top.

'Oh Mia, tell me, what is it?' It was the first time someone had asked what was going on.

Of course she couldn't tell her, not like this. Nor could she tell her about David. 'It's Dad...' She left the sentence hanging, unable to do that to her mother.

Danni pulled back from Mia. 'What do you mean, your dad?'

Mia realised her error. She just meant that he hadn't cared enough to ask if she was okay. What if her mother probed and she caved? The mood she was in, it was just a matter of time before she told her mother about the affair, about the two-year-old son, about the duty he felt towards his new family. She had dropped herself and her father into the shit. Now what?

'Is there something going on with your father?' Her mother's dark eyes piercing her daughters.

'No, Mum, I'm just having a bad day is all. I have to go and do my homework.' Mia ducked back up the stairs, not looking back at her mother. She realised that she and her father needed to get their stories straight for when her mother asked for an explanation. She was going to go outside to find him but then decided that it was a terrible idea. Her mother would be watching her. So she went to her room instead. She picked up her phone and sent a message to her father.

Mum saw me crying. Told her I had a bad day but you're going to have to tell her soon. I'm not covering for you any more.

She pressed send and waited. Her father must have had the phone in his hand because he immediately replied, begging.

Please Mia.

He still hadn't asked her what was wrong with her and she wanted to tell him, *fuck you very much for not caring*. He didn't want to get involved; clearly he had his own shit going on.

David. How on earth was she supposed to sit in his class and not say something? What would he say to her? How would he treat her? As if she didn't have enough going on with her father and his bullshit. She looked around her room and had the strong urge to destroy the entire thing. Pull the photos from the wall and smash the glass against the edge of the bed, tear her posters down and shred them into a million pieces, but that would bring her mum running, so she settled for screaming into her pillow. She heard footsteps running and she froze. Her mother had heard that. The door burst open and Alexandra stood there, naked fear on her face.

'Are you okay, Mia? What's wrong?' Her eyes were wide and her mouth open.

'Yeah,' she said wearily, 'I'm just tired is all. Bad day at school.'

Alexandra came over to her and hugged her tightly. 'You can always talk to me,' she said, sounding older than her nine years.

'Thanks, sis.'

Alexandra walked out the door, and Mia knew that she would have to do something sooner rather than later. She could just tell her mum and be done with it, let the chips or pieces or whatever fall where they may. Could she do that to her mother and her siblings? Could she do anything to stop it? She'd yet to talk to her dad properly about what he would be giving up, yet from the conversation she'd overheard him have with his mistress, he already knew what he was giving up and he didn't care about them enough to stay. He was leaving regardless.

Mia was devastated over the future loss of her father and it hurt her deeply that he hadn't just cut the cord and left already. It would make it so much easier, rather than not knowing when the axe was going to fall. On top of all the David stuff, she felt betrayed by the two men who were the closest to her. One was leaving and they both were lying to those they loved the most.

28

Joe paced the gravel square near the front door. He kicked the grey chunks of rock, sending them flying in random directions. His text message had gone unanswered, so he decided to call her.

It rang and rang. 'Answer, God damn it!' he whispered angrily. The phone went to voice mail and he left a terse message to call him back as soon as she could. He stayed outside, waiting for her to call back. He knew that she was punishing him for taking his time leaving his family when he said he would, but it wasn't as cut and dried as she thought it was. His phone, on silent, vibrated in his hand. He turned it over so fast that he almost dropped it in his haste to answer it.

'Hello?' he said breathlessly.

'What do you want, Joe, because you seem to be making your choices very clear.'

'It's not like that, you know it isn't.' He hated the pleading quality to his voice.

'Tick tock, Joe, this offer goes away soon and so do I and our son.'

'I want you,' he growled into the phone.

'Then prove it. Leave her, leave *them*. I won't wait around forever.'

'Yes, I know and I don't want the two of you to go anywhere. I love you.'

'I love you too,' she said before abruptly disconnecting their call.

Joe wanted to smash his phone, much like his daughter wanted to smash her room.

The day his son had been born was one of the happiest of his life. He'd been waiting for the phone call all day, and when it had finally come, he had no one to share it with. He had told a suspicious Danni that he was just in an extremely good mood. His kids rejoiced that their father was happy again for a day. It didn't last long, of course, as he worried about how the hell he was going to see his son. He loved his kids, all four of them, but it was time to make a choice. He'd had nearly two decades with Danni and their children, now was the time to leave. He wanted Joe Junior, he wanted *her*.

Joe tried to spend weekdays with her as much as he could, but weekends were the hardest. It's when she wanted to see him the most, but Danni knew that he didn't work weekends and, with no extra cash coming in, he couldn't say he was working. Danni worked some weekends and he tried to get away then, but she asked him to watch the kids.

'I don't want to babysit,' he had whined.

'It's not babysitting when it's your own kids, it's called parenting.' And with that, she had stormed off to work. The best Joe could do was a phone call, which she was less than impressed with. Of course, when he did manage to disappear, Mia now knew where he was going. But he didn't think she would say anything. Not yet, anyway. He had a little bit of time left.

He had gone up to Mia's room one afternoon, ready to reward her for keeping his huge secret. He pushed open her room, she had her headphones on. He touched her on the shoulder. She turned at his touch and scowled.

'What do you want?' she'd asked, pulling off her headphones, disgusted by him. It showed in her glare.

'I have a present for you,' he said awkwardly. 'I saw this and I thought of you.' He pulled out the latest smartphone. 'You've earned it.'

'I've earned it? Are you kidding me? Why, because I'm keeping your dirty little secret?'

'Well, yeah,' he said scratching his chin.

'I don't want your bribes. I'm not interested... *Dad.*'

'I can't tell your mum yet.'

'Well you have to tell her soon. She knows something is up.'

'I can't just come out and say "I don't love you and I'm leaving you" all in the same breath.'

'You don't love her any more?' Mia asked, shocked at his confession.

'I kinda do, but my... girlfriend wants me to choose straight away. Mia, you have to understand, she's going to take my son away from me. She's going to move, leave town if I don't move in with her.'

'So what? What do you think Mum is going to do? She's going to lose it. Have you even thought about that? About Alexandra and Noah? About me?' She fought back the tears.

'Yeah, but your mum's a strong woman, she'll cope. Besides, I need to spend time getting to know my other son. I'm done here.'

'You're done here? Fine. Then fucking leave already.' Mia turned and walked out of her bedroom, disgusted, passing her father with the phone still in his hand. 'And take your bribe with you.'

Dinner was a sombre affair. He kept looking at Mia and she alternated between ignoring him and throwing daggers his way. If looks could kill, he'd be diced into pieces and buried in the back yard. Danni was puzzled as she watched her husband and daughter locked in a silent battle of wills. When Mia's eyes met Danni's, they were filled with tears.

Joe knew that he had to talk to Mia again. Plead his case to her one last time. Later that night he rapped on her door. 'You awake, Mia?' He opened the door.

She was in her pyjamas, sitting up in bed reading. 'What do you want, Dad? It's late. Actually, let me guess, more presents for me if I don't tell?'

'No. No more gifts, but I do need to talk to you. I love you Mia, I really do, but I can't stay. I've made my decision and it's final. I've been with your mother since we were teenagers, it's time to move on. To experience new things. I've been given an ultimatum and I've chosen.'

'If you're going to leave, then just fucking leave!' she almost shouted. 'Stop dragging it out!'

Joe sighed. 'I am. I'm telling your mother next week. All I ask is that you keep my secret until then.'

Mia said nothing and Joe left her room, closing the door gently behind him. He didn't see Danni standing at the bottom of the stairs watching her husband sneaking out of their daughter's room just after midnight.

29

Weekends were the worst. Her dad would work a double shift and Beth would have people come to the house. Older guys and girls.

Beth would corner Danni in her room, hissing at her to stay hidden. 'Don't you dare embarrass me. You hear?' Never mind their mother passed out drunk in her room might be considered an embarrassment.

Danni spent the time writing in her diary, one that no one knew about. Danni kept a record of the abuse that occurred, when and what. She wasn't sure who would ever see it, but it made her feel better. Maybe someday someone would take an interest in her, read her diary and she'd get taken away from this lonely place. She didn't even care if she was placed in a group home. Couldn't be any worse than how she lived now. Her parents didn't even bother to keep up the pretence of loving her at home but they seemed to care what everyone else thought. That's why Beth wasn't supposed to hit her across the face or anywhere that people might see the bruises.

Danni was busting to go to the toilet. She snuck down the hallway and was about to open the toilet door when it opened inwards suddenly.

A tall, good looking older boy stood in front of her.

'And who are you?' he asked, giving her the once over, obviously liking what he saw.

'*That* is no one,' Beth said as she strode down the hallway, like an enraged bull.

'Is this your sister?' he asked.

'She's no one. Let's get back to the party.' She grabbed onto his arm and propelled him down the hallway. She turned back and hissed at her. 'Piss then get back to your room, got it? I don't want to see you again.'

She came out of the toilet only to find the boy waiting for her, casually leaning up against the wall.

'Donovan! What the fuck are you doing?' Beth demanded. 'Do you want to watch her, or touch these titties?'

With a smirk toward Danni, he turned and left, following Beth down the hallway. 'How young is she?' she heard him ask.

'Too young for you. You need a real woman, Donovan. Come have a drink with me.'

He took off after her sister with the promise of breasts and booze. Danni reached the sanctuary of her room. She pushed the chair up against the door and went back to what she had been doing: holding the small knife in her hand. Beth would never see it coming.

* * *

The next Friday night, Danni returned home late after staying to help the teacher pack up the classroom. Danni snuck into the house, seeing that Beth was setting up for another one of her parties. By eight o'clock, she could feel the bass vibrating through her bedroom walls. The party was in full swing. If only she could climb through her bedroom window and escape. If only she had friends that she could go and hang with. If only...

Opening the door, the smell of booze and pot hit her nose like a brick wall. The lounge and kitchen were almost invisible because of the smoke weaving around people's heads, like wraiths. She coughed lightly, hating the smell.

Once in her room, she very quickly changed out of her school uniform, just in case Beth came barging in while she was in her underwear. She put her sneakers on and retrieved the knife from its hiding spot, tucking it into her sneaker and pulling her trouser leg over it to hide it. She never knew when she'd need to protect herself so she kept it close to her at home.

The party kicked up a notch, and Danni, trying to read within the thumping walls of her room, wondered how her mum managed to sleep through it all. Oh, she knew, she got rip roaring drunk.

Danni was sitting on her bed with her back against the wall, where she felt safest. She found she did it at school too, sat with her back against the wall so no one could sneak up on her and attack her. Her door banged open with so much force it rebounded off the wall, leaving a crescent dent in the paintwork that Danni would surely be blamed for. Beth stood in her doorway, the noise and smoke leaking in around her, invading her personal space.

'What do you want, Beth?' she asked warily. She didn't want a fight, but Beth had that look in her eyes. She was spoiling for one.

'You're coming with me,' she snarled at Danni, that look in her eyes. Beth marched across the room and grabbed Danni's arm tightly, her painted talons digging into the soft flesh of Danni's upper arm, leaving marks. Danni wouldn't be surprised if she had bruises tomorrow. Beth dragged her along the hallway and she thought she was taking her into the lounge, no doubt to humiliate her in front of her friends, as if they didn't think she was already a loser. Instead, she took her to her room, swinging open the door and shoving Danni into the darkened room. Danni stumbled into the room, hands out in front of her, trying to get her bearings. Beth slammed the door and once Danni turned around and worked out where the door was, she tried to open it.

Someone was holding the handle from the outside, she was effectively locked into Beth's room. But why?

'Beth? Let me out!' She banged on the door, the sound lost in the music from down the hall.

Then the lamp behind her clicked on, illuminating the room. Danni was too scared to turn around. She grabbed at the door again.

'Let me out, Beth! Please!' she yelled over the music. The hammering that had started in her heart when she was plunged into the darkened room had ratcheted up a notch, her whole body thrummed with terror.

'Come on, Danni, be nice to me, sweetheart,' she heard the deep, honeyed voice say behind her.

She recognised that voice. She turned. It was Donovan.

He was sitting on the edge of the bed close to the pillows. He patted the space beside him, encouraging her to come and sit by him. She turned and pulled on the doorknob, but Beth was still holding onto it.

'Enjoy yourself, little sister!' she laughed wildly.

Danni knew what being locked in the room with this boy meant. He wanted sex and if she said no, then he'd probably rape her. Her eyes were wide, her mouth dry, making a clicking sound when she swallowed, and she felt the beginnings of a headache brimming behind her eyes.

'Please...' she begged.

'I won't hurt you. I promise I'll make you feel good. You've never been with anyone before, have you?' he asked softly. 'That's what Beth said, anyway.'

Danni couldn't answer, her body had seized up on her. Donovan stood and casually walked over to her, reaching out a hand, cupping her cheek. 'You're so beautiful, Danni.'

'Don't touch me,' she said in a voice that barely carried the distance between them, trying to turn her head away

He gripped both her shoulders, spun her around and pushed her toward the bed. She fell, bent over then felt a hand on the back of her neck.

'Oh yeah, you're gonna feel so good. Hold still baby, this might take a while.'

Danni heard him undoing his belt, felt him pulling his jeans down. His hand pulling roughly at her jeans, her underwear. He was panting hard, like he'd run a race that he hadn't yet begun. She felt his fingers on her skin. They were cold, icy cold and she couldn't for the life of her figure out why. The coldness reminded her of when she was locked in the shed at the back overnight during winter, her hands and feet near frozen.

She felt him press up against her, she could feel his hardness. He flipped her over, ripping down her underwear and admiring the view.

'Virgin pussy,' he said, like it was some kind of rite of passage. He lunged at her, pulling on her hair and positioning himself above her. She could see the sweat popping on his forehead, the pimples that dotted his cheeks, the beer breath that washed over her face as he panted. He pulled back to push down his underwear and she sat up so fast that he ripped out a chunk of her hair.

She pushed him off her and quickly bent down, grabbing the knife from her shoe. She held the plastic grip, no hesitation, and stabbed down into the flesh of Donovan's hands. Danni stabbed him again and again, his cries becoming louder and louder. Then, in a frenzy, she lashed out, stabbing him wherever she could. He lowered his hands to cover his genitals as Danni stabbed him over and over.

The door flew open and Beth rushed in. 'What the fuck is going on?' Then she saw the half-naked Donovan covered in blood.

'Oh shit! Danni, what have you done? *Fuck!*' She kicked the door closed. Then she grabbed the weapon that was slick with blood from Danni's hands and shoved it in her pocket. 'You bitch! All he wanted to do was fuck you!' Beth said, backhanding Danni. She fell to the ground, then stumbled to her feet, pulling up her pants, desperately trying to cover herself.

Donovan was moaning, holding his bleeding crotch. The music thumped, the bass drumming, drowning out his cries.

'Shit, we've got to do something.' She snapped her fingers in front of Danni's face.

'*Fuck*, how could you do this to me? I'm gonna go to jail, you stupid bitch. Shit. Help me drag him out the window. Now. Danni! Now, God damn it! I should let you suffer for this.' Beth's face was dangerously flushed, her eyes black pinpricks as she slapped Danni's arm to get her attention.

Danni, hands covered in blood, obeyed the command in her sister's voice without question, absently wiping her hands on her pants, leaving streak marks. Donovan was groaning loudly, bending over the end of the bed, turning his hands over, staring at the blood.

'Shut up, Donovan, we're going to get you help, but I've got to do something first.' She cocked back her arm and hit him square in the face. He dropped to his knees, clutching his nose, crotch momentarily forgotten. Beth stuffed a pair of her underwear in his mouth then wrapped a dressing gown belt around his head tightly, holding the gag in place. Beth grabbed one arm and hissed at Danni to take the other. She moved robotically and took hold of his other arm as Beth dragged him towards the window. Of course, her window wasn't nailed shut.

'Get out the window, Danni. Grab him.'

Danni climbed out of the window and grabbed the torso of the bleeding, barely struggling, moaning Donovan and held him tightly while Beth shoved the rest of him through the gap.

'Hurry, up to the shed. Fuck, he's heavy,' Beth groaned as they took an arm each and dragged Donovan to the shed slowly, breathing heavily. Beth kept checking towards the lounge room window, but the curtains remained closed. Beth reached the door to the shed and dropped Donovan, his weight resting uncomfortably on Danni's shoulder while Beth fumbled with the handle before finally opening the door. Danni staggered under his weight and fell, Donovan dropping heavily to the ground. Beth grabbed Donovan's arm, angrily murmuring at Danni to do the same. They shoved him inside where he rolled onto the floor, knocking over petrol cans and tins of paint. A long-forgotten project of their father's, painting the house. Six tins of paint and a tin of paint thinner rolled around, banging into the prone boy. His hands were cupped between his legs, Danni was disembodied from her surroundings, not really comprehending what was going on.

'Get in and close the door, stupid. Want people to see us?' Beth pulled Danni inside then grabbed at her hair. 'What to do, what to do. Donovan, I'm gonna take that gag out of your mouth but if you scream no one will hear you and I'll let my sister finish what she started. Understood?'

The semi-conscious boy nodded.

Beth undid her belt and took out the gag. Donovan was silent, hardly conscious now. Looking around, Beth's eyes wild, she picked up a can of thinner and unscrewed the lid.

'Danni? Danni, we have to get rid of the body.'

'Why?' she said absentmindedly.

'Well, for one, you just stabbed the shit out of him, but I can't count on you not to tell the police that I organised for you to be raped. *Fuck!* Why did you have to stab him? You've made life harder for us both. You need to swear that if you're questioned, I had nothing to do with this, neither did you. Understand me? I'm not going down for this and the only way that's gonna happen is if you talk. So don't talk, okay?' Danni was in shock but she could hear the fear in Beth's voice as she tried to convince Danni not to say anything, but Danni was beyond caring now.

Beth upended the tin on top of Donovan and around him, the fumes threatening to suffocate Danni. She coughed, covering her mouth with her hand, trying to be quiet but she needn't have bothered, the sounds from the party covered up any noises they made. In her confused state, even Danni realised that ultimately Beth was looking out for herself. Beth would be blamed for this, and the whole truth would come out. The abuse, the attempted rape. Danni could bury her if she wanted to.

Beth took a packet of crumpled cigarettes out of her pocket and a lighter out of her back pocket. She lit it, exhaling jerkily. 'Get out, Danni.'

Danni moved slowly, as if she was walking underwater, then she felt Beth give her a hard shove and she all but fell out of the shed. She turned and watched as Beth flicked the cigarette into the shed then closed and flipped the lock, trapping Donovan inside.

He started to scream as Beth pushed Danni back down the grass and inside through the window of the house. She turned back after Beth slammed the window; the shed was alight. Danni couldn't hear screaming, but she could imagine the skin melting from his body, the excruciating pain he would feel until his nerve endings burnt away. Danni turned, dropped to her knees and vomited.

Then her world went dark.

30

Danni hadn't seen Beth since the day she'd given her the key to the shitty motel and driven off. Beth had said she didn't want them in her life, and Danni was fine with that.

Beth may have been nothing but a manipulative, nasty, abusive bitch to her, but for now, Danni needed her, needed her charity. It made Danni's blood boil to have to take anything from that woman, but it had to be done, for her sake and Mia's.

Danni parked outside the café and took a couple of deep, calming breaths before walking inside. The café was on the corner of the intersection and was an old-fashioned place. The booths were vinyl, red and white striped tablecloths, decorated with kitsch salt and pepper shakers and a random unlit tea candle in the centre. Beth sat in the corner booth, staring out of the glass shop front across the street. If she had seen Danni, she didn't acknowledge her or turn to greet her. It was as if Danni didn't exist. Danni stood in front of the table, hitching her bag onto her shoulder clearing her throat, trying to grab Beth's attention.

Danni shifted her footing and cleared her throat again. 'Beth?'

Beth still ignored her, and Danni felt like a young girl again. She grabbed the salt shaker while she waited for Beth to turn and talk to her but it took a good while before Beth finally turned her head and stared at

Danni. She had a look of disdain on her face, her mouth sneering at her, her eyes narrowed in anger. Danni still didn't know what she had done to incur such wrath and hate this many years after they'd last seen each other.

'Beth. What am I doing here?'

'When I call, you come. Same as always. Nothing's changed there, has it, little sis?'

Danni felt rage building up inside of her. Patient, yet coming, building within her like a blossoming flower.

'So, what am I doing here?' she repeated. Danni wondered why she had even bothered coming at all. She was a grown ass woman, and her sister hadn't been a part of her or her life in years, so what was the point?

'Didn't you hear me, you're here because I called you. There are some things that we need to discuss, and I thought it was about the right time to do it.'

'You mean weeks after I lost my family, you absolutely have to talk to me? Where have you been all this time? Where have you been all these years?'

'We need to talk about the money, Danni.'

'What? The money you lent for the room and the spending money? I'll pay you back when I can,' she said sighing, running her hand through her dark hair. She hadn't bothered to brush her hair this morning. It was a tangled mess, the total opposite to her manicured sister.

'That's not what I wanted to talk to you about.'

'About what, then?' Danni said, not comprehending what Beth was talking about.

'Money, yes. Specifically the insurance money. When it comes through, I want half of it.' She said it so calmly, like it was no big deal.

Danni sat there, looking at her, dumbfounded, she literally could not find the words, while Beth sat there, admiring her nails and waited for Danni to catch up.

Danni laughed, a barking sound that seemed out of place. 'What?' Danni asked finally. 'What are you on about?'

'Are you fucking deaf?' Danni shrank back, transported right back to when she was young, shrieked at by her older sister. 'I said I want that money and you're going to give it to me.'

Danni just stared at her sister, still not understanding what was going on. Her face obviously reflected her confusion.

'Fucking hell, you're still a stupid bitch. Ever wonder if Joe was being faithful to you? Being a good husband?'

'That's none of your business. Why do you want to know, anyway?' Danni's mind flashed back to the night she saw him leaving Mia's room. *Was* he a good husband? She thought about the rumours. No, he wasn't a good husband.

'You're doubting him,' Beth said, twirling her long, straightened hair in her hand. Actually, she looked good. Good enough that Danni looked down at her donated jeans, top shop top and jacket and felt inadequate. 'You never were good enough for him you know. We all knew it.'

'Look, if this is going to turn into one of those bitter rants about how Joe should have been yours, then I'm leaving,' said Danni, half-standing up.

'Sit the fuck down!' hissed Beth, her hands slapping the table. 'There's something you should know,' Beth said, flipping her hair back over her shoulder as if she was annoyed.

'Oh, so I'm going to get life lessons from a child-abusing, sadistic bitch—'

'Your precious Joe was cheating on you.'

Danni stopped talking. She had heard the rumours, of course, but to actually be told it flat out still hurt.

'You were just too dumb to notice. Now close your mouth, you look like a hooker waiting for her next client.'

'Joe never cheated on me,' Danni said, knowing it wasn't true, but not willing to let her sister have the upper hand. Besides, she didn't know; not for sure.

'I can see the wheels in your brain turning so let you help me out. Your beloved husband Joe, who you married so young, has been sticking his dick wherever he likes for the better part of two decades.'

Danni looked up at Beth, who had a smug look in her eyes, and

Danni stared at her blankly for a minute, then let out a faint exhalation. 'You?'

'You're damn right, me. It should always have been me. I've been with him on and off for years. He'd come to me, whining about his life, how he felt trapped, suffocated by his kids, by you, especially. You never even stood a chance against me.'

'He never divorced me, Beth. He loved me and he loved his children. You have nothing, your shrivelled pathetic heart doesn't know what love is. He would never have left me for you. You have nothing.'

'I have his son.' Her eyes met Danni's and she knew that Beth wasn't lying.

There was dead silence as Danni digested the bombshell. Beth seemed to savour her victory, drawing out the silence until finally Danni spoke.

'What did you say?'

'I said,' Beth said, speaking very clearly, 'that I have his son. We've been together for three years solid now and yeah, we had a baby. His name is Joseph Junior. He's adorable, looks just like his daddy.' She twisted the knife that she'd plunged into Danni's heart for good measure.

'I can't believe this. How could you stoop this low?'

'Me? You trapped him first with Mia, and then Alexandra, and then that other one. He was dying inside, anyone could see that; he'd lost weight, he wasn't sleeping as much, he had lost his love for life, then we had the baby and he promised me the moon. Said he'd divorce you, but I didn't expect you to have the hold over him that you did.'

Was it her or Mia?

'So finally, I gave him an ultimatum, choose one of us and fuck the other off. He chose. He chose me and made me promises.'

'If he chose you, why was he in bed with the weekend before the fire?' Danni asked.

Beth looked annoyed. 'He was giving the kids one last weekend before he ripped the plaster off and changed their lives forever. Then the fire happened and neither of us got him.' She actually managed to mimic tears then acceptance all in the space of a few seconds. 'Anyway,' she said, back to business. 'I'm going to have half the insurance money from the house, since it was half his and he was all mine.' Beth smiled slowly, the corners of her lips turning upwards. 'Okay?' She grabbed her bag and was about to leave the booth.

'Over my dead fucking body will you get a cent from Joe's estate. He had a will and you weren't in it, so fuck off.' Danni stood up, faced off with her sister for a moment before turning and leaving, bag held close to her chest. Beth had pierced her heart with her words, which Danni knew to be true, but she was counting on that money to get a small house in town and put the rest away, not giving to a home wrecking whore like her sister. That money was their future, hers and Mia's.

Danni made it inside the car before the tears began falling. She banged the steering wheel and wanted so badly to scream. Of all the people he could have cheated with, he chose her sister. Why? Why would he do that, knowing what Beth had done to her for years?

She hated her sister for what she'd said. Could it be true? Joe could never answer her questions, never refute the claims, never confess about Beth and her bastard child. *Fucker.*

* * *

Danni drove around aimlessly for a while, bawling, the tears stinging her already swollen eyes. Joe had been seeing Beth for three years? For three years he'd lied to her, lied to their family. How could she ever forgive him for that? And his son, Joseph Junior, he was leaving them, her, his other three kids for this child. This faceless child who had contributed to her husband wanting to leave them.

If Joe wasn't dead already, she'd have killed him.

How dare Beth demand half of the insurance money that she was going to use to set up her and Mia. After all she'd put Danni through, the taunts, the abuse, the hatred.

Finally, Danni remembered that Mia was back at the motel by herself. She turned the car around and headed back into town. Unconsciously, she had been heading to the farm. When she pulled into the motel car park, she grabbed hold of the rear-view mirror and turned it on herself. She looked a mess. Like she'd had a real kick to the teeth, which she supposed she had. Her eyes were swollen, her teeth bared like a wild animal, which matched the look in her eyes. Wild. She had to calm down for Mia's sake.

Mia. Always on her mind. Even more so than her other children. Alexandra. Noah. Over and over so she could pretend they were still here. How she missed them, Noah's cheeky giggle, Alexandra's mothering way. The tears came again. She swiped at her eyes angrily, opened the door, slammed it with much more force than was necessary and locked it.

She took a deep breath and walked inside. Mia wasn't curled up on her bed. She was sitting on the edge facing the door, waiting for her.

'Where have you been?' Mia asked, then cleared her throat after her voice cracked.

'Mia, darling. It's so wonderful to hear your voice.' Danni dropped her bag and walked over to her quickly, cupping her face in her hands. Mia tried to turn her head away but Danni wouldn't let her, staring into her eyes for a moment longer before she let her go. She paced in front of her daughter, trying to decide how much to share with her.

'Do you remember Beth?' she asked, nearly walking a hole in the threadbare carpet as she paced up and down.

Mia regarded her with blank eyes. 'I remember, she drove us here,' she said quietly.

'She claims that she and your father were having an affair for the past three years, that they have a son together. She's just trying to get under my skin, yet again. What a fucking lie!' she yelled, clenching her fists and squeezing her eyes closed briefly. It was all a show though. She knew it could be true but couldn't accept it just yet.

'It's not a lie.'

Danni stopped pacing and stared at her daughter. 'What?'

'She's telling the truth,' she said in a whispered voice.

'What? Tell me what you know.' Danni's eyes were intense as they focused on her daughter.

Mia scooted back further on the bed. 'Dad – he was having an affair with her. I learned that they had a baby boy. He was leaving us for them. *He was leaving us.*' Her bottom lip quivered. She looked so young and vulnerable.

The full force of Mia's words hit Danni like a blow to her stomach. She couldn't breathe. Spots appeared in front of her eyes, and her breathing, when it did start again, was shallow and unsteady. When she could talk, she said, 'You knew about this?'

Mia nodded.

'For how long?'

Mia looked away, 'A few weeks, maybe a month.'

'Mia, you didn't tell me. Why?'

'I don't know. Dad said he was going to talk to you and asked me to give him the space he needed to find the right time. He begged me, Mum. I didn't know what to do.' Mia stuck a hunk of hair into her mouth and began chewing on it.

'Oh, baby. I can't believe he put you in that position.'

'Then he was gone. Like really gone.' Mia began to cry quietly. Danni went to wrap her arms around her daughter, but she shrugged her off again. Danni couldn't seem to get through to her no matter how hard she tried. It was like there was a pane of glass between them; she could see her but not reach her.

31

Sports day was always a huge source of anxiety for her. Julie and her posse never let up on her, they just kept coming at her until they could break her. Some days she felt like an ice sculpture, ready to topple over and shatter into a million pieces, melt away into nothing. She couldn't tell her parents. She couldn't tell anyone. She was all alone.

Changing into her bathers, she cowered in the corner, trying to make herself invisible to the other girls, who were laughing.

A couple of the girls looked at her as Julie made her way over to her. There were some sympathetic glances, but no one came to help her. She was only half dressed and felt exposed. Julie stopped in front of her and said in a nice voice, 'Hey freak. Where'd your tits go?'

Everyone could hear but, despite her frantic glances around the room, they all turned away, some looking guilty, but none helping her.

'She's got no boobs,' Julie said with disdain, thrusting her own large chest in her direction. 'You're such a baby. Come on! We're going to go swimming,' she said brightly, snapping the strap of her bathers. Her two friends were wearing identical grins. She quickly pulled up her bather top, hiding the barely-there buds of breasts. Julie put a hand on her shoulder and propelled her towards the door out to where the swimming pool was.

They didn't have one at their school, so they caught a bus down to the local pool, and she always scrunched herself down in the front seat, making herself small. Then the humiliation of getting changed into her bathers, then letting people see her scrawny, underdeveloped body. It was pure torture, although not as bad as changing back into her school uniform.

Julie pushed her way through girls, using her as a battering ram of sorts. She quietly and desperately apologised to all of them as she touched them, hoping someone would step in and end this madness. But of course, no one stood up to Julie. She ruled their class and that was that. She pushed her towards the pool, ever closer to the edge. Julie didn't know that she had a deep fear of water, having almost drowned in the river during a camping trip when she was younger. She remembered the swirling of the murky water, pulling her under, violently turning her this way and that with the current. She thought she was going to die that day until the strong arms of a stranger dragged her to safety.

The edge of the pool loomed closer and closer. Inch by inch Julie pushed her forward. She looked frantically around for help, a teacher, a lifeguard, but none were watching her and she knew if she called out, she'd be in for so much worse. So she let herself be pushed ever closer to the edge. She stared down at the clear water just as Julie gave her an almighty shove. She landed in the pool with a splash and immediately began thrashing about. She looked towards the edge of the pool, so tantalisingly close, just as Julie jumped in beside her with a whoop. Julie grabbed her by the shoulders and pushed down, shoving her under the water. She began to panic, opened her mouth to scream, but only water rushed in. She gulped it down in an effort to not breathe but holding her breath made her lungs burn and tears streamed from her eyes, mingling with the chlorinated water.

She was back in the muddy water, thrashing about, not able to get out of the current. Julie popped up for air, let her up for a second where she grabbed a deep breath before being dragged down again. She tried holding her breath, eyes wide, looking into Julie's eyes, which were half closed, staring at her, her mouth stretched into a smile. It was terrifying; Julie was getting off on this.

She was running out of air and feared she would be drowned while the people from her class looked down at her, not helping. She could see their blurry faces when she looked up, distorted by the water. Not one of them helped her. She would have to help herself. She grabbed Julie's wrists and tugged at them, releasing the grip on her shoulders, shoving her down. As she flailed her arms in an attempt to get to the surface, she felt Julie grab her ankle. She kicked out with her foot and felt it connect with something hard that jarred the bones in her foot. She managed to wade her way through the water, the faces fast becoming clearer. She pushed through the surface, her head bobbing out of the water, gasping for much needed air. She flailed about and tried to swim her way to the edge, reminded again of the swirling current of the river.

Julie popped to the surface right beside her. 'You broke my nose, you bitch!' she yelled, blood streaming from her nose, colouring the water pink.

Teachers came running after seeing the blood in the water. 'Oh my God, Julie, what happened?'

'She kicked me in the face!' Of course she didn't say that she had tried to drown her first.

The teacher crooked her finger at her. 'Was this an accident?'

She nodded her head, close to tears. Everyone was staring at her, witnesses that didn't want to be involved. The teacher could see she was about to cry but put her arm around Julie and walked her away. Julie looked back at her and narrowed her eyes. She knew she was in for it now.

32

Sweating and grunting, the man on top of her thrust into her like a freight train and she loved every minute of it. She felt powerful, in control, sexy. She knew that picking up a random stranger at some unknown bar and going home with him was risky, but this wasn't her first rodeo. She had no friends to tell them where she was going, but she didn't feel she needed to. She could protect herself.

He rolled her over so she was on top, now she had *all* the power. The stranger finished in record time. She crawled off him and pulled her underwear on, annoyed that he had come so quickly. Now she felt empty inside. Empty and alone. She finished getting dressed and left, slamming the door behind her.

She came face to face with a woman, blonde, plain but pretty in her own way. 'Who are you?' she asked, gesturing to the house she had so recently left.

'A friend.'

The blonde stared at her. 'Who were you visiting?' she asked, eyes narrowed.

'Um...' She had no idea what his name he was. They had never got that far.

'Did you just screw my boyfriend?' the girl asked hysterically, her bag slipping from her shoulder to land on the floor with a soft thump.

'No, I was just—' She never even saw the fist coming. The girl punched her across the cheek, causing an explosion of pain. Finally, she felt something.

'Well, shit,' she said as she aimed a punch at the girl's eye. Her fist connected and when the girl dropped, she took off walking at a fast pace, heading for the corner so she could catch a taxi home.

Yes, finally she felt something.

Fulfilment.

33

Danni sat on the leather couch, her mind drifting in and out. She was sitting beside Michelle, otherwise she would have taken off by now. She did not want to be sitting in the waiting room of Dr Parson's office. She did not want to see a head shrink, a doctor, another person telling her how she should feel, asking questions that she didn't want to answer and analysing those answers. She didn't need the added stress and extra layer of drama; she'd had enough of that to last a lifetime. Michelle prattled on beside her, perhaps sensing her reluctance.

'I have to see the doctor after you, for a quick chat, so you'll have to wait out there for me. Okay?' she said brightly.

Danni played along and gave her a tentative smile. 'No problem.'

'Danni?' She looked up at her name being called, her stomach churning. She felt like crying. She didn't want to go in. She would find out her secrets. No one would like her, she kept repeating this mantra over and over.

'Danni?'

Michelle smiled at her, encouraging her to stand up and go in. Danni felt helpless, the tears beginning to build in her eyes, yet she went in anyway.

Danni had no idea how long she had been in the doctor's office, her mind seemed to drift in and out. She asked her questions as she knew she would, but she scarcely remembered answering them. She did remember tears and then anger, but not much else after that. She was guided out of the office by the doctor and Michelle helped her into a chair to wait while she went back in. Danni sat there for who knew how long, still in shock, until Michelle came out. She gave Danni a brilliant fake smile that she could see coming a mile off then said brightly, 'How about we go home now, Danni?'

Funny thing was, Danni couldn't seem to remember now what had been said or asked of her, and clearly Michelle knew but wasn't willing to bring it up with her. As her guardian she was supposed to know everything, Danni guessed, not just feed, clothe and provide her with a roof over her head.

When they finally pulled into the driveway, Danni was exhausted. She just wanted to sleep for a week but when she opened her bedroom door, she felt that something just wasn't... right. It felt like the room had been disturbed somehow. Had Michael done a check of her room to make sure she hadn't brought drugs into the house? She began to catalogue her meagre possessions; she didn't plan on staying here long so she didn't have much. Soon she and Joe would move in together and start their lives with their baby. She rubbed her stomach, imagining she could feel the burgeoning life growing within her. She opened her underwear drawer. One for each day of the week plus a spare. And one pair was missing. One guess as to who had taken that.

Incensed, she stormed across the hall and barged into Andrew's room. 'You think it's funny to steal other people's shit? Well, do you?' she demanded when he didn't answer.

'I... I... don't know what you're talking about,' he stammered.

'I don't like people stealing my stuff and I hate liars.'

Michelle appeared in the doorway. 'What's going on?' she asked, 'I can hear you down the hallway.'

'He took a pair of my underwear. I counted,' accused Danni, breathing heavily.

'I'm sure that's not the case,' Michelle said, frowning at Danni. 'Andrew would never do that. Would you, Andrew?'

'No, Mum, of course not. Maybe you miscounted, Danni,' he said in a sweet as pie voice.

'I did not miscount,' Danni said through gritted teeth.

'Okay, okay, let's defuse the situation, shall we? Danni, perhaps you miscounted, and Andrew, stay away from Danni's room and we won't have any more of these... misunderstandings. Why don't you go back to your room, Danni?'

Danni went back to her room but she could hear the low rumble of Michelle's voice through the walls. What was she telling him? What they'd talked about today or how she was crazy to react like that about the loss of a pair of underwear? She just hoped Michelle didn't tell him whatever the psychologist had said to her. It remained to Danni just a blur of leather couches and winged back chairs, this year's magazines and fresh linen air freshener.

Half an hour later, there was a knock on her door. 'Come in.'

Andrew poked his head around the door frame. 'Just wanted to check that you're okay,' he said, showing fake concern. 'Mum told me what happened to you today. Must be hard going to see a shrink. I wouldn't like to.'

'What do you want, Andrew?' she said with a sigh, rubbing her temples.

'Oh, nothing. Just wanted to show you something.' She looked up; he was holding the missing pair of underwear.

'You little fucking creep,' she said as she flung herself off the bed.

'Uh-uh, Danni. I'll just hide them and say you attacked me then my parents won't want you here any more and you'll be back to the group home. You want that?' Cockily, delivered with glee, but he had Danni over a barrel.

'Fine, keep them, I don't care,' she said flippantly.

He looked almost crestfallen at the thought that she wouldn't play his game. Danni had enough dramas going on. Joe hadn't been at school for two days and as far as she could tell, neither had Beth. Was it a coincidence? She'd ask him next time she saw him, since his phone kept going to voicemail.

'Fuck off, Andrew,' she said as she closed the door on the teen grasping her underpants. How many of the other girls had he played inappropriate pranks on?

34

She'd never wanted kids. Never wanted to bring another life into this fucked up world. There were enough losers with kids and she sure as shit wouldn't be one of them. A deadbeat mum without a deadbeat dad. So, when she found out that she was pregnant, her brain immediately switched gears. Who could the father be? Could it have been the guy she'd fucked at the party? The guy she'd screwed in the bar toilet? Or the guy she'd picked up at the supermarket then ridden in his car? So many men, so many options and those were just the ones she could remember. There were many more hazy nights filled with booze and grinding, hands all over her body. Who knows who else she'd slept with?

They made her a whore; she was just living up to her reputation.

Now she was knocked up, no idea who the baby daddy was. Not that it mattered, she wasn't keeping it anyway. No fucking way, there was no room in her life for a baby. She'd have to change everything about herself and she was too selfish to do that. Thinking about the life growing inside of her made her angry. She picked up a vase and threw it at the wall, glass raining down on her, leaving some small cuts. *Fuck*. She was selfish. She didn't want to quit drinking and sleeping around.

She thought about adoption for a split second, and decided against it. She couldn't carry it then give it away. That wasn't fair to anyone, plus, if she carried the baby, no one would want to screw her any more. A whore, that's what she was. Someone to fuck then leave. Never tell them your real name or real phone number, and never take them home. Three rules to live by. She pulled out her phone and looked for the nearest place that she could find. For another moment she wondered what a baby would look like in her life. Would she be a good mother? One that would nurture her child? Nope. She'd screw this baby up no end. No bloody way.

* * *

She walked up the steps to the flat, squat building that held doctors who gave abortions to people like her. Her hand found its way to her stomach for the briefest of seconds. It was time to be rid of her predicament. Like now.

Four hours later, she walked out of the boring, unassuming building, slowly making her way to her car. She had an ache in her stomach, which she blamed on her little problem. A problem that was now done and dusted.

Vowing to no longer think about the baby, she went home to her shit heap of a unit and lay on her bed, sheets crumpled from her sleepless night the night before. She'd been dreaming about this guy she'd met a few weeks ago at a bar in town. She didn't want to think about him; everyone thought she was Miss Pump and Dump, but he had her intrigued. She was actually imagining what might be if things were different.

As she lay on her bed, she looked at her phone and urged it to ring. She had given him her real phone number. She hadn't meant to when he'd asked for it, but there was something about this guy. He'd noticed her at the end of the bar and just like in the movies, he'd come over to buy her a drink. He was hot and she needed validation.

'Thanks for the drink,' she said in a seductive voice, whispered into his ear.

'You're the most beautiful woman here.'

She blushed prettily underneath her makeup. His deep voice gave her the shivers, and electricity coursed through her. The thrill of the chase. 'And you're a walking cliché,' she countered. 'Hey, want to get out of here?'

His hand touched her, then he lightly ran his fingers up to her thigh. 'That answer your question?'

She returned the favour by sliding one finger from his knee, then ran a circle round the crotch of his pants. She could feel he was hard.

'Want to go to your place?' she asked, remembering her own rules.

'Actually,' he said, holding up his hand, 'I'm married. But I'd love to get your number. I'll even give you mine.' She wasn't shocked that a man that good looking was married, she just didn't care.

Whether it was the shots, the desire or the man himself, she gave it to him. Her real number. Her smile had slipped a little upon hearing that he was married, but she loved a challenge. She grabbed a napkin and scribbled her number down, passing it to him. He stuffed it in his pocket.

'Where's your car?' she asked.

'I'm married, remember?' he said, twirling the wedding ring on his finger.

'So what? I won't tell if you don't.'

He smiled slowly, her insides tumbling with desire. He stood, and, as she did the same, he put his hand on her elbow and led her through the crowd. Once outside she looked around, blinking in the sudden darkness, hot from being inside with all those sweaty people bumping up against her.

'My car's over there,' he said quietly. She wondered if he came quietly too.

He held open the back door and she climbed in, the leather cold on her thighs but she figured she'd be warm enough soon. They hadn't exchanged names, but she decided that if he asked she would tell him her real name. He didn't ask, instead, he laid her down on the cold seat and began to kiss her with passion. Then that was it, no more foreplay, he just thrust himself inside her, pumping away, and she wondered if this was how he fucked his wife. It didn't matter. She'd show him a better time than he'd ever had. Them getting caught fucking in the back seat of his car just added an extra layer to the experience. Then he surprised her by wrapping his hands around her throat and squeezing harder as he grunted and came inside her. He pulled out and she sat up. He gave her a lingering kiss. She took this to mean that he had enjoyed their encounter that she didn't want to end.

'I have to get home.'

'To your wife?' she said cheekily. Bet he never choked her out.

She waited for three days for him to call. She resisted texting or calling him. Maybe he was busy with work, or the wife. That must be it, she probably had him on a short lead. On the fifth day she could wait no longer. She picked up the phone, looked at the number and dialled with a nervous hand.

'Crisis Line, do you need a friend?'

She held the phone loosely in her hand.

'Hello? Do you want to talk about something that's bothering you? Hello?'

Slowly she dropped her phone into her lap. She shouldn't have been surprised, but right now she felt shock, then emotionally empty. It was a feeling she knew well but never to this degree. She had felt confused, but now she knew what she needed to do.

She went to her shower, turned on the hot water and stood under the cascade. Her hand slid down her stomach, fingers massaging the insides of her thighs before she parted her legs and began to touch herself. She came, panting hard with desire.

Sated for now, she dressed. Now it was time to go on the prowl. She smiled, a slow and calculated smile.

* * *

She watched as he bought a drink for the woman with the long curly red hair, then he touched her high on the thigh. He was certainly bold; she'd give him that. He obviously didn't recycle his conquests, choosing a new woman every time he came to the bar.

She felt like tapping the redhead on the shoulder and warning her, but she didn't. She wanted to teach him a lesson he wouldn't soon forget. She felt like she needed to gain control again, the upper hand, especially after what he did to her. The woman stood up, heading towards the bathroom, maybe getting cleaned up for him. Touching up her lipstick maybe, running her hands through her hair. Maybe she was going to sleep with him, maybe not.

Knowing that if they did fuck, they'd probably soon adjourn to the car for a quickie, she only had a limited window of time. She hid between two cars as she watched him walking towards his car, alone in the dark, no doubt waiting for his date. Or maybe she'd ditched him and he was going home alone. Either way, she stood up from behind a car, sliding the silver knuckle duster over her right hand, and followed him in the dark. Once she was right behind him, she said, 'Hey.'

He turned around, obviously not worried by the female voice and said, 'Hey, I know you.'

'Yeah you do,' she said as she drew back her right arm and punched him in the face. She felt satisfaction as she heard the crunch of bone and saw the spurt of black blood as he fell to the ground, gripping his nose, moaning. She smiled as she looked at the knuckle duster covered with blood. She looked down at him. She was going to punch him in her face again, going so far as to pull her hand back, then she changed her mind. He'd learned his lesson. 'Next time you screw a woman, don't screw her over.'

35

She forgave him, how could she not? After all, he was the father of her baby. They were going to be together, forever, one happy little family and no one, not even her sister could take that away from her. She walked down the hallway at school, thinking about the plans she'd had to get out of this place, run far from her life and leave it all behind her. Joe had the same dreams. To get away from who he was and make something of himself. Had she trapped him in this town, with her, unconsciously? No, she loved him, and this baby was a representation of their love. He loved her too.

'Hey, bitch, you know yet that I fucked your boyfriend?' Beth said, suddenly appearing in front of her. She hadn't even seen her; she was in a world of her own. One of changed lives and forgotten dreams.

'Go to hell, Beth.'

'So now that we're not at home, you think you're the alpha now? That it? I could beat you down anytime I wanted to. What do you have to say about that?' She stood so close to Danni she could smell the mint on her breath.

'Don't care,' Danni said, feeling no fear. In fact, her blood started to simmer under her skin and she felt another headache pulsing in the base of her neck. She had the urge to watch her sister bleed.

Out of nowhere, Beth slapped her. The slap left her skin singing with pain and Danni instantly responded by wrapping her hands around Beth's neck and squeezing. Out of the corner of her eye, she saw people coming out of a classroom and stop to stare at the sight before them. Beth's face had started to turn a blush shade of red and she was clawing at Danni's hands, trying to pry them free.

'Hey! Get off her!' someone cried, but did nothing to help. Maybe they were scared of *her* now.

Danni leaned in close to Beth, putting even more pressure on her throat. 'Don't you ever come near me or Joe again. I am the alpha now, *bitch*,' she whispered before she was wrenched from behind, the hold on Beth broken. Beth collapsed to the floor, coughing and panting. There were red marks around her throat. Danni whirled around, ready to dish out the same justice to whoever had stopped her, but it was a male teacher. Scowling, he said, 'Right, both of you, the principal's office, now.'

They talked to Beth first who croaked out a bullshit tale of being attacked by Danni. She out and out lied to the principal. When it was Danni's turn to speak, all she had were threats and a slap.

'She tried to kill me!' cried Beth, huge tears rolling down her cheeks.

'We have a no bullying policy here at the school and we enforce it, young lady,' the principal said to Danni when they were sitting in his office, his fingers under his chin. 'You'll be suspended for one week and it will go in your permanent file. Do you understand, Danielle?'

She nodded.

'Beth, do you want me to call the police so you can lay charges?'

Beth looked panicked for a moment.

'Uh, no. No police.'

Yeah that's right, run and hide, bitch.

That was usually what Danni tried to do, but this time she had power coursing through her. What was she going to tell Michelle? Her headache, which she noticed had gone away for a while was now back with vengeance, throbbing from the base of her neck to the top of her head which was woolly, her mind unfocused.

She left school at recess after trying unsuccessfully to find Joe to tell him what had happened. He could be anywhere, so she just left, feeling both dejected and strangely elated. Danni walked back to the house, rehearsing in her head what she was going to say, but when she opened the front door, Michelle yelled, 'Is that you, Danni?'

'Yeah, it's me.' She trudged into the kitchen where Michelle was sitting, mobile in front of her on the table.

'I just had an interesting call from your principal.'

'It was self-defence.'

'You were choking a girl,' Michelle said, totally shocked.

'It was my sister, Beth. And she started it.' She knew how petulant she sounded, but oddly enough, she cared what Michelle thought. She was the only mother figure she had.

'So that makes it okay? I don't think so. Now tell me, what was going through your mind? Sit down, Danni, we need to talk about this and I'd rather do it before the boys get home.'

Michelle seemed intent on getting to the bottom of why she had tried to squeeze the life from Beth's body. At least there'd be a visual reminder on Beth's neck of what Danni could do if pushed too far now. Absently she rubbed her belly. Did evil transfer? She wondered. *Was she evil?*

'Why did you try to hurt your sister?' Michelle dived right in.

'Well, I'm guessing you've read my file and my case worker would have told you about me, right?'

'Yes, I'm aware of your background.' A look of sadness came over her face as she looked at Danni. 'I'm sorry you've had such a traumatic childhood Danni, but it doesn't excuse what you did today.'

'She really did slap me first, you know. She's always hurting me, this time she just held back and I didn't.'

'And then what happened?'

'I don't know, something just came over me and I found my hands wrapped around her throat. I'm not even sure how they got there. I swear I'm good. A good person, I mean.'

Michelle leaned forward. 'I believe you are a good person deep down, Danni, but you have some serious work to do on yourself to be a better person. I want you to be that person.'

What Michelle said made sense to Danni and she wondered why she had attacked Beth. She'd hit, kicked, pulled out her hair and much worse before yet a simple slap and some nasty comments had set her off? Why was that? Was she finally able to protect herself? Was she fighting for her child? Had her experiences hardened her? She didn't want to be a hardened person, yet at the same time, she knew that she'd do anything to survive and absolutely anything for her unborn child. Again, her hand snaked its way across her belly, an action that Michelle saw.

'You okay?'

'No. Actually, I'm feeling kinda queasy after today. What I did...' she trailed off. 'I might go lie down if that's okay. But thank you for caring. Makes a nice change.' And that was the truth. Someone giving an actual shit about her was a new thing for her. She lay down on the bed, kicked off her black school shoes and made a silent promise to her baby.

I will always be there for you. I will never harm you in any way. Nothing but love from me, kiddo.

* * *

Michelle checked in on her later, sitting on the edge of Danni's bed. 'You know, you can tell me anything, I'll always listen and I won't judge.'

Danni had the uncomfortable sensation that Michelle could look into her soul and see that she was pregnant. Michelle didn't say anything but she'd left the door open for Danni to say something to her. If she did, she was worried that they'd take her away and put her in some dark, dank place for pregnant teens. At least, that was her nightmare. She would have loved to have a mother to ask things about the baby, but until she was eighteen, in just under a month, she had to keep it to herself. She'd tell Michelle after her birthday. Admit that she was having a baby.

Joe would have to get a job. Luckily, in their town, rent was cheap. He already had a car so that was one thing. Car, a place to live, food and baby stuff. She had it all figured out. Joe should try to look for a job now, get a jump on the job hunting before he graduated and everyone was looking for a job. Danni wouldn't be finishing year eleven. How could she? She'd have a new born baby to take care of.

36

Joe saw her after lunch. She was walking ahead of him slowly, like maybe she wanted to be caught. He ran up behind her and tapped her on the shoulder. She turned.

'Jesus, what happened to your neck?' he said, staring at the red welts on Beth's neck.

'Your fucking girlfriend happened,' Beth croaked out. She had been advised to go home but she would never pass up a chance to be the centre of attention and marks on her throat plus her difficulty in speaking made for added delight when she told the story of how her sister had tried to kill her in the hallway. By the end of the day, everyone would think Danni was a dangerous freak. She would be just the way Beth liked her, isolated. No friends, no chances left and suspended from school.

'Did you say or do something to her?' He watched as her eyes dropped to the floor. The Danni he knew only retaliated when seriously provoked or backed into a corner. He just knew that Beth had done something to her.

'Okay, so I may have slapped her, but she totally overreacted, don't you think?'

Joe shook his head. 'I can't believe I ever fucked you.' He stormed off, hearing Beth pleading behind him to stop. She ran after him, grabbing his arm.

'Don't leave me Joe. I'll die without you.'

'You never had me, Beth, you were just a piece of ass. I love Danni, have since the beginning. You just can't compete, so why don't you leave me and her alone from now on?'

He left school early, blowing off the afternoon and drove to where Danni was now living. He'd dropped her off before but had never been inside. He knocked on the door and a nice-looking middle-aged woman opened the door.

'Yes?'

'Hi, Mrs Johnson?'

'Yes.'

'I'm Joe Brooks, I'm Danni's boyfriend, I was wondering if I could see her, please?'

Danni, who must have seen his car pull up, appeared behind Mrs Johnson. 'Hey, Joe,' she said as the woman stepped to the side.

'Why don't you two go and sit out the back where it's more comfortable.'

'Thanks, Michelle,' said Danni and gave her a smile. Joe followed Danni inside the nice home and out to the back patio.

He waited until they sat down next to each other. Joe grabbed Danni's hand and said, 'I heard what happened today with Beth and the suspension. Why didn't you fight it? You could have just got you caseworker to show them your file and they would have believed self-defence. Now you're not where I can see you every day.'

'You really care that much?' She seemed surprised and he began to evaluate how good a boyfriend he'd been. He now regretted ever sleeping around on Danni, especially with Beth, she just had a sexual pull over him. He was surprised that Danni hadn't dumped him already, but he guessed she was as stuck as he was. They only had each other now, and the baby.

Goddamn, he was going to be a dad. Everything that could go wrong ran through his head. But the person he wanted to speak to most after

Danni was his mother. She needed to know in case something happened to her that she was going to be a grandmother.

'Of course I care about you. Danni, I've loved you ever since I saw you sitting alone at lunch. I remember asking Beth who you were, not knowing that you were related.'

Her name tainted the sweet moment between them. Danni put her hands in her lap so he couldn't touch her, and he could have kicked himself. She knew he'd slept with her recently and he knew that Beth had rubbed it into Danni's face already. She was that kind of vindictive person. If Joe was honest, she was a horrible person and he made a promise to Danni and himself to never go near her again. He brushed her hair from her face.

'Look, I have to go, babe, but I'll come by and see you in a couple of days, okay?'

'Sure,' she said, looking dejected. He stood up and pulled her up gently by the arm too. He kissed her lovingly and whispered in her ear, 'I love you, Danni.'

'I love you too, Joe. I guess I'll see you in a week when I'm back at school.'

She looked down, so he said, 'Want me to come see you Wednesday?' Her face lit up so he vowed to keep his promise to her. All of them.

* * *

Joe drove home, taking the corners way too fast. Now that he'd made the decision to tell his mother, he just wanted to get it done, besides, he was late checking in on her. One day he was going to have to confess to Danni what went on in his home. How sick his mum actually was and what his father was like. A loser. Joe refused to be like him. He was adamant that he'd be a good husband and father. Once Danni turned eighteen shortly, he was planning on asking her to marry him. He was sure that she'd say yes, especially when she wanted to build a life together.

He pulled up at the front of his house and when he opened the door, he was hit by the smell. Rushing into his mother's room, he saw her lying there, covered in vomit.

'Shit, Mum, what happened?'

Her eyes were puffy and her nose was red from crying. 'He left you like this? Where is the bastard?' Joe demanded.

'He went out a few hours ago. I was feeling sick but he didn't leave me a bucket, so this happened.' She weakly held her hand up.

Right, it was time for him to confront his father about what he was doing to his mother. She deserved so much more than this fucking bullshit.

'Okay, Mum, let's get you cleaned up.' There was dried vomit on her chin, so he tenderly wiped it off with a warm face washer before changing her sheets, giving her a sponge bath and putting her in a clean, soft nightgown.

She looked at him with imploring eyes. 'I'm sorry you have to do this, Joe. I'm so sorry.'

'Mum, would you stop apologising. I love you and I'm happy to do this for you.'

She turned her head to the side and let out a weak sigh. 'I just want you to leave this place, Joe. Never look back. As soon as you can.'

Joe realised that he was about to lift her up and break her heart in one go. 'Mum... Mum, there's something that I need to tell you. I won't be going anywhere. I won't be leaving town for the city after I graduate. I'll get a job and stay here.'

'No,' she breathed.

'My girlfriend Danni is going to have a baby. You're going to be a grandmother.'

He waited for her to speak, the warring emotions plain as day on her face. Elation and devastation. It looked like she didn't know which to focus on first.

'She's amazing, Mum. She goes to school with me. She's smart and pretty and she's having my baby. I'm happy, Mum.'

Finally, his mother smiled. 'I'm going to be a grandmother?' There were tears in her eyes as she spoke.

'Yeah, Mum, you are.' He held her hand gently as she cried. He leaned over and pulled out a tissue, wiping her eyes which immediately welled up again. He was grateful to Danni for giving his mum a reason to smile again.

* * *

Joe waited in the darkened lounge, ready for when his father came home so they could have a little heart to heart. A little father-son bonding time. When he finally did stumble in sometime after midnight, Joe could smell the booze on him as he fumbled with the light. Before he could turn it on, Joe was up in a flash and slammed his baseball bat right into his stomach. His father groaned loudly, then dropped to his knees, vomiting on the carpet, the sour stench lingering in the air. Joe could hear him wheezing for breath. It reminded him of his mother sometimes when she couldn't breathe. Joe flipped on the light so his dad could see who'd hit him. His father looked up at him from his now kneeling position.

'The fuck?' he managed, vomit dripping from his chin. He wiped it with the sleeve of his shirt.

Joe hauled him up and threw him into his recliner chair. His father tried to struggle out of the chair but Joe pushed the bat into his chest so he was forced to sit still or be hit again.

'This little chat is long overdue,' Joe said, towering over the seated and unsettled man. There was a look of real fear in his eyes.

'What's this about, son?'

'Son? Since when have I been your son? I've been doing your job for years and it stops now. Got it? I'm talking about Mum. You take care of her properly, the way you're supposed to, or I'll dob you in. You get me? And while you're at it, you're to stop seeing your girlfriend. Dump her. Your wife, my mother, is your only priority now. Do you understand me?'

His father let out a coughing bark.

'I don't want to have to have this conversation with you again, okay? Next time, I'll really hurt you.' It wasn't a threat, he'd do it. He'd do anything for his mother.

The wheezing man nodded quickly, looking at the bat gripped tightly by Joe's side. Maybe once he could intimidate his son, but not now. Joe was going to be a father and a father should sort shit out. Well, that's what he believed, anyway.

Joe helped his father to his feet. 'Go check on Mum before you go to bed, all right?'

'Yes Joe,' he said meekly. Joe allowed himself a small smile of victory. Things were finally changing.

37

Danni's phone rang, vibrating in her pocket. It was on silent so as to not disturb Mia, who was resting on the other bed. Danni didn't recognise the number, but then again, she had no numbers in her new phone except Susan's, whom she hadn't heard from since the funerals. She walked out of the room, easing the door closed behind her.

'Hello?' she said, standing outside their room.

'Is this Ms Brooks?' asked a disembodied woman's voice.

'It's Mrs,' and again she wondered whether people who kept referring to her as Ms did so because she no longer had a husband or if it was just an oversight.

'My apologies, Mrs Brooks. My name is Katherine Walker with Trust Insurance.'

'Are you ringing about my claim for my house?'

'Yes, I am,' she said in a strong voice. There was a small pause. 'I'm afraid to inform you that Trust Insurance has rejected your claim. The police have concluded their investigation and we have been informed that they have found the fire was the result of arson by person or persons unknown, so Trust Insurance will not be paying out your claim.'

'What? You can't do that! What will we do for money? Please, you need to reconsider. Surely there's something we can do. I lost my house and I lost my family, please, help me.' This could not be happening. She was begging, desperate for help.

'You are certainly welcome to appeal the decision, Mrs Brooks, but I must caution you, this is the decision we've come to after two separate investigations reached the same conclusion as the police, and that was that someone deliberately set fire to your house, therefore voiding your insurance. I'm sorry for your loss. Remember, you can appeal the decision with our office,' she said calmly.

'Fine,' snapped Danni. 'Thanks for all your fucking help.'

'Goodbye, Mrs Brooks,' she said with finality, probably used to being sworn at.

Danni wanted to storm back inside, slam the door and rail at the insurance company, but she didn't. So it really was official now. Someone had definitely set fire to her home, murdering her family and leaving her and Mia without a cent, a home or their family.

She went back inside and sat on the chair, elbows resting on the small round table in the cheap motel room, deep in thought. She needed to plan her next move. What the hell was she going to do without the insurance money? She had counted on it to get a small place for her and Mia, somewhere safe for Mia to recover. She had savings in the bank, but not enough. Not nearly enough.

She looked over at Mia. 'I think it's time you went outside, honey. You haven't really been outside since... since the funerals.' Even then she had barely been outside and ever since, she had stayed cooped up in the dark room. Danni felt guilty about the times she'd had to go and leave her on her own, but she still had things to do. Luckily, she had been able to access her bank accounts and had a new licence and credit cards, so although this place was a mess, it had become *their* mess, thinking that she might have heard back from the insurance agency by then.

Thinking about the insurance money automatically made her think of Beth, her stomach turning. How dare that bitch demand anything of her, let alone the hard-earned money she and Joe had paid in case of a tragedy. It was to get *her* family on their feet. Beth wasn't her family. She had never been.

'C'mon Mia, there's a table and chairs just outside the front door.

Come and sit with me. You're wasting away and you need some sunshine.'
Danni was pleading now.

Mia gave her a mournful look then slowly unfolded her legs like a
praying mantis, getting off the bed and following her elated mother
outside. Danni pulled out a chair for Mia and she sat down gingerly.
Danni sat across from her and reached her hand across the table for
Mia's, hoping she would meet her halfway now that she had seemed to
show some interest in living again. Mia didn't move her hand.

'Please, sweetheart. Just... let me help you. Let me love you.'

Danni was aware of the two people walking past staring at them,
probably thinking, *There's that poor widow.*

She didn't want to be known as that poor widow. She was a survivor,
someone who had survived the unimaginable. She wanted to be known
as Mia's mum, not some tragic figure. She missed her children so much, it
was like there was a hole in her heart, never to be filled again.

'What do you want to talk about, honey?'

Mia just shook her head.

'Okay, why don't I start? This may upset you but it's Noah's birthday
next week, so why don't we go and visit his grave today, lay some flowers
and maybe leave a toy truck there as well. What do you think?'

'Mum,' she said, finally talking to her since she'd told her about
finding love elsewhere. 'I can't. Can you?' She went to reach out for
Danni's hand, thought better of it and pulled her hand away. Danni
wanted to cry.

'I think I have to; I think *we* have to. We didn't go to their funeral, love.
It's time.'

Mia looked up at her, tears in her eyes as she whispered, 'Okay.'

Before Mia could change her mind, Danni ushered her daughter back
into the motel room and tried to encourage her to change. Danni placed a
pair of jeans and a top, much like the outfit she was wearing, onto Mia's
bed. Mia looked at it for a moment then changed slowly. Danni turned
around to give her privacy. Soon enough, they were in the car, heading to
the nearest petrol station to fill up the tank and buy a toy truck for Noah's
grave.

Danni was afraid Mia was going to bolt as soon as she left the car, but she was pleasantly surprised to find her still sitting in the passenger seat when she came back. 'What do you think of this?' Danni asked, showing Mia a bright blue truck with red flames down the side. Noah loved collecting trucks and had an extensive collection of them. Danni drove to the cemetery, neither one looking at the other, nor talking, somehow knowing that neither one of them could handle it. Danni's nerves were frayed, close to breaking with the approach of the first of the important dates since her family had died.

She kept her eyes firmly on the road in front of her, trying not to think about her dead son. Danni's mind wandered while she drove, the weak sun blinding her, bouncing off the recently rained on road, throwing startling shapes into her eyes. She pulled down the visor to cut some of the glare and wished she had some sunglasses. She risked a quick glance at her eldest child, only child, who was staring out of the side window so Danni couldn't see her expression, but her hands were clenched into tight fists in her lap. She was dreading this trip as much as Danni was.

Danni pulled up in the car park then realised that she had no idea where her family were buried.

'Mum, I can't. Take me back, please. Please,' Mia pleaded.

'But we're already here, love. All we have to do is find their graves.'

'I can't. You don't know what it's like, being the only one. You think you do but you don't. Take me back,' Mia demanded, tears behind her raw emotions.

'Mia, please, we need to do this for both of our sakes. We'll be together.'

'I don't want to go!' screamed Mia, her voice crashing around the car, stunning Danni into silence for a long moment. 'Don't you get it? I don't want to see them! To be reminded that I'm alive and they're not.'

'Okay, I'll take you back, but sooner or later, we're doing this, understood?' she said in a firm voice.

Mia ignored her, looking back at the window at the rows and rows of head stones, some crumbling, some new.

I'm sorry, she whispered to her family. *I'll come back when I can.*

She felt the pull of the dead and the pull of the living. Making up her mind, she fishtailed the car out of the gravel parking lot in an effort to get Mia back to the motel as fast as she could. She chose the living.

They arrived back at the motel about fifteen minutes later. As they walked into the room, Danni put her hand on Mia's shoulder. 'I'm sorry I forced you to go. I shouldn't have. I guess I just wanted you to deal with your pain.'

Mia walked off and sat down on the bed facing the wall. Danni had lost her yet again. How could she have been so stupid? Mia's shoulders hitched as she silently cried. Danni, heart breaking, sat beside her, but didn't touch her.

'I loved them, Mum. But I just left them. I let them burn. How am I ever supposed to forgive myself?'

'What happened wasn't your fault, sweetheart. It may not have been an accident, but it wasn't your fault.'

Mia stopped crying abruptly, turned and stared at her mother. 'What do you mean it wasn't an accident? Wasn't it faulty wiring or something?'

Danni didn't know if she should tell her, but she didn't want there to be any secrets between them any more.

'Um, I've been informed by the insurers that the... fire wasn't an accident. It was... deliberately lit and they used an accelerant to make it burn faster.' She looked at Mia, tears shimmering in her eyes.

'I don't understand. Someone wanted to kill us? Who would want to do that?' She was deathly pale, her dark eyes like empty sockets in her wan face.

Danni went to put her arms around her to quieten her down, but Mia was having none of it, pushing her away. 'What the fuck, Mum?'

'Language,' Danni retorted without thinking. She sat there in stunned silence, Mia looking at her, before they both burst into laughter. Suddenly Mia clamped her hand over her mouth, cutting off her laughter, then burst into tears. This time, when Danni went to hug her, Mia let her.

Danni didn't know how long they sat locked in each other's embrace, she seemed to lose track of time again, but she knew it was nice, Mia hadn't let her hold her like that since the night of the fire. Not with any real feeling, anyway. Was this bonding the beginning of the road of forgiveness for Danni? With all her heart, she hoped so.

Now that Mia knew about the arson and the attempt on her life, Danni didn't know if Mia would fall back into her own world or not. But Mia stayed with her long enough to eat a sandwich and have a drink of water before she went to lay down.

Danni had a sudden flash of memory, sitting on a leather couch in what she knew was a waiting room, but she could remember nothing more about it. Perhaps she should seek some help for Mia down the track when she convinced the insurance company to change their minds. Someone had deliberately lit the fire. She believed now that it wasn't Oliver. Then she had a thought: what if it was Beth? Did Beth hate her enough to murder her children? She dismissed the thought almost as soon as it crossed her mind. She wouldn't risk hurting Joe, her satisfaction was in taking Joe away from her, her future was tied to Joe. No, Joe was her golden ticket. Beth wanted him for herself and their son. Danni stiffened with anger at the thought of Joe having a love child, with Beth no less.

Danni wondered how many times he had come from Beth's bed then laid next to her. It made her shudder. How many times had he lied to her? The 'extra' hours at work that yielded no money, the late nights with 'friends', had all that time been spent with his mistress? She felt sick, her stomach churning. She looked over at Mia; what a burden for a young girl to keep. How dare Joe have expected her to keep his dirty little secrets.

38

It was the last thing Danni wanted to do. Her mouth was dry, like she'd put cotton wool in there, her teeth clenched in nervousness making her jaw ache. Danni knew that she needed to get this done, to underline it once and for all. After today, she would plan her next move. It was like she had been in freefall since the fire, and, if she was honest with herself, before the fire. She hadn't been right in ages; she could acknowledge this now that Joe was gone. Pulling her bag closer, she found the scrap of paper with a phone number on it.

Mia was, as usual, on the bed, facing away from her, but she wasn't asleep. After spending so much time in a small space observing her daughter, she knew when she was awake and when she wasn't. 'Mia?' No response. 'Mia, honey, I have to duck out for a bit, I'll be back soon.' Danni knew Mia had heard her mother, but she still felt conflicted about leaving. But no, this had to be done.

Danni gently closed the door behind her and half walked, half ran to the car. Once inside, hands shaking, she dialled the number, not knowing what to expect. Each ring was like a stab to the heart.

'It's me,' she said when the line connected. 'I need to talk to you.'

'Have you got my money?'

'I need to meet with you.'

'Fine,' snarled Beth, and Danni remembered all the things she hated about her sister. 'The same café as last time, half an hour.'

Danni responded to the words and the tone of voice and felt herself slipping away from the conversation. 'I'll see you soon,' she said before hanging up. After sitting in the car, deep breathing for a few moments, she started the engine. As Danni drove to the café, she wondered why her sister hated her so much. Why she'd tortured her as a child. She never did understand and she was sure as shit never going to get any answers from Beth.

Arriving at the café, Beth wasn't there yet, so Danni chose a booth and waited. Why had Beth paid for a motel room and given her a car? Danni instinctively knew that it would be a case of 'a means to an end' with her. She just wanted the insurance money as soon as she found out that Joe was dead. Did she mourn him, she wondered? Did she lose sleep over his death? Seemed like she was quick enough to want to profit from it.

Danni ordered a coffee from the older waitress and, when it came, she absently shook two packets of sugar then poured them in, watching the patterns the granules made as they fell deep into the coffee cup. Finally, she stirred it, mesmerised by the swirling patterns her spoon made.

Beth slid into the opposite side of the booth without warning, startling Danni. Danni looked at her sister, really looked at her. She was wearing tight jeans, a skin-tight white top that Danni would never had dared to wear on the farm, long, blush-coloured fingernails and red lipstick over a well made-up face. She was getting old, only just holding onto her looks. It looked like she was going out, not catching up for coffee and demanding insurance money from her estranged sister. Is that what she always looked like? Is this one of the reasons that Joe fell in love with her? Beth made an effort with her appearance? Was that what he wanted? Her mind flitted back to the open laptop. Did Beth do those kinds of things for him? Immediately Danni wanted to be sick, but would not back down to Beth, not now. She was a grown woman; she had come to finish things and she would.

Beth rapped her polished nails on the table, the sound grating on Danni's nerves. It was a habit that Beth had had since she was a teenager. 'Where's my money?' she asked without preamble.

'Want a cup of coffee, Beth?' Danni asked politely.

'No. I want my fucking money.' Rage behind the hissed words. 'Now.'

'Well that's a pity,' Danni said sweetly, 'because there is no fucking money.'

'What? What do you mean?'

'The insurance company told me that the results of the police investigation and their investigation reached the same conclusion: the fire was due to arson and they're not going to pay out on the claim.'

'What?' Beth said again. She seemed confused, then again, her plans had just been blown out of the water.

'Yeah. It's made me wonder if we were randomly targeted or if it was someone with a grudge.' She looked pointedly at her sister.

'Please. If I wanted to kill you, you would have been dead years ago.'

'And Joe?'

'What about Joe?' Her eyes narrowed. She didn't like the insinuation.

'He hadn't left me yet, maybe you got sick of waiting.'

Beth laughed. 'You think I set fire to your dump of a place? Damn thing looked like a fire hazard anyway, not surprised it burnt down.'

'Now how would you know?' Danni demanded.

'Lumpy bed, too. Really bad for your back, Danni,' Beth said, watching her reaction.

'You were in my house? In my bed?'

'Once or twice. That piss you off?'

Danni breathed in then let it go. 'The only thing pissing me off is you. I don't have any money coming, so there's no reason for us to speak again.'

'I want money from Joe. He owes me that. I have a child to look after.'

'Well, so do I.'

Beth stared at her for a long moment, her eyes unreadable before saying in a low voice, 'This isn't the last you've seen of me.'

Danni paid for her coffee and hopped into the car. Would she ever be shot of Beth, or would she haunt Danni into the grave? She drove back to the motel on autopilot, turning where she was supposed to, no idea if she was driving at the speed limit or not. It was like she wasn't in control of her own body.

Mia was just coming out of the bathroom when she walked in. 'Sorry, sweetheart, I didn't want to leave you, but something came up that I had to deal with. Hopefully it's all taken care of now. You feeling okay, honey?'

For a moment, she thought it was going to be the same as every other question, every other day. 'Yeah,' Mia said.

Danni crossed the distance between them and folded Mia into her arms, trying not to hold her too tight. 'I'm glad you're coming back to me, love. I know you've had a traumatic time of things and I wish I could make it better for you. I will do my best to help you as much as I can.' She pulled back and looked into Mia's dull eyes. 'I promise.' Mia didn't say anything, just moved back to the bed and lay down.

Her phone vibrated in her bag, so she grabbed it and answered it without thinking.

'Remember Donovan?' said the voice on the other end, soft yet vicious, barbed wire wrapped in velvet.

'What?' she said.

'Donovan? Ring any bells?' Beth snapped.

'I don't know what you're talking about.' Danni had a vague recollection of a party, the bass thumping, giving her a headache, her sister, a dark room. That was it and she had a feeling that that was all she wanted to know. She didn't know who this Donovan was.

'I'll keep your secret, as long as I get my money. I guess the farm was worth around five hundred, so I want my two-fifty, and soon. Joe's life insurance. You'll be getting a pay out from that even if the house insurance won't pay out. I want my share. Understood?'

'Beth, I barely have enough to make ends meet as it is, and you want me to give you money that I don't have.'

'Joe promised to take care of me,' she snapped.

'Yeah? He promised to do a lot of things. Like to not fuck my sister. But he wasn't exactly the dependable type, oh, and he's dead, so you won't be getting a cent out of his widow, so fuck you.' Danni hung up the phone, breathing hard. She knew she had probably just started another war with Beth, the first in a decade and a half, but any money she had or received was to go to her and Mia. Mia needed stability. Her daughter needed her own, safe place. Danni put in a long call to the insurance agency to plead her case but was transferred around so many times that she eventually hung up. She had told several of the insurance people what had happened but none of them seemed sympathetic to her plight.

Putting the phone down, Danni hung her head in her hands and resisted the urge to cry. She would stay strong. She would work something out, somehow. She had enough money to stay in the motel a while longer, but not enough to rent a house and pay bond. She could go back to her job, but what would she do with Mia? She needed someone to watch her. Every idea she came up with came with its own set of problems.

A slight pressure on her shoulder made her jump. She looked up to see Mia standing in front of her.

'We'll be okay, Mum. You'll work it out.'

At the sound of Mia talking, tears ran down Danni's face. 'Oh, Mia, stay with me this time, beautiful. Don't slip away like a dream, stay.' Mia went to the bathroom and washed her hands, running them over her dirty and matted hair. Danni had tried brushing it for her but she wouldn't take a helping hand when it was offered to her. She was like Danni sometimes, too stubborn for her own good.

Mia's show of love lifted her up, made her want to get through this whole mess with as little pain as possible.

The phone rang again. Danni didn't want to answer it, but the buzzing in her hand wouldn't stop and it was driving her crazy, like a bee caught in her fist. It made her want to throw the phone but then she remembered that it could be the insurance agency. It was a no caller ID number. Danni picked it up.

'Don't you dare talk to me like that, you little bitch!' screamed her sister. She wasn't calling from her mobile, maybe her house phone, a blocked number?

'I have nothing to say to you,' hissed Danni, stepping outside the front door, closing it gently behind her.

'Oh, yes you do. If you want me to keep quiet about a certain young man, then you'll find the two hundred and fifty thousand Joe owes me.'

'I don't even know what you're talking about, Beth.'

'I still have the knife you used on him, your fingerprints, his blood,'

Beth said quietly. There was silence on Danni's end as she tried to remember what the hell her sister was talking about. 'Jesus, you really don't remember, do you? Well, let me enlighten you. You stabbed a man almost to his death, then dragged him up to the back shed, and you set him on fire, Danni. He died. You did that.'

Danni drew a shocked breath. 'I don't understand. I could never do a thing like that. You're wrong,' she said desperately.

'All it takes is for me to anonymously send the knife to the police and you're fucking done for. No way out for you. It's still an open homicide, they never charged anyone for his murder, obviously, or you'd be in jail.'

Danni was speechless. There's no way she did that. No way. She decided to bluff. 'Go ahead, then. Send what you think you have on me, but you'll never get any of my money.' Danni pushed her hair out of her face, picked up and tossed around by the wind, tucking it back behind her ear. Of course, she didn't have any money either and had no chance of getting any, but it bought her time to come up with a plan.

Run.

The word just slid into her mind. It wasn't the worst idea. She could trade in the bomb of a car for another bomb, take Mia and what money they had and just leave. Drive until Danni felt they were far enough away from Beth's reach and hide there. There were worse plans, like stay in town and be arrested for something she believed she didn't do and leave Mia all alone in the world. She'd go into the foster system, just like Danni had. Her mind went back to Michelle, her foster mum. She was a lovely woman, and Danni wondered what became of her and her husband. What happened to creepy Andrew? She didn't think people like that just changed overnight. You were who you were. Andrew would be a man now, and although she didn't really care what he was or who he was, something niggled at her, a memory she couldn't quite capture. Easing herself back into the room, she pondered her next move. Yes, she thought it best that they run, and soon. She could only hold Beth off for so long.

She looked over at her daughter's form. Mia rolled over, Danni still looking at her.

'Who was that on the phone?' Mia asked quietly.

'No one for you to be concerned about, love. Have a little rest.' Beth had mentioned life insurance, which they had let lapse... a year ago. Since Danni had got a job, they had planned to reinstate it, but, like everything else, it was added to the to-do list but hadn't managed to get done. Danni sighed, wiping her hand over her face. She was utterly exhausted. She'd barely had any sleep since the night of the fire, maybe averaging three hours a night. She had nightmares about her burning children when she did sleep. She had barely any money and a vulture of a sister threatening her with arrest and prison. Not to mention, an almost comatose daughter who desperately needed psychological help, help that she couldn't afford just yet. Fuck, life was hard right now. She'd give anything to have someone to share the load with. Her mind went to her husband, his cheating really shouldn't have bothered her, as in the end, she was planning on leaving him anyway. She still didn't know for sure what had gone on with him and Mia. Was it just him trying to get her to keep her secret, or was it more sinister? She thought back to the website, and the girl who was barely older than Mia. Shaking her head, she cleared her mind. Joe was gone, dead, he couldn't hurt Mia any more. She had to focus on the future, but it was hard when Beth kept dragging her back down the path of the past.

'I love you, Mum,' whispered Mia from the other bed, so quietly, Danni might have missed it had she exhaled.

'I love you too, baby.'

39

While Danni Brooks was thinking about him, Andrew Johnson was thinking about her.

Andrew had a secret. One that he'd never shared with anyone. He knew about Danni's family dying in a fire, he'd kept tabs on her all these years, knowing that she'd married her high school sweetheart and had a baby. She had been pregnant when she'd been living at his house but had not confided in his mother. Once she left after she turned eighteen, she had married Joe and had moved out to an old farmhouse. They'd ended up having two more children, another girl and a boy. Andrew had driven up to the road a number of times, but he could just see the top of the house.

One day, he waited until both Danni and her husband Joe had left the house, and had parked his car beside the road and then run down the driveway. He was surprised to notice that there were bars on the ground level of the house. He tried all of the windows but he couldn't get in. The doors were locked tight. Danni and her husband obviously worried about security and they were right to. If he could have, he would have gone in and looked around at where she was living these days. He was looking through the window when he was startled by a growling behind him. He turned slowly to face a medium-sized dog. He thought it was a Rottweiler.

'Hey boy, how are you? Are you a good doggy?' he said in a sing-song voice. The dog wagged his tail hesitantly. Andrew spoke to it again, trying to make friends. 'I'm going to go now,' he said, taking a small step backwards. He then turned and slowly began to walk down the driveway, careful to keep his stride measured and not too hurried. Halfway down the driveway, he looked over his shoulder. The dog had followed him part of the way then stopped. Andrew took the opportunity to walk a little bit faster until he reached his car. He did a U-turn and headed back to town. He had seen where she lived and knew that he could provide a much better life for her than this minimum wage husband of hers ever could.

* * *

Andrew needed to talk to Danni, he needed to unburden himself and she was the only person he could speak to about this. His parents had been huddled around the table, talking in hushed voices, yet he was used to eavesdropping on his parents, and he liked hearing about the foster kids, it was interesting. They were discussing Danni. It seemed they were always whispering about Danni since she had arrived.

He stayed behind the kitchen wall, completely enthralled by what his mother was telling his father. His mouth popped open and suddenly he understood. It was shocking news that would upend Danni's world, if she could remember it. His mother had said that she had already completely blocked out her visit, but that the psychologist had told his mother everything. Andrew would keep this information to himself, waiting for the right time to tell her. After he read about her unfortunate house fire and her losing her family, he wanted to see her. He wanted to hold her and tell her everything would be all right, that he'd take care of her. He just needed to find out where she was so he could organise a catch up.

He was following her story online and even though it didn't say exactly where she was, it did say that she was staying at a motel and if people wanted to donate money or goods, they could call Susan Patrick, who was spearheading the campaign to get her back on her feet. He took a chance and called the number at the bottom of the screen.

'Susan Patrick speaking.'

'Hi, Ms Patrick, my name is Andrew Johnson. I'm an old friend of Danni Brooks, actually, I was her foster brother for a while back when she was in her late teens. She was Danni Douglas back then.'

'Oh, hello Andrew, how are you?' The woman at the end of the line sounded pleased to hear from him.

'Listen, I want to offer my emotional support to Danni. I care about her very much, but I'm afraid we fell out of touch over the past few years. I'd like to find her and offer my condolences in person. Are you able to tell me where she is?'

Susan sounded relieved. 'I was hoping some friends or family would come forward to help her cope with her devastating loss. You're the first person who has offered to do so. I'm not sure if I should pass on her details or not, she's been so upset, poor thing,' she said, pausing, 'but having family around might really help her heal, so I guess since you're basically family it's okay. She's at the motel, here in town. Should I let her know you're coming?'

'No, I'd like to just pop round and see her on my own, if you don't mind.'

'Of course, Andrew, I'll give you her number as well. Thank you for contacting me and good luck with helping Danni. She needs all the emotional support she can get.'

'No problem.' Andrew hung up, smiling. Now he had her phone number and where she was staying. He only had to decide whether he called her or just showed up at her door. He mulled over it for another two days, weighing up his options.

Then he decided.

40

It was so easy to pick up men. It was like shopping for clothes. You see something you like, you eye it up and down for a moment, deciding if you want to try it on, then you make your decision to walk out of the store with it hanging off your arm. Men are visual creatures and she was hot, dressed provocatively and was always up for a good time, and she looked like it too. Any guy, married or not, was hers for the picking.

She didn't often hear no, and on the rare occasions she did, it just made her go harder for the yes. She always got the yes in the end. When she met the tall studious man in the café, he was sitting at a small round table, laptop in front of him, looking at the screen intently. He had a pen between his lips, which she thought odd because there was no paper in sight. The café was crowded and the only way to have a place to sit was to double up on tables. She made a beeline for his table, narrowly beating out a mousy-looking woman who huffed then went and found another table. This one was hers.

'Hi, may I share your table?' she asked, speaking slightly louder to be heard over the din.

He looked up, surprised, as if he hadn't noticed how busy the space was around him.

'Uh, of course. Please, sit down.' He immediately began staring intently at his computer again, pen back in his mouth.

'So, you're a writer?'

He looked up again, surprised that she was speaking to him. 'Yes, fiction writer, but I'm afraid I'm a little stuck right now, hence my trip to the café. I thought a change of scenery might help me through this block, but no luck so far.' He smiled a goofy smile, as if unaware of how attractive he was. She would screw him, she decided. There was something about him, something that reminded her of what it was like to be good. They exchanged names before she said, 'Maybe I could help?'

'That's nice of you, but I don't think so.'

'C'mon, let me try. I love to read.' *Lie.*

He explained that his storyline was about a widower who couldn't move on from his wife's death, and who had no one to turn to help with his grief. There was more to it, but she was more interested in watching his full lips as he spoke.

'That one's easy,' she said. 'He gets over her by getting under someone else.'

'I beg your pardon?' he said quizzically.

She tried again. 'He goes out, finds a very willing and attractive woman and fucks her. Then he can move on.'

He blushed, the colour creeping up his neck. Was it the storyline or the use of the word fuck? She didn't know.

'I don't think people do that in real life,' he said eventually, after clearing his throat twice.

'Trust me, they do. Men are simple creatures, not too hard to unravel. They need to be wanted and don't like being without a woman. Surely you have a girlfriend and can relate?'

'I'm single.'

'I find that hard to believe,' she said, beginning to set the bait. The blush coloured his face again. 'Look, why don't we go back to your place and I'll give you the exact scene you need, okay? Blow by blow.' She dropped a wink and smiled at him.

'I have a deadline,' he stammered.

She let out a small sigh. 'I told you the next part of the story and I offered to give you the material you needed. Want to take me up on my offer or what?' He looked around, as if checking that no one else was hearing her proposition him for sex, as if it was a dirty thing.

'Um... okay, I guess that would be fine.'

Fine? She'd show him she was better than fine.

A quick taxi ride later and they stood in his apartment. It was beautiful. Immaculate, even, and she knew she was going to have a great time messing up his bed. He was shy, nervous, so she took off his clothes for him. He was muscular under the track pants and hoodie, his cock hard and ready to go.

'Lay down,' she commanded as she pulled a condom from her purse, expertly rolling it down his cock with her mouth.

'Where'd you learn to do that?' he asked, slightly in awe of the ravenous woman on top of him.

'I've picked up a few tricks here and there,' she smiled. 'Now relax.'

Fifteen minutes later, as he strained from fucking her hard, he yelled, 'I'm about to come!' She smiled. They were all the same. *Joanne!*' he shouted as he came inside her. He had remembered her name, she thought, shocked. *Her real name.*

She climbed off him. 'Now that's the next part of your book,' Joanne said, beginning to put her clothes back on, mission accomplished. Actually, he'd ended up being pretty good, knowing his way around the female body. 'Don't forget to write it, dirty act by dirty act.'

He leaned over the side of his bed and grabbed his laptop. As she left his apartment, she could hear him furiously tapping away at the keys. She went home feeling good. Happy, even. It had been a long time since a man had called out her real name during sex. She used a fake name so often that sometimes she almost forgot that she was known as something else. *Joanne.*

41

She awoke with a start. She hadn't slept last night, so she'd fallen asleep in health class, the second to last class of the day. She hadn't felt it when Julie had taken a pen and drawn a penis on her face near her mouth, droplets heading towards her lips. When she woke with the bell and her classmates saw her, they laughed and pointed. She could guess what they were laughing about. She wiped her hand over her mouth, nope, no drool, and her heart sank. She quickly went to the toilet and looked in the mirror, squeaking with shock. *Who...* Then she remembered that Julie was in the class with her. She pulled out a bundle of paper towelling, ran it under the water and began scrubbing. She had to rub so hard that her face went red and began to feel raw. Finally, the ink was off her face, and her skin was glowing red.

She stalked off to find Julie to give her a piece of her mind. She didn't normally engage in retaliation, except that time at the pool, and that was because she feared for her life. No, she was normally passive to the point of being walked all over. The bell rang for the next class. Julie would have to wait. She glimpsed her in the crowd as they went their separate ways but there was no way she was letting this go, not this time. She was sick of being the laughing stock of the school. People who she didn't even know would chuckle at her expense and she couldn't handle it any more. She had been pushed beyond breaking point. No more. She had to do some-thing. She had no friends, so it wasn't like she had anything to lose and as she sat in the last class, she began plotting her revenge. Once she happened upon an idea, she wondered why she hadn't thought of it before. It was so simple yet so humiliating, all at the same time. She couldn't wait for the bell to ring so she could put her plan in motion.

She would go directly to Julie's locker and wait for her there. She just wished she had a phone on her, but she figured that enough people would whip out their phones or use the ones already in their hands. It was going to be a doozy. She waited very impatiently, watching the clock tick off the seconds, paying absolutely no attention to what the teacher was saying.

The bell finally rang after what seemed like an eternity and she hurried against the sea of humanity so she reached Julie's locker before she did. She made it and leaned against the locker. She received a few looks, people knowing the history between the two of them; they were probably wondering why she was waiting for her, what would happen.

'What are you doing standing against my locker?' Julie roared, barging through the crowd towards her.

The kids gathered, the tension hanging in the air like the ozone smell before a storm. Everyone knew that Julie picked on her, so they wanted to see what she did to her. She would have the last laugh.

As soon as Julie was close enough, she stepped forward and, before Julie knew what hit her, quick as a flash, she pulled down her gym shorts so she was on show to everyone. No pants, no underwear. Naked as the day she was born. The cameras caught every humiliating second.

'*Christine!* No!' shouted one of Julie's friends, but the damage had already been done. The crowd roared with laughter as Julie frantically tried to pull her pants up. Julie started to cry, great heaving sobs, before pushing through the crowd, running.

Christine had the last laugh.

42

Danni woke up in a panic. She could smell smoke and could hear the cries of Alexandra and Noah. She was trapped by the sheet, fighting with it to free herself. She was covered in sweat, her face flushed. Quickly she hobbled over to Mia to make sure that she was real, that she was alive. Danni reached out with a trembling hand, afraid to touch her as much as she wanted to. Eventually, she unfroze, wondering how long she'd been standing there. Long enough that Mia had sensed her, rolled over in her bed and was facing her, a blank look on her face.

'Sorry, honey, I had a terrible nightmare about Alexandra and Noah. I dreamed that you were gone too. I just wanted to make sure you were okay. I couldn't stand it if something happened to you too. I would just die, Mia. Do you understand that? I can't live without you.'

'Yes, Mum.'

Danni went to the bathroom and looked in the mirror. There were dark circles under her eyes that looked bruised, her eyes themselves were bloodshot and her hair was a tangled mess. Instead of brushing her long hair, she swept it up into a messy bun high on her head. After splashing her face with cold water, she felt a bit more human, the smudges under her eyes receding so she looked reasonably normal.

Once dressed, she was trying to coax Mia into the shower, as it had been a while, her grief ran that deep, but it was no use, short of dragging her there. It might actually come to that eventually, thought Danni. She dressed, leaving Mia in her pyjamas. It was what she was more comfortable in, anyway, and who was going to see her? She stayed in the room all day every day.

Her phone, which she was beginning to hate, rang. She quickly silenced it before looking at the screen. No caller ID. That meant it could be Beth, or it could be someone else. Only Susan's number was stored in there, that and Trust Insurance's, who'd knocked back her appeal yet again. She really was screwed now. Running away sounded better and better each day. She was brought back to the present by the vibration in her hand. The damn phone was still ringing. She took it outside.

'Hello?' she said warily.

'Danni?'

'Yes, who's this?'

'It's Andrew.'

She wracked her brains trying to think of any Andrew that she knew.

'I'm sorry, I don't know any Andrew. How did you get this number?'

'Susan gave it to me. I'm Andrew Johnson, from your foster family.'

Again, the smell of leather, the softness under her fingers, the hushed voices.

'Oh, Andrew,' she said without much enthusiasm. After all, he had been a fourteen-year-old creep back then. Could he blame her for not being more excited?

'Before you say anything, I just want to apologise for my behaviour in the months that you stayed with us. I was cheeky and unkind.'

Not the words she would have chosen.

'I would have apologised sooner, but I lost track of you.' *Liar.*

'What do you want, Andrew?' she asked, sighing slightly. She didn't have time for this. She had to plan their escape from Beth's watchful eye and vengeful heart.

'Actually, I want to see you, I mean, to talk to you. Can we catch up somewhere? I can come to you if you'd like.'

'No,' she said quickly. Mia needed to rest and their motel room afforded no privacy from her daughter. She had no idea what he was going to say, so she needed to pre-empt it. 'I'll meet you somewhere. Where and when?'

'How about we meet at the park? By the pond in an hour and we can have a real catch up.'

'Fine, Andrew, I'll see you then.' She hung up the phone, wishing she could just throw it out the window. Pity she couldn't. However, she *would* dump the phone as soon as they left town, just so she couldn't be tracked. She hadn't expected Susan to give out her phone number, but Andrew had probably sweet-talked her. She really didn't want to see him, remembering the cocky and pervy fourteen-year-old boy who stole her underwear then lied to his parents about it. She wondered what he could possibly have to say to her.

'Mia,' she said from across the room. The girl rolled over and looked at her mother. Progress. 'I have to go out again. I'm so sorry I keep leaving you like this, but I think it's important. And... there's something else I need to talk to you about. Um... we're going to be going on a little trip for a while, actually, indefinitely. Beth is making life difficult so I thought it would be easier to leave town for a while, maybe for good. How do you feel about that?' She waited, holding her breath.

'What is she doing?' Mia asked softly.

'She wants money, love. Money that I just don't have since the insurance company won't pay out. She's asking for it because of promises your father made to her.'

'Let's just go, Mum, there's nothing for us here any more.'

Danni knew Mia was right. The graves of her family were here but she couldn't let that dictate her life. The two of them had to get out and start again.

'Okay then, I'm going to meet an old acquaintance, he was my foster brother once and he might want to help us, who knows.' She smiled at Mia reassuringly who returned it with a watered down one of her own.

Danni grabbed her handbag, slinging it over her shoulder and, with one final look at Mia, left the room. She drove to the park, lining up the car next to a dark blue sedan. She then walked down the concrete path to the seat by the pond.

Andrew was there, waiting. He looked like she remembered him, just older now. When he saw her, he jumped up and opened his arms. What was she to do except step into his hug? He hugged her gently, but for much longer than was necessary. When he finally pulled back, he motioned for her to sit down.

'Wow, you look amazing,' he started by saying.

She knew she didn't. She hadn't washed her hair in god knows how long and she needed a shower. The bags were still under her eyes but, right now, she didn't give a shit what she looked like or what he thought.

'Thanks,' she murmured gently. 'Andrew, why am I here?' She needed to start packing, buy a map and work out where the hell they were going. She shouldn't have wasted time being here. She should have told him no; she didn't have time for a catch up.

'I wanted to discuss something with you.'

'What is it?' she asked, trying to hurry the conversation along.

'I'm not sure if you know, but my dad died a few years ago, and my mum just recently.'

'Andrew, I'm so sorry. I didn't know. I haven't seen your mum in such a long time.' She had fond memories of her one-time foster mum. She had been so nice to her after her horrific experiences at her own house. House, not home. It was never a home.

'Yes, well, thank you, Danni. Anyway, I've been cleaning out the house getting it ready to put it on the market. I found something that might... upset you.'

'If it's my underwear, we both know you took it,' she said, trying to lighten the mood.

He had the decency to look away. 'No, it's not that and I'm sorry about that. I was young and stupid. Tell me, do you remember going to the psychologist when you stayed with us?'

Danni had the flash again of the feel of a leather couch underneath her legs, sticking to her skin. 'I'm not sure,' she said quietly. 'Why are you asking, Andrew?'

'Well, Mum went in after you and was told exactly what had happened in your session. She put on a bright face for you, but inside, she was terrified. When she arrived home, you went to your room and

Mum and Dad sat down and started talking. I heard some interesting things so later, once I'd grown up a bit, I befriended a woman – actually, I seduced her – to gain access to your patient files. I didn't quite believe what I heard my mother and father discussing. I had to hear and see for myself. I got your file, it was a DVD. I watched it. Actually, I watched it twice. The second time, I recorded it. I have a copy on my phone, Danni.' He was speaking very quickly and she was having trouble keeping up with him. 'I think you need to watch it. It's enlightening. It will help you understand the truth about yourself. Actually, I encourage you to watch it, I really do. You can call me when you're ready to watch it; here's my number in case you didn't store it in your phone.' He stood up, as did she, and was putting her hand out for a handshake when he pulled her into another one of his long hugs. It was clear that he still had a thing for her. He flashed her a smile then walked away.

The whole conversation had been veiled and odd and Danni didn't know what to make of it. Danni dropped back onto the bench seat, wondering what the hell to do. When she allowed herself to think about it, she had always felt a little different. It wasn't just her upbringing, the abuse from Beth, she had always felt like that. The way sometimes she was meek, and at other times she fought like a rabid dog, the loss of time and the feeling of fuzziness in her head. It baffled her and, if what Andrew was saying was true, then he had answers. Answers she wasn't sure that she wanted. She felt violated. Why would Andrew watch anything about her? It seemed weird and creepy, but then she remembered the kind of kid he was. What secrets did the video hold? Andrew had made it sound like it would show her the reason she was the way she was. Did she want to know?

Yes.

As she drove back to the motel, Danni kept looking at her phone, lying on the seat next to her, waiting, wondering. She wanted to know what had been said about her. She didn't remember going to the doctor but reasoned that she must have, the leather couch... it had the feel of a doctor's waiting room, the fear and the anxiety that she felt when she remembered the feel of the leather. She also remembered the pile of National Geographic magazines stacked on the stained wood table. Little bits were coming back to her but not what happened inside the office. The waiting room was as far as her mind let her go. So, what really happened in there? And why had Andrew cared so much, back then and now? Was he truly looking out for her? Did he have her best interests at heart?

Finally, she made it back to the motel. She opened the door to find Mia asleep on her bed, arms wrapped around Danni's pillow. She looked almost peaceful except for the two lines in between her eyes that had formed there since the fire. Shock, grief, loss. Danni wasn't exactly looking her age these days either. She looked down at her clothes. Her staple jeans which really needed a wash and the sunshine yellow top, complete with something, food perhaps, crusted at the bottom. She really needed to take better care of herself and Mia. Do some washing, go to the supermarket for supplies, find a place to run to. Find another car. There were so many things to do before she they left this place and put it in their rear-view mirror. All of this before Beth came after her again, threatening her with something she didn't even know was the truth.

Danni threw her bag onto the small round table and went to brush her hair and wash her face, wiping off the grime of the day, wiping Andrew off her. He had given her his number, which she had no intention of using unless he could help her get out of town. He was wearing a nice suit, maybe he had a good job and was willing to help out someone he obviously still had a crush on. It couldn't hurt to ask. She'd probably have to endure many more hugs, but she could put up with it if he staked her the money to get away. With that in mind, she decided to give him just one call. Couldn't hurt to ask for the money, right?

'Danni, hi. So good to hear from you so soon.' She could hear machinery pounding in the background and she could barely hear him. She heard him say, 'Just hang on and I'll go outside so we can talk.' She heard his footsteps and gnawed on a fingernail, wondering if she was doing the right thing. Then all was quiet. 'Sorry about that, I'm at work, afternoon shift.'

'I'm so sorry to bother you at work, Andrew, I didn't know.'

'It's fine, Danni, really. I'm free tonight if you want to talk about the video. You and me, together again, just like the old days.'

Danni cringed on the other end of the phone with his words.

'I have something else I'd like to talk to you about. You remember my sister Beth?'

'Yes, the one who damaged you so much that you ended up at our house. I remember her,' he said warily, probably wondering where this was going.

'Well, she's trying to blackmail me to get insurance money out of me, but the insurance company and the police ruled the fire as arson, so my policy doesn't cover it. She wants two hundred and fifty thousand dollars from me.'

'Danni, if you're asking me, I don't have that kind of money.'

'No, you misunderstand, I'm not asking you for that amount of money, but I have to get out of town, away from her. I need help getting a car and have some money to live off until I can settle in and find a job. I'd pay back every cent.'

'How much do you need? Five thousand? Would that do?'

Danni couldn't believe her luck. Here was her fairy godfather in the form of Andrew offering her the loan and for more than she had wanted. She wasn't going to knock it back. 'That would be great, thank you so much, Andrew.' She was almost giddy with excitement.

'There's one string attached, though,' he said, and her heart sank. 'You have to go out for dinner with me, then I'll give you the money.'

Danni was silent, weighing it all up. She needed to leave, and what was one little dinner in the grand scheme of five thousand things? 'Okay,' she said.

'I assume you want to leave as soon as possible, so how about we go out for dinner tonight? We can talk about the money then.'

Again, she hesitated. 'Okay,' she finally said.

He gave her a time and place, and just before he hung up he said, 'It's a date.' She wanted to correct him, that it was a thank you for helping her out, but he was already gone.

Sitting down next to Mia, she shook her awake. 'Mia. Mia? Wake up love, I have something to tell you.' She watched as the chocolate eyes, so much like her own opened, and focused on her.

'Darling, I have found a way to get us out of this hellhole once and for all. A friend is going to lend us the money to get as far away from here as we possibly can. I'm going out for dinner with him tonight to say thanks and get the money.'

'Him?' she asked, her voice just above a whisper, still sleepy.

'Yes, him, my foster brother, Andrew. I think he's really matured over the years, especially if he's going to lend me the money to get out of here.'

'Be careful,' Mia said before rolling over.

Danni knew she was right. She did have to be careful. Andrew had picked a restaurant in the next town over. She knew it but had never been there: small, intimate, expensive. She didn't have much of a choice in the way of dressy clothes so chose a black maxi dress and ballet flats from the wardrobe. *Thank you, Susan.* It would have to do, although she did make an effort with her hair. Danni washed it and braided it, reminding her of her youth, which in turn reminded her of when Beth had cut off her plait. She frowned at the uninvited memory as she unconsciously touched her hair.

Danni drove to the restaurant as the sun was beginning to wane. The shadows crept forward, easing out of the corners where they had hidden all day. It was a little cold, so she swung a bolero jacket over herself and shrugged her arms into it. She wanted to pull it over her chest as the dress was a little tight at the bust. She hoped Andrew wouldn't see it as a come on. Taking a deep breath, she walked inside the restaurant, scanning the tables for Andrew.

He waved, then stood up so she'd see him. He was wearing a dove grey suit, and had clearly made an effort, like this was a proper date. 'Andrew, hi,' Danni said, beginning the ass-kissing.

'You look amazing,' he replied, his eyes dropping immediately to her breasts before pulling her into his arms, inhaling the clean scent of her hair, 'and you smell delicious.'

Danni pulled away and gave a nervous laugh as she sat down at the table. Back corner, low lighting, it would have been romantic if she hadn't been there with him. She slung her bag over the back of the seat. It was the one she'd been using every day but it didn't matter. She was almost broke and was still living off the charity of others – she couldn't afford to be picky. She had hoped that he'd brought the money with him and that she and Mia could leave tomorrow morning.

'Come, let's order something to eat,' Andrew said, tucking himself back under the table. Danni was a little more unsure, perching on the edge of her seat, as if ready to run at any moment.

'So, do you want to talk?'

'I have more pressing things going on, like leaving this place once and for all.'

It was the perfect intro for him to give her the cheque, but instead he said, 'They do a really nice seafood basket here.'

She wanted to yell at him, to ask him if she could just have the money so she could get the hell out of there.

'So, Danni, apart from the messy and unfortunate business with your family, how have you been these past two decades?'

Messy? Unfortunate business?

It seemed like he wanted a trip down memory lane. 'Actually, Andrew, I was wondering if you brought the money or cheque with you? I really need it.'

He reached into his back pocket and pulled out his wallet, looking inside. 'Oh shit, I must have left it on the kitchen counter at home. I'm so sorry, Danni, you're going to have to follow me home if you want the cheque.'

It sounded like a threat just to get her into his home. She suppressed a sigh. 'Okay, we'll go to your place and get it.' She made a move to stand up.

'Hang on, Danni, let's enjoy dinner together first, all right? It's not often I get to dine with such a beautiful woman.' He winked at her, actually winked. Did he forget that she was a recent widow?

'I'm sorry, Andrew, I guess I'm just not in the mood.'

'Well, maybe I'm just not in the mood to give you the money,' he snipped.

Danni looked him so hard in the eyes that he dropped his head. Joe had always called it her death stare. He'd been on the receiving end enough times to coin the phrase.

'Just one drink then,' he almost pleaded.

She relented. 'One drink, then your place, then I am getting the hell out of here.'

'Well you don't have to make it sound like such a chore,' he pouted. 'I'm trying to help you, what with the loan and the video that I have. I was serious when I said you should watch it.'

'Sorry, I don't mean to sound ungrateful, but I really need to get going. I will watch the video but I just don't have the time right now. Maybe you could message it to me sometime and I promise that I'll watch it.'

'How about this?' he countered. 'We have the drink at my place, you can pick up the cheque and be on your way.'

Of course, Danni was wary, but she was also desperate. 'Okay, let's go.'

Andrew paid for his one drink and told her to follow him to his place. The whole way she wondered just how far she would go to secure the money to leave. She pulled up behind him in a quiet residential street. At least someone would hear her scream if she needed help. She smiled at her paranoid thoughts, not entertaining them as real.

She slammed her car door, and a lone dog barked down the street as she followed Andrew into his home. It was meticulously clean but not decorated. There were none of the knick-knacks that made a home. No paintings on the wall, no framed photos of family or friends. She found it odd that there was no photo of his departed parents. That was one thing she desperately wanted. Photos of Alexandra and Noah.

'This is... nice,' she said diplomatically, watching as he put his keys and phone on the kitchen bench.

'I know, I know, it's such a bachelor pad but I just haven't found the right woman to decorate my walls, if you know what I mean.'

Oh, she knew what he meant. He was still as creepy as ever.

He rummaged around in the fridge looking for the wine, then popped back up, bottle of champagne in hand. There were two glasses already on the bench, which had Danni wondering if maybe this had been a set up from the start. He poured her a full glass then handed it to her.

'Here's to old friends,' he said, clinking his glass against hers.

'To old friends,' Danni repeated and took a sip. It was expensive, she could tell that, not like the twelve-dollar bottles of wine she and Joe bought. It was unlikely that he had this just lying in his fridge, glasses out and ready.

'Shall we sit on the couch?' he asked, even as Danni drained half her glass in one long gulp.

'Almost finished. Andrew, how about that cheque?'

'Danni, I'm beginning to feel that you don't want to be around me. That all you want is the money. I just want to be your friend, but I feel that you're not going to let me be.'

'Andrew,' she sighed, 'I don't have time for friends. I have to leave, tomorrow. Please, are you going to give me the money or not?'

'I wasn't planning on it,' he said slowly, smiling at her without mirth.

Her heart deflated. He wasn't going to give her the money.

'What?' she whispered.

'I said, I wasn't planning on it. I just wanted to get you back here.' He lunged at her and she dropped her glass as she nimbly jumped out of his way. The glass hit the floor with a high-pitched crash. He charged at her with his arms open, intent on tackling her to the ground. She dodged to the left but he managed to get a hold of her hair, pulling painfully at the scalp as he dragged her backwards. Danni opened her mouth to scream but was silenced by a punch to the stomach. She hadn't felt this way in years. The pain, the fear, the inability to breathe. Being the victim didn't suit her any more.

In the next moment, she turned on him and pulled him to her, catching him completely off balance, which is right where she wanted him. She threw her hand straight out and connected with her target, his throat. He started to cough and splutter, letting go of her hair to clutch his throat. Danni grabbed his mobile off the kitchen counter and ran to the front door, unlocking it and ripping it open. She flew across the road, slamming herself into the driver's seat and locking the doors. Danni peeled off down the street, desperate to get away from him. The car screamed around the corner, her heart hammering in her chest. Once she had driven a few streets away, the adrenaline started to wear off and she began to shake. Danni pulled the car over to the side of the road and waited until the shaking and the tears subsided and she felt okay enough to drive back to the motel. Her body might have been betraying her, but her mind was clear. Andrew had given her perspective. They needed to get the hell out of town. Andrew probably knew where she lived, and Beth certainly did.

Danni broke the speed limit driving back to Mia. It was time to move on. And quick.

43

'Mia! Mia!' Danni yelled as she barged through the door. She saw her lying on the bed, facing the wall. 'Mia. Get up, pack your bag, we have to go. Now.' Danni turned around and started throwing clothes into her bag. Once she'd finished, she turned back to face her daughter. She was standing, but that was it. She wasn't packing, she wasn't doing anything.

'Mia, did you not hear me? We have to get going.' Mia didn't move.

'What happened, Mum?' she asked, her voice barely audible from across the room.

'Nothing, baby, it's just time for us to leave is all.'

'In the middle of the night?'

'Yes, damn it, in the middle of the night! Now pack your things.' This time Mia began to move, picking up clothes and slowly putting them into the bag. Danni flew into the bathroom and swiped all of the toiletries into the bag. They didn't have the five grand, but they would make it work. They could still run. They *had* to run.

She felt the weight of Andrew's phone in her pocket. Quickly she pulled it out and touched the front screen. It was pass code protected. *Damn it*. How was she going to get into it now? She quickly stuffed it into her handbag and grabbed Mia's packed bag and her own.

'C'mon Mia, to the car, quickly,' Danni said, pushing her daughter towards the door and out into the car park. Danni opened the back door for Mia, watching as she folded herself into the seat carefully. Danni slammed the door and ran around to the driver's side, throwing herself inside and locking the doors. She turned her head this way and that looking for Andrew. What if he'd come to the motel, what if he was going to follow her as they fled?

She reversed out of the car park, tyres crunching on the gravel. Danni had no idea where she was going, anywhere far from here. She drove, weaving her way through the streets until she reached the old highway. She wanted to keep off the main roads in case he found her. Did it count as paranoia if they were really out to get you?

Danni drove for hours, the headache building up, the pressure behind her eyes hurting her, making her wish she had painkillers in her bag. Danni was driving with her mind going in and out. She tried to remember what happened when she was at the psychologist's office, but all she could remember was the waiting room, then nothing. Why couldn't she remember what happened past that room? What did Andrew know that she didn't? Did Andrew's phone hold all the answers?

There was one way to find out for sure: watch the damn video. Mia was asleep behind her in the back seat, her head lolling to one side, bumping off the window every now and then. Danni kept checking on her in the rear-view mirror. She had been passing semi-trailers for the whole time she had been driving. They must have used the old highway so they could push the speed limit and not get caught by the police. Their trailers rocketed past her, and she was doing well over a hundred. Danni had taken the highway so Andrew couldn't find her. If he came after her, he would assume that she'd linked up to the freeway. Danni kept driving for another half an hour before she could no longer take it. She was tired, her eyes gritty and when she looked in the mirror, for a moment, she saw another face before her vision cleared. She was so damn tired, she was hallucinating. That was not good. Danni pulled over onto the verge, tyres flattening the weeds that poked up through the cracked bitumen.

She grabbed Andrew's phone and looked at it. She had no idea what the password for it was, of course. She could guess forever and never get it right. Then she had a thought, and typed in her own name. Suddenly it opened and all of the icons popped up. She was stunned. Who used the name of a girl you barely knew from nearly two decades ago? Even so, she was grateful, and scrolled through until she found the photos. There was a separate folder with her name on it, but she was too scared to open it. What would she find? Nothing good, she was sure of it. Looking at the information, she discovered that the video was nearly an hour long. Was she ready for whatever secrets it held?

Mia was still asleep so she decided that she *would* watch the video. Danni pressed the play button, feeling apprehensive and uncertain. The picture was grainy and the voices a little tinny as it was a recording of a recording. Danni turned up the volume to full, quickly making sure she hadn't woken Mia.

'Danielle? My name is Dr Parsons. Do you prefer Danielle or Danni?' The doctor smiled reassuringly at the young girl.

'Danni,' she mumbled.

'Okay, Danni. I would like to talk to you for a little while. Is that all right?'

'Yes.' Danni watched her seventeen-year-old self chew on her nails, nibbling at them in fear. Danni didn't know if she could actually watch the video or not. She had no idea what she would find. Would it help or hurt?

'Danni, tell me a bit about your childhood. Did you have a good childhood?'

Young Danni looked down at her hands in her lap, one finger now bleeding at the quick.

'Danni, tell me about your childhood,' the doctor pushed gently.

'I... I...' she stumbled. 'I didn't have a very good childhood. My family was... uncaring, no that's not right, they were *evil*. They never loved me. Especially my older sister, Beth. She was always hurting me.' She opened up quickly. No one ever had ever asked her how she *was* like this before.

'What kind of things did your sister do to you?'

'She cut off my plait once. She used to punch and kick me all the time. I have healed fractures and breaks that were never set properly because my parents wouldn't take me to a doctor in case they got caught.' The more she spoke, the more she felt the electricity building in her body. She needed a release. An outlet, she felt like she might explode with... anger? Longing? Fear? She didn't know.

'Danni? Danni, are you with me?'

'Danni's not here. You're talking to me now,' answered a voice different to Danni's. As Danni watched, her whole demeanour changed. She leaned back comfortably in the overstuffed chair, uncrossing her legs, spreading them a bit wider than was necessary, a deliberate and provocative act. Dr Parsons scribbled in her notebook. Danni watched, horrified, but she couldn't look away.

'Who am I speaking to?' the doctor asked.

'You want my name? I don't normally give out my real name, but sure, I'll play along. I'm Joanne.'

Joanne? Where did she know that name from?

'Joanne, then. What role do you play in Danni's mind?'

Joanne laughed loudly. 'What role? Fuck, you do sound like a doctor. All right doc, I'm her protector. I take care of her when she can't take care of herself.'

'Like when?' the doctor said, staring intently at the young girl before her.

'Like when her sister would beat her up. When Danni fought back, that was me. When she attacked Beth, that was me, all me. Danni doesn't have the balls and I, well, I have them and more.'

'What do you mean by that?'

'I gave her a life; I made her strong and desirable. She needed that.' Joanne tossed her hair that she'd taken out of the braid Danni had done that morning. She was looking at herself, but it wasn't her. She was a different person. Danni watched in horror, unable to tear her eyes away from the grainy screen. She wanted to believe that she had been joking. That she had been putting it on for the doctor, but deep in her heart, she knew it was true. The name Joanne resonated with her, in her soul. She knew her.

'Joanne, how often do you come out?'

Suddenly her voice changed from the sultry, adult voice to a small, soft, younger voice.

'Hi,' she said simply, pulling her legs together neatly.

'Hi, yourself. Who am I talking to?' Dr Parsons asked, seemingly unconcerned with the fact that she was talking to someone else now.

'I'm Christine,' she said, sitting back in the chair and crossing her legs neatly, hands clasped in her lap, smoothing down her skirt primly.

Christine.

'Nice to meet you, Christine. Is there anyone else in there?' Dr Parsons asked, still scribbling on her notepad.

'No,' Christine said absently, looking round the room at the decor. 'It's just me and Joanne.'

'Do you and Joanne talk to each other, Christine?'

'Jo and I talk, but Danni, beautiful, innocent Danni doesn't know we're here.' Her voice was a song like a bird would sing, high and lilting. Danni was fascinated by her voice, her demeanour. So different from her own.

Danni watched as her body, but another person, spoke for her. Danni was both horrified and fascinated. These people lived inside of her? The more she thought about it, the more she understood – the blackouts, the time loss, the driving somewhere and not knowing how she got there, the ups and downs. The dots started to connect up. It was true.

Dr Parsons was talking again. 'Christine, can I talk to Danni now?'

'Danni doesn't want to come out to play, she's scared.'

'I know she must be very frightened, but I need to speak with her. Please.'

'Okay, but don't you hurt her,' Christine said sweetly, 'otherwise Joanne will come out. You don't want that.'

Danni watched as the little girl disappeared and the real Danni, her, came back. She knew it was her by the way she sat, uncrossing her long legs. Her hand went up to her hair, touching the long loose waves before pulling them back into a messy bun.

'Danni?'

'Hmm? Yes?'

'Do you remember anything we just talked about? Any of the questions I just asked you?'

'You didn't ask me any questions yet,' she watched herself state.

She had had no idea who was living inside her head, but she had seen for herself.

Joanne. Christine. Two somebodies. A woman and a girl. How long had they been there and why didn't she know about them?

On the video Danni looked at the clock. She checked again, then looked at her watch. Dr Parsons noticed her looking with a frown on her face.

'Wondering where the time went?'

'Yeah. I just sat down, didn't I?'

'No, you've been here but you haven't been here. Tell me, besides the abuse you suffered at the hands of your sister, did anything else happen to you?'

The heaviness of his body, the blood, the smell of smoke, the screams, her blood-slickened hands.

Yes, something happened.

Dr Parsons could obviously see something written on her face. 'Do you want to share what happened?'

Danni was back to biting her nails, something she was also doing in real life as she watched the video with all the interest of a rubber-necker watching a car crash as they drove by slowly. She couldn't look away.

'I don't think I can. She'd kill me.' Poor choice of words.

'All right. Danni, during your childhood, you have suffered much abuse, but there was one event, one so bad, so devastating that it caused your mind to fracture. One person became three people. You, Joanne and Christine.'

'What? What do you mean? What are you saying? I don't understand.'

'I spoke with a woman named Joanne and a girl named Christine. They know about each other but your mind is protecting you from knowing about them. I'm telling you this so you understand that your mind works differently to other people's. That's why you do things you don't remember doing, you black out, you do things without any particular reason, right? Time passes and you don't remember where it went or what you were doing?'

'Yes,' she whispered.

'Well, these are the times when one of these women takes over.

They're protecting you. It means that one or more other personalities live within your mind. They each have their own personalities; Joanne told me she is in her late teens now and Christine is halfway through high school. Do you understand what I'm saying to you, Danni?'

No, she couldn't. The younger Danni on camera became very agitated, then began to cry. Danni in the present shook her head in confusion. This couldn't be possible. Could it? Again, she mentally ran through her life, the times when she did things without remembering, so many other things that all added up to the doctor being right, but if so, why did she never remember that conversation? Did she deliberately delete it from her mind or did someone else? Joanne or Christine? Had they stolen this memory too? Why? How many more memories had they taken from her?

Maybe one of them had taken over when the doctor spoke, or she couldn't handle the truth, so she just shut down mentally.

Christine and I are right here, a voice said. Danni felt panic rising inside her, so she switched off the video by stabbing at the button on the phone. She didn't want to listen to another word. She'd heard the details she needed to hear. But the voice. It wasn't from the video, it was inside her mind.

She had two other people living within her. She had to try and wrap her head around it. How would this help her moving forward? Danni was scared.

We can help. Just let us in.

'No, no, no,' whispered Danni, not wanting to wake Mia. She put her hands over her ears as if she could block out the voice in her head.

Danni, please. It was the little girl's voice. *Christine.* Danni pulled the car back onto the road, driving way above the speed limit, trying to outrun something that was a part of her. She began to cry, something she hadn't done much of, still in shock from the death of her loved ones. Alexandra. Noah. Joe. Did they ever realise that she was three people? Did Joe? The closest person to her? Had he known, or suspected, that she was different? Was that one of the reasons he was leaving her?

44

Mia didn't know why, but she woke suddenly from a deep slumber. She'd been dreaming about being a famous ballerina, something she'd wanted to be when she was much younger. Now she wanted to be a veterinarian. The radio was playing softly in the background. 'Oh, What a Night' filled the room. She loved the golden oldies channel. They had great music back then. Sometimes she thought she was an old soul caught in the body of a seventeen-year-old. Did the radio wake her? Unlikely, she had it on the same volume every night, number three.

Something was wrong.

She could smell something that she couldn't identify at first, her tired and sleepy mind refusing to process it. It took her a moment. Petrol. She could smell petrol. It was strong and growing stronger by the minute. Her brain kicked into gear and she felt her heart start to hammer. Why was there petrol in her room? She threw back the covers that had tangled around her body and went to open the bedroom door so she could see what was going on, but when she tried to open the door, she found it locked. Since when had her door ever been locked? *There was no lock on her door*, her mind screamed.

She heard a noise, a small snicking sound, and suddenly she could smell smoke. Black, oily and greasy. It snuck its way under her door and she jumped on the bed. What could she do? She was too scared to remember that her dad was just across the landing. She couldn't even let out a scream, such was her fear. Perspiration broke out on the back of her neck and she could feel the heat coming in from under the door along with the smoke. Thick, black smoke that began to make her choke, and she realised that she could just open her window. The flames were licking at the worn carpet now. She had to get out.

Mia jumped off her bed, over the flames, and tried to open her window. It wouldn't budge. She lifted it again with all her might, making a primal grunting sound, but it wasn't opening. She screamed in frustration. In horror, she watched the flames roar higher, eating at the walls, the floor, the furniture. She looked out of the window at the night beyond longingly. Freedom.

Then she unfroze and kicked into action. Mia picked up her desk chair and threw it at the window, the sound of breaking glass not heard over the sudden swell of flames. Quickly, Mia moved over the windowsill, being careful of the shards of glass that threatened to cut her, the flames making her more desperate. She rolled out onto the hot veranda roof, burning underneath her bare feet. She looked over the edge, at the drop to the ground. She had no choice. Looking out from her vantage point, she saw something so horrific that her already reedy breath caught in her throat.

She saw her mother, on the back lawn, just standing there, watching the house burn, and she realised something. Her mother was laughing.

45

The driver's side window was rolled right down, the cold air buffeting her face, cooling her cheeks. Goose bumps adorned her arms. It was like she needed to be uncomfortable, needed to hurt, to feel. She drove down the highway, thinking about how hers and Mia's lives were going to change yet again for the second time in just a few short weeks. They had finally left the shitty motel they had lived in and were speeding towards probably another in a long line of shitty motels. Their lives were going to be hard until they settled and she found a job, but first they had to get far enough away that neither Beth nor Andrew could track them down. Sweat pricked her forehead, dried by the night air. She had no idea why her face was sweaty; sweat was also pooling in the small of her back. She rubbed her back left and right on the chair, trying to dry it.

Danni thought about Alexandra and Noah. Her sweet little babies, taken all too soon. She had almost forgotten what it was like to hear their laughter, the sight of them under the sprinkler slowly fading. Was this a true death? When no one remembered what you were like? She looked at the sleeping Mia, head bent at an awkward angle, and smiled sadly. What a legacy to put on such young shoulders. She was now everything to Danni.

She thought about Joe, but she promised herself it would be the last time she indulged herself. His lie had hurt her more than she cared to admit. Through all the ups and downs, she had thought that they still loved each other, were in love still. He had taken their weddings vows, said so long ago, and had made a mockery of them and her. And with Beth. Banishing Joe to the deep recess of her mind proved easier than she thought, it was like she had scrubbed her hard drive, all memories, both good and bad, just... gone.

What she had seen. She knew it to be true. Joanne and Christine. Wrestling control of Danni's mind. How many times had Danni's personality been taken over by one of the people in her mind? Who was she and where did she end and they begin? Questions she'd never find answers to, she feared. Another semi-trailer barrelled past them, rocking the small car. Dust flew over the windscreen, momentarily obscuring her view. Frantically, she flicked on the wipers to clear her vision, then used the water to wash away the dead bugs. She watched as the wipers smeared the tiny corpses all over the window. A parent should never have to bury a child, let alone two. The thought caused pricks of pain behind her eyes which then welled with tears. They flowed down her face faster than she could wipe them with her hand. They made it hard to see through the darkened night. It wouldn't do any good for them to crash.

Pull over, the voice suggested, but Danni ignored it, she didn't want others to be in control of her any more. *She* was in control goddamn it. Her life might be in free fall, but it was *her* life.

Let us help you. Pull over.

She didn't know how they could possibly help but she mumbled, 'Go away,' quietly anyway.

A large four-wheel drive flew past her, followed by another semi-trailer, again rocking the car so much that she had to hang onto the steering wheel tighter. She was so tired, emotionally and physically. She felt like she hadn't had a good sleep in over a month. She guessed she hadn't. All the stress with her family's deaths, the insurance company's refusal to pay out, Beth, and now Andrew, had taken their toll on her. She had lost weight, was tired yet couldn't sleep and was a nervous wreck, jumping at shadows. She sometimes wanted to be like Mia, oblivious to what was going on around her. Off in her own world, where the pain and guilt couldn't touch her. She wanted it all to end, but she could never do that to Mia.

So she kept driving, blinking a few times to try to get the grit out of her eyes. They had to keep moving.

A loud blare of a deep horn brought her back to reality. The car had wandered across the double white lines. The semi's rumbling blast warned her to get back on her side. Heart hammering, she quickly yanked the wheel, swerving back into her lane. She put a hand on her chest to stop her heart from beating so fast. Her phone rang and, in the close quarters, it sounded like a scream, and she jumped with fright. She quickly silenced it and wondered who was calling her so late. Adrenaline coursed through her veins, making her grip the wheel tighter. Danni didn't look. She looked in the mirror at Mia, but she hadn't stirred with the phone ringing. In fact, she hadn't moved in hours. Danni reached behind her and touched her wrist, feeling for a pulse. She found one and breathed a sigh of relief.

Driving through the black of night, Danni decided to put the radio on. She listened to the news and a couple of old songs that she sang softly to. The next song that came on was 'Sherry' by the Four Seasons. It reminded her of one of Mia's favourite old time songs, 'Oh, What a Night'.

Danni was instantly transported to a different time. A time and place that was very familiar to her. Danni was in her bed, the old springs digging into her back, Joe's loud snoring beside her. He had woken her up yet again and she had the urge to smother him with his own pillow. She was so tired and she had to work tomorrow morning, not to mention get the kids off to school. Once she had woken, she realised that she'd have to go to the toilet and soon. She was busting. She reached for the dressing gown in the dark and folded it around her, tying the belt up tightly. She realised that it was Joe's but she didn't care, she'd give it back to him before he woke up.

Danni walked quietly across the landing. She went into the bathroom, careful not to close the door. Once closed, the broken knob held you prisoner until someone set you free. She didn't want to yell the house down for someone to come and rescue her. Once she had washed her hands, she stared into the bathroom mirror. She leaned forward and breathed on the mirror. She drew a love heart. No idea why, she just felt like it.

Danni walked back across the landing to the cupboard door next to Mia's room. She opened the cupboard quietly on its oiled hinges. Oiled by her a week ago.

Danni grabbed out lengths of polyurethane rope and a box cutter. She could hear a song playing on the radio from Mia's room. 'Oh, What a Night'. She hummed along with the song, enjoying the peace and quiet that the early hours of the morning afforded her. She nodded her head along with the beat. Putting the rope and box cutter on the small stained wooden landing table, she reached back into the cupboard and grabbed a jerry can, the liquid sloshing around. She could smell the pungent petrol, even though the yellow lid was on the nearly-full red plastic container. This was it.

Danni walked over to Noah's room first. He looked so sweet and innocent lying there, a teddy tucked up under his neck, gripped firmly in his arm. She kissed him on the cheek and stroked his hair. He slept with the door open, always, a hangover from his nightmares when he was younger. When he had nightmares, he would scream the house down and Danni would run in and comfort him, holding him and stroking his hair until he fell asleep. Joe didn't agree with her methods, but she didn't give a shit. She opened the cap of the can and poured a line from the middle of his room out into the middle of the landing. She blew a kiss to her youngest.

Next, she walked into her daughter's room. Alexandra, her middle child, ever the peace maker, was lying with the cover pulled almost over her head. Danni leaned down and gave her a kiss on her hair, moving the blanket slightly, running her fingers down her soft cheek. She murmured in her sleep, a wordless sigh that Danni couldn't understand. Again, Danni uncapped the can and ran a length of petrol to the middle of the landing, meeting the one from Noah's room. She whispered, 'I love you,' to Alexandra.

Danni headed to the opposite side of the house, slowly walking into Mia's bedroom. Her first child, seventeen now, almost a woman. She didn't give her a kiss or stroke her hair as she had the others. She didn't want to wake her. Danni's eyes felt like they had sand in them, so she rubbed them hard, but ended up making it worse. Mia's radio had changed songs now, but there was still a golden oldie on. Mia said she found them comforting and relaxing when she was drifting off to sleep. Like she had done to her other children's rooms, she opened the jerry can and drew a line of petrol out onto the landing, linking it up with the others, a pool of petrol soaking into the threadbare carpet where they converged.

She saved the best for last, heading towards her own bedroom. She stood quietly at the bedroom door, listening to her husband's loud breathing, interspersed with even louder snoring. The noises that always woke her up nearly every night. She thought back to Joe coming out of Mia's room late at night, the frostiness between the two, Mia pushing the boundaries with her father. It all added up. She didn't want to think it, but she remembered the website. Determined, she walked into the room, confident that Joe wouldn't wake up. She coated the floor around the bed with petrol and poured some on him for good measure. She had to make sure that the job was done properly.

She thought back to when they were first married, the love, the promises, the future. All gone now. Nothing left.

Putting the jerry can on the floor where all of the lines of petrol met, she picked up the rope, woven tightly together. The best rope she could find for the task. She started with her bedroom door, tying the rope around the door handle, securing it with zip ties that she had found in Joe's shed. Danni then ran the rope to Alexandra's room, repeating the process, and then to Noah's room, tying off the last of the rope. She tested the doors; they were now locked securely from the outside, intertwined. There was no way they were getting out unless one of them had a knife, but by then the petrol would have lit their rooms, engulfing them in smoke and flames. She walked over to Mia's room and repeated the process, tying the rope to the hall cupboard, zip tying it off, so even if she could open the door a bit, she'd never be able to get out.

Smiling, she pulled a box of matches from the waist band of her pyjamas, put there at some time in the night. Walking down to the second step, she pulled two matches from the box, struck them against the rough side, the sound deafening in the near silent house. She held the matches for a second, watching the flame burn towards her fingers and inhaled deeply before she flicked them towards the middle of the room. Instantly, the fire whooshed as it connected with the petrol, flaming blue for a moment before an oily black cloud started to fill the landing, snaking out towards the bedrooms.

Danni ran down the stairs and out the front door, knowing it would lock behind her and she wouldn't be able to get back in. She quickly walked over to the dog's kennel and unclipped Pooch's collar from the chain. The dog ran in circles around her legs, yipping and trying to lick her hand but she kept pulling away. Eventually he gave up and trailed after her silently, nudging her leg every now and then. Maybe she wanted the company, or maybe she didn't want Pooch to burn, too.

Danni went around to the back of the house, feeling the heat as she turned the corner. The smoke boiled around the house. She couldn't see Noah's or Alexandra's rooms from her vantage point, but she could see Joe's and Mia's. Danni stared intently at her bedroom window, waiting for Joe to appear, on fire. He had had petrol doused on him and she wanted to see him burn. *Needed* to see him burn.

Suddenly she was rewarded. Joe's flaming body appeared in the bedroom window, screaming, yet making no sound at the same time.

He hadn't even tried to open the window, but had he tried, he would have found that his had been nailed shut, as had everyone else's. Nobody would be able to get out now. Suddenly she heard a faint scream cut through the roaring night. Danni turned to see her daughter, Mia, at the window, her face a mask of terror.

The girl moved into action, throwing her desk chair through the window, breaking the glass. The sudden rush of oxygen fanned the flames even higher as they licked the ceiling, coming ever closer to the teenager. She jumped through the window and stood on the veranda for a long moment, watching her mother. Danni looked at her and began to laugh as she watched the look of terror on Mia's face turn to one of shock.

Mia slid over the veranda and dropped heavily to the ground.

46

Danni saw all of this flash before her eyes. She cried out, screamed, banged her hand against the steering wheel and pulled over in a hurry, the car screeching to a stop, rocking on its suspension. With the engine still running, she stumbled out of the car, fell to her knees and vomited on the ground, over and over, until there was nothing left inside her. She put a hand on her stomach which was seething with pain, bile coming up her throat, vomiting again. She was clammy to the touch. Her hands were shaking, and her mouth tasted foul.

You're welcome. Joanne.

I'm so sorry, Danni. Christine.

Joanne's voice filled her head again.

Now you're free.

'Why?' she yelled, the question echoing through the night.

Damaged goods. You would never have come back from it and you should never have had children. You're damaged, Danni. You forget, I can see into your heart, Joanne replied. *You're rotten.*

Danni screamed. So loudly that she hurt her own ears, the scream ripping at her throat as she clawed her neck, drawing blood, primal and fierce. She stumbled back into the car, revving the engine and took off so fast that the tyres spun and she fishtailed all over the road. She gripped the steering wheel so tight that her knuckles were white and quickly began to ache. It was only when she looked over at the back seat that she realised.

Mia wasn't there.

She slammed the car to a stop on a small rise. Her engine, ticking loudly, filled the night air as Danni yelled her name, checking the back seat again for her daughter. Where was she? Where was Mia?

'Mia!' She cried over and over until her voice was hoarse.

Suddenly she was standing back on the lawn behind the house watching it go up in flames. She was smiling as she watched Joe disappear from view, no longer able to stand up. She didn't want to go around the corner to see if Noah and Alexandra had fared any better, she had a feeling that the smoke had put them to sleep and no fire had touched them. She thought of Joe, coming out of Mia's room and her absolute belief that Joe had been abusing Mia.

Danni flashed back to her own youth. She remembered, now. She had been locked in a room with a boy who was trying to rape her. She had stabbed him over and over before Beth came in and took control. Danni had been made to help carry the wounded boy to the back shed, full of paint tins and flammable paint thinner. Beth had lit a cigarette and thrown it into the shed then locked the door. The boy had burned to death, the fire consuming him.

That was the night that Joanne and Christine had made their first appearance. Joanne knew. She knew that being abused as a child followed you, haunted, hunted you through the rest of your life, tainting every experience you ever had, making you suspicious of everyone and everything. Joanne was right, she should never have had children. They weren't safe around her.

Danni stopped screaming as she finally understood what they were protecting her from.

Mia was never real.

She had died in the fire with the rest of her family.

You're free now, Danni.

* * *

Danni never saw the headlights blazing into her car, never heard the sound of the air horn pumping, never heard the squeal of the exhaust breaks. Suddenly, there was a jarring impact, the sounds of metal screeching against metal, burnt rubber scenting the air and someone screaming in agony.

Her body ricocheted against the seatbelt and back again half a dozen times, breaking ribs, parting flesh, spilling blood. Danni, accepting of her fate, looked into the spiderwebbed rear-view mirror. She saw her beloved children, all together again, waiting for her. Mia smiled serenely at her. She whispered, *I love you.*

As the car flipped, skidding along the road, pushed along by the semi-trailer, Danni's gaze was still fixed on her eldest daughter. 'I love you too,' she whispered.

ACKNOWLEDGMENTS

This book centres around the mental health and wellbeing of a woman, a mother. Women's mental health is a cause that I feel deeply connected to. Many women are fighting a daily battle with mental illness and most of the time you would never even know it. They hide their pain, paste a smile on their face and get on with their lives, all the while fracturing on the inside. If you see someone struggling, ask them if they are okay, you could make all the difference to them. Be kind to each other and always remember, it could be you one day that needs help.

On a lighter note, I'd like to thank the team at Boldwood Books, you're all amazing and I thank you all for your help. I am truly grateful to you all.

I'd also like to thank my family and friends for their everlasting support, I couldn't do it without you, and of course you, my lovely readers. I hope you have enjoyed my book and if you have, don't forget to tell a friend. Drop by and say hi on my socials and keep an eye out for my next book.

Kirsty x

www.kirstyferguson.com

Twitter.com/kfergusonauthor

Instagram.com/Kirstyfergusonauthor

Facebook.com/authorkirstyferguson

Bookbub.com/authors/Kirsty-Ferguson

MORE FROM KIRSTY FERGUSON

We hope you enjoyed reading *The Silent Daughter*. If you did, please leave a review.

If you'd like to gift a copy, this book is also available as an ebook, digital audio download and audiobook CD.

Sign up to Kirsty Ferguson's mailing list for news, competitions and updates on future books.

https://bit.ly/KirstyFergusonNewsletter

Never Ever Tell, another gripping novel from Kirsty Ferguson, is available to order now.

ABOUT THE AUTHOR

Kirsty Ferguson is an Australian crime writer whose domestic noir stories centre around strong women and dark topical themes. Kirsty enjoys photography, visiting haunted buildings and spending time with her son.

Visit Kirsty's website: https://www.kirstyferguson.com

Follow Kirsty on social media:

twitter.com/kfergusonauthor

instagram.com/kirstyfergusonauthor

facebook.com/authorkirstyferguson

bookbub.com/authors/kirsty-ferguson

ABOUT BOLDWOOD BOOKS

Boldwood Books is a fiction publishing company seeking out the best stories from around the world.

Find out more at www.boldwoodbooks.com

Sign up to the Book and Tonic newsletter for news, offers and competitions from Boldwood Books!

http://www.bit.ly/bookandtonic

We'd love to hear from you, follow us on social media:

facebook.com/BookandTonic
twitter.com/BoldwoodBooks
instagram.com/BookandTonic

Lightning Source UK Ltd.
Milton Keynes UK
UKHW041808060223
416534UK00002B/128

9 781804 262184